DEATH OF A SOPRANO

A JOSEPH HAYDN MYSTERY

NUPUR TUSTIN

Foiled Plots Press

Death of a Soprano
A Joseph Haydn Mystery
Foiled Plots Press

Copyright © 2023~Nupur Tustin
Cover Design by Karen Phillips

Published by Foiled Plots Press

ISBN 979-8-9863995-3-9

Typesetting services by BOOKOW.COM

Acknowledgments

Many thanks to Solveigh Rumpf-Dorner of the Österreichischen Nationalbibliothek in Vienna. Without her invaluable help, it would have been impossible to flesh out the characters of Archduke Ferdinand Karl, his older brother, Leopold, Grand Duke of Tuscany, and Maria Beatrice D'Este.

I will confess I've taken some liberties with the Archduke's character. For story purposes, I've given him something of a past.

The information Jeremy Gray, artistic director of the Bampton Classical Opera, kindly provided me for the previous Haydn Mystery, *Murder Backstage*, proved helpful for this one as well. Thanks to his advice, I was able to locate a libretto of the opera Haydn performs in this novel: *L'infedeltà delusa*.

Needless to say, this particular opera wasn't written by Greta's beau, Karl Schulze. The librettist is **Marco Coltellini** who makes a cameo appearance along with the composer **Gluck** in *Murder Backstage*.

Finally this book would not be in your hands were it not for my husband's loving provision of all my needs and to God who blesses us all and through whom all things are possible.

ALSO BY NUPUR TUSTIN

JOSEPH HAYDN MYSTERIES
A Minor Deception
Aria to Death
Prussian Counterpoint
Murder Backstage
Death of a Soprano

CELINE SKYE PSYCHIC MYSTERIES
Visions of Murder: Prequel
Master of Illusion
Forger of Death

SOPHIE'S ADVENTURES
The Pompadour Necklace

ANTHOLOGIES
Murder in Vienna: A **FREE** Joseph Haydn Mystery
Murder in the Sun: A **FREE** Women Sleuths Mystery
The Baker's Boy: A Young Haydn Mystery
In **Day of the Dark,** Edited by Kaye George
The Christmas Stalker
In **Shhh. . .Murder!,** Edited by Andrew MacRae

FREE Mysteries Available from NTUSTIN.COM

A Note on the Nobility

Titles can be confusing. Here's a short primer:

His Imperial Majesty: Emperor Joseph was Emperor of the Holy Roman Empire, a loose coalition of German states and principalities. It had taken considerable maneuvering on the part of the Emperor's mother, Maria Theresa, to ensure the Habsburgs retained control of this title, which was coveted more as a status symbol than for any real power it conferred upon its holder.

Her Majesty: Empress Maria Theresa, ruler of Austria and the Habsburg hereditary lands. For political reasons, the Empress had refused to be crowned empress of the Holy Roman Empire along with her husband, Francis I. She appointed her son, Joseph, co-regent of the Habsburg lands when Francis died.

His Imperial Highness: The title accorded to all Archdukes of the Habsburg family. In this novel, it refers to Archduke Ferdinand Karl.

His Grace: Leopold, technically also an Archduke, was Grand Duke of Tuscany. He succeeded Emperor Joseph in 1790, reigning for only two years before he died and was succeeded by his son, Francis II.

His Royal Highness: The Duke of Modena insisted upon being addressed thus.

Her Ladyship: Maria Beatrice D'Este, daughter of the Duke of Modena, and the bride of Archduke Ferdinand Karl.

His Serene Highness: Prince Nikolaus Esterházy was Prince of the Holy Roman Empire. The Prince is a recurring character in the Joseph Haydn series.

Her Serene Highness: Prince Nikolaus's wife, Marie Elisabeth. She plays a supporting role in *Aria to Death*, the second Joseph Haydn Mystery.

Chapter One

Was it time to call for Archduke Ferdinand Karl? Joseph Haydn plucked his gold timepiece out of the pocket of the baggy Pierrot costume the musicians were to wear for the morning's entertainment.

He had barely bent his head to glance at the watch when the rapid drumbeat of approaching footsteps assailed his ears.

Startled, the Kapellmeister raised his head in time to see the tall figure of Leopold, Grand Duke of Tuscany, storming into the antechamber where he sat, waiting for the Archduke.

"Your Grace?" Haydn rose. Why was the Grand Duke here? He had supposed His Grace to be with Prince Nikolaus, Haydn's employer, ready to sail across the Neusiedlersee to receive the bridal party.

"Ah, Haydn. There you are." The Grand Duke rearranged his stern features into a smile. He inclined his head toward the Archduke's door. "Where is my brother? The bride and her father will soon be here. Is he within?"

"Attending to his correspondence, I believe," Haydn replied with a nod. So the Archduke's valet had loftily informed him when Haydn had knocked on the door fifteen minutes ago to summon His Imperial Highness to the festivities planned for his bride-to-be.

"His Imperial Highness will be ready no sooner than a quarter to the hour," the valet had said imperiously.

"B-b—" Haydn had begun to protest only to have the door firmly closed in his face.

The bride and her father would arrive at nine, the hour at which Haydn himself was to conduct the music for her reception. He could ill afford to stand around waiting. But he'd been given no choice.

The Grand Duke's lips tightened. "Ferdinand's correspondence—such as it is—can wait."

The Archduke was a notoriously slow writer. So slow that rumor had it an opera in Prague had been delayed two hours while His Imperial Highness dealt with his letters. But it was likely not the speed—or lack thereof—of his brother's writing that was causing the Grand Duke's current anxiety.

Eszterháza, a remote outpost in Hungary, was as far from any kind of temptation as it was from Vienna—and civilization. Nevertheless, the mail coach delivered letters to this remote place. It was quite possible to carry on a clandestine correspondence wholly undetected.

Haydn had worried about the possibility as well. But even though he'd been charged—by the Emperor, no less—with the Archduke's well-being, it was not his place to demand to see the Archduke's letters.

His Grace strode toward the door and hammered his fist upon it. As before, the valet appeared at the door, an annoyed frown on his face.

"His Imperial Highness—" he began, his nose in the air, only to be cut short by the Grand Duke.

"Stand aside, man! I am his brother." Beckoning Haydn to follow him, the Grand Duke pushed his way in. Then, turning to the valet, His Grace dismissed him with an airy flick of his fingers.

"Leopold!" The Archduke rose hurriedly from his writing desk. Papers were strewn on it, and crumpled sheets littered the black lacquer wastebasket in the corner. "There was no need to barge into my room. I was on my way."

A slim young man, the Archduke bore a startling resemblance to his oldest brother, Emperor Joseph. They had the same light blue eyes—although the Archduke's eyes had not the coldness and cynicism that habitually marked the Emperor's gaze.

At this moment, they were blazing defiantly at the Grand Duke. Seeing Haydn, however, the Archduke acknowledged him with a curt nod and smile.

"I'm glad to hear you were." The Grand Duke cast an appraising eye over his younger sibling's richly embroidered beige coat and the black trousers with a band of gold and orange encircling the bottom edge. "You look presentable enough," he commented, leading the way to the door. "You are finished with your letters, I trust."

"Oh, never fear, brother." A glint of amusement and determination sparkled in the young Archduke's eyes. "It is all taken care of."

What had been taken care of, Haydn wondered as he waited for the Archduke to go on ahead of him. They were at the threshold when he noticed a crumpled piece of paper fall from the Archduke's tightly closed fists. He was about to retrieve it, but the Archduke adroitly maneuvered him out of the door, and closed it.

"Leave it! Surely one of the servants can pick it up. I gather we have no time to waste."

Haydn hesitated. He had the distinct impression he'd been deliberately prevented from looking at the missive. Was the Archduke carrying on a cloak-and-dagger correspondence with the paramour he'd been separated from?

He looked to the Grand Duke for direction.

But although His Grace frowned, he didn't admonish his brother for his slovenliness. Nor did he appear to think anything else was amiss.

"No, we don't," he simply agreed and hurried down the hallway.

Haydn pursed his lips. Should they have stayed behind to examine the note, whatever it was? What if the Archduke was planning some kind of escapade, some way of avoiding the inevitable nuptials?

The embarrassment such an incident would afford to His Imperial Highness's mother, Empress Maria Theresa, and to Haydn's own employer, Prince Nikolaus Esterházy—who'd offered to host the betrothed couple's first meeting—was not to be thought of.

Haydn was still pondering the situation when they stepped out into the strong sunlight of a late summer day. It was beautiful—even here in Eszterháza where mosquitoes and fever abounded, it was a lovely day.

Roses in varying shades of delicate pink lined their way, their sweet aroma scenting the pleasant breeze that playfully encircled them.

Down below, the enormous swan boats that would convey the Archduke to his bride could be seen, moored firmly to the shore. The floating island —decorated with flowering bushes and palm trees—where the musicians would be stationed strained at its ropes.

The Grand Duke surveyed the scene with an approving smile.

"The bride will find much to please her here," he said, turning to Haydn. "Esterházy has outdone himself."

"Let us hope she finds the groom just as pleasing," the Archduke remarked as they hastened toward the grassy bank where the entire village was gathered. His tone was bitter. "Did you know, Haydn"—His Imperial Highness turned toward the Kapellmeister—"that she has sworn to become a nun if she doesn't find in me a suitable mate?"

That the bride had made some stipulations, Haydn had known, but what exactly she had demanded, he hadn't until now been aware. He was about to assure the young Archduke that Maria Beatrice D'Este, heiress to four states, was certain to find him pleasing, but His Imperial Highness went on without waiting for a reply.

"She wrote to Mother telling her so. Would you believe it, Haydn?" It took Haydn by surprise that a chit of a girl—how old was she? About twenty-one?—should have undertaken to write thus to the Empress, her future mother-in-law. But no doubt as heiress to four states, she had some claim. "And what must Mother do, but jump to her demands."

"She will find all to her satisfaction, no doubt," Haydn murmured soothingly. He had no desire to get drawn into petty matters of state. He was a musician, not a statesman.

"She had better, or you'll be taking Holy Orders, Ferdinand," the Grand Duke warned his younger brother. The grassy slope was steep here, and His Grace sounded breathless as he hurtled down it.

"I thought being a younger son released one from the burden of ruling," the Archduke retorted, his nimble steps taking the incline more gracefully than his brother. "Isn't that what Mother told Max?"

"It doesn't relieve one from every duty," his older brother remarked sharply. He glanced over his shoulder at his brother. "As the youngest, Max is destined for the church. Is that where you wish to go too?"

"No!" The Archduke shuddered, and Haydn, bounding down the incline behind him, shuddered along with him. There was a time when his parents had strongly desired that Haydn enter the church. He had managed to persuade them that the strict regimen and celibacy involved were not for him.

But at least he'd been given a choice in the matter. And no one had suggested he take a wife at that age! Heaven preserve him, His Imperial Highness was barely seventeen—little more than a lad.

Yet his destiny was set, his choices limited to marrying a woman he'd never met—and who was making demands before she'd even wed the groom —or entering the church.

As for Archduke Maximilian, the Empress's youngest—he appeared to have even less say in his future. Haydn fervently thanked the Lord he'd been born to a poor wheelwright and his wife, a cook, rather than in a palace. Far better to be poor and free than to be a prince only to have one's entire existence arranged at another's whim.

He felt a reluctant sympathy for the young lad. He himself might have been tempted to cut loose. Would certainly have cut loose, he reflected with chagrin, recalling the small revenge he'd exacted on Kapellmeister Reutter as a young choirboy.

Expelled for cutting off a fellow choirboy's pigtail, Haydn had slyly exchanged the musical setting of the Kyrie for the Gloria in a mass to be sung before the Empress. The singers had stumbled through the mass, scrambling to fit the words to the music.

Haydn's mouth twitched. The memory of Reutter's subsequent embarrassment had warmed many a cold, wintry Viennese night for him.

His life in those days had been a constant struggle. But it had all been worth it—the intense hunger, the bone-shaking cold, the dire poverty. Unlike the Archduke, Haydn had possessed a dream no one could deprive him of.

"I trust Your Imperial Highness will enjoy the music," Haydn now said, attempting to divert the young man from the burden he must endure—and from any shenanigans he might have planned to escape it.

The cobblestone path flattened out, meandering through the thick grass down to the edge of the lake.

"Signora Pacelli will be singing some of the Italian madrigals Your Imperial Highness selected." The Archduke fortunately took a keen interest in music. It was the only aspect of the entertainment that had sparked his attention.

But if Haydn thought mention of the prima donna would raise the Archduke's stormy spirits, he was mistaken.

"Signora Pacelli, Signora Pacelli." The Archduke waved an imperious hand through the air. "Have you no other singer but her? One tires of her voice."

Tires of her voice! Haydn repeated the words incredulously to himself. His prima donna had a breathtaking range of both emotion and tone. How could any connoisseur of music tire of the incomparable Lucia Pacelli's voice?

Even the Grand Duke seemed surprised. "Since when have you tired of her voice, Ferdinand?"

It was but the other day that the Archduke had gushed his praises of it.

The Archduke shrugged, his blue eyes colder than Haydn had ever seen them before, his lips a thin, tight line. He looked more than ever like his oldest brother, the Emperor.

"It palls—like everything else. Where is my boat, Haydn?"

Chapter Two

"You are barely on time, Herr Kapellmeister!" Peter von Rahier's angry hiss startled Haydn into dropping the rope around the long, curving swan neck that formed the prow of the Archduke's boat

His Imperial Highness was fortunately already in the boat, for it immediately glided away from the shore.

"Herr Rahier!" Curbing his irritation, Haydn spun around, bumping into the white suit trimmed with gold that covered the Estates Director's tall, elegant figure. Rahier had always tended to treat him like a subordinate—assuming a position of authority he did not in actuality possess.

But it would not do to air these petty concerns before their imperial guests.

"*Guten Mor*—" he began.

But the Estates Director ignored Haydn's attempt at a greeting.

"What were you thinking?" he fumed on, apparently unaware of the Grand Duke's presence. "Your tardiness—"

"Is not his fault," the Grand Duke interrupted the Estates Director's tirade. "And we'll be later still," he went on, as a trumpet sounded in the distance, announcing the imminent arrival of the bridal barge, "if we have to listen to your recriminations."

"Your Grace." Rahier wiped the ire off his face, replacing it with an unctuous smile. "Let me hail your boat for you." Turning toward the water, Rahier flicked his fingers peremptorily, gesturing the waiting boat forward.

"Call the floating island to the shore as well," His Grace commanded, stepping over the enormous white swan wing that formed the side of his boat. "Haydn here needs to get on board."

Beckoned onward, swan-shaped boats tugged the island into position. An oarsman in traditional Hungarian garb—wide-legged black trousers that flared out toward the ankles and a white linen shirt—moored it to the post set deep into the grassy bank.

A second trumpet blared as Haydn gripped the bow his Konzertmeister, Luigi Tomasini, held out to him and climbed onto the floating island.

"It's just as well you appeared when you did, Joseph," Luigi said to him in a low voice. "Rahier has been sniffing around us all morning." Turning to the shore, he called aloud to the Estates Director who was still staring at them disapprovingly. "We are all here and accounted for, as you can see, Herr Rahier. May we leave?"

His mocking tone must have further angered the Estates Director. For, determined to assert himself, Rahier let his sharp blue eyes rove over the performers arranged by the bushes and palms of the floating island.

"I don't see Miss Lidia," he sniffed. "Where might she be?"

"Her services are not needed this morning," Haydn replied. "Although that is none of your concern," he couldn't resist pointing out. "She is with Paolo."

He tipped his chin toward the shore where the tall English soprano could be seen helping a frail man—Lucia Pacelli's husband—down the grassy embankment.

Rahier's lips tightened as he gazed at Paolo Pacelli's ill-fitting Pierrot costume. Why Paolo insisted upon receiving his livery and wearing it, Haydn would never understand. But for Lucia's sake, he humored the cranky older man.

Rahier sniffed again. "Another useless member of your orchestra who does nothing to earn his keep. But your prima donna must be kept happy at all costs, I suppose."

Haydn ignored the snide insinuation—although truth be told he'd done his soprano far more favors than she deserved. He gave her a quick glance.

Looking pale and uneasy, the beautiful Lucia clung to a palm tree. A moment later, the spasm of pain on her features passed and she straightened up again.

Seeing Haydn looking her way, Lucia smiled. "I am all right, Joseph. It is just the infernal swaying and bobbing of our platform that plays havoc with my insides."

A surge of anger swept through Haydn. His prima donna frequently forgot herself in private, addressing him by his given name. He didn't usually mind, although it was a bitter reminder of a single, almost fatal indiscretion. But to do so in public, before the other performers and the Estates Director—who'd just hinted at a clandestine relationship between them—was unforgivable.

Had she been similarly over-familiar with the Archduke? Was that why His Imperial Highness had suddenly sworn off her?

His lips stretched into a tight smile. "It is no matter, Signora Pacelli," he said, deliberately formal. "Since you are not well, Fräulein Leon can take the madrigals today."

It satisfied him to see Lucia's mouth drop open as her young rival, Narcissa Leon, pushed her way forward and smiled broadly all around.

Luigi seemed stunned as well. "Are you sure that is wise, Joseph?" he whispered with an anxious glance at the Archduke's boat.

"I have no doubt about it," Haydn assured him. "His Imperial Highness claims to tire of her voice. A fresh, young talent will revive his jaded appetite."

"Very well." Luigi subsided, bringing his violin up to his chin in readiness. But the expression on the Konzertmeister's features remained skeptical, and he looked around, undoubtedly in search of Haydn's younger brother.

Johann Evangelist could always be counted on to sway Haydn's mind, and had he been on the island, he may well have prevailed. But Johann was fortunately in the opera house with the other singers, preparing for the premiere of their opera buffa that evening.

⊷•••⊷

"Hey, du!"

The peremptory tone caught palace maid Rosalie Heindl's attention. She spun around, one hand still on the cleaning cart she was wheeling out of Princess Marie Elisabeth's room.

Her lips tightened when she saw who it was.

"Yes, what is it?" She put her hand on her hip and balefully regarded the Archduke's valet. He was a skinny runt of a boy with a thin face, a narrow forehead, and gleaming strands of dark hair combed stiffly back over his head.

How dare he hail her like that! She might be a common servant, but so was he.

"His Imperial Highness wishes his room to be cleaned. You'd better get to it. Swiftly," the valet added, his eye roving up and down her form contemptuously. In years, he was no older than his master—barely a lad of seventeen or so.

Rosalie would've dearly liked to box the pimply-faced lad's ears, but his master was a guest in the Esterházy Palace. She'd only get herself in trouble if she picked a fight with His Imperial Highness's servant.

"Very well." Rosalie tamped down her indignation. Cleaning guest rooms wasn't part of her job. She'd only taken on the additional chore—like all the other palace maids—because they were short-staffed.

She was about to trundle the cart back to the servant's hall when the young valet spoke again.

"I am hungry. I wish to eat."

"Then take yourself to the kitchen." Rosalie hadn't heard Clara Schwann —lady's maid to the Princess—step out of Her Serene Highness's suite. "It's what all the other servants do."

Arms folded across her chest, the lady's maid regarded the valet, whose eyes widened as Frau Schwann continued: "You've been here long enough to know where that is, haven't you, boy?"

"Err-yes." The valet hurried to the door the lady's maid was pointing to.

"You mustn't let a young pipsqueak like that order you about, my dear." Frau Schwann turned to Rosalie after the valet had left. "Put them in their place—the sooner the better, I say."

"Yes, Frau Schwann." Rosalie nodded obediently. But it was easy for Frau Schwann to say, she thought. A middle-aged plump woman with graying hair, she'd served as Princess Marie Elisabeth's lady's maid ever since Her Serene Highness had arrived at the palace as a young bride.

Naturally, she carried an easy air of authority. Rosalie had only occupied her current position—Principal Maid to the Musicians—for six months. She wasn't accustomed to lording it over other servants. Neither was Greta, her fellow servant. But Frau Schwann was right; they'd both better get used to it.

Rosalie bent toward her cleaning cart, about to wheel it back into the cleaning closet—she could hardly take it upstairs where the Archduke's suite was—but Frau Schwann gently pushed her aside.

"Let me take that back for you." She sighed heavily. "If His Serene Highness had any sense, he'd hire more servants. God knows, we need them. But until the Princess can prevail upon him to do so, we'll just have to help each other. Here, you get whatever supplies you need and go upstairs."

"Thank you, Frau Schwann!" Rosalie bobbed her head gratefully, picked up a broom, dustpan, and the basket in which she was collecting paper for Greta, and ran up the stairs.

The Archduke's suite was a mess. The coverlet was half on the bed, the other half trailing on the parquet floor. Pens were strewn on the small nightstand by the bed and books lay scattered on the floor next to it.

Sighing, Rosalie set about putting the room to rights. There were wine stains on the carpet—the Archduke had been drinking in bed. Empty bottles were under it. Couldn't his valet have taken those to the kitchen?

Well, there was nothing she could do about the carpet. It would have to be replaced with a fresh one, and she had no time for that now. She dabbed at the crimson stains tarnishing the white areas as best she could. Fortunately, they blended in with the pattern of roses on the black and white background.

The ash stains were worse. Had the Archduke been smoking cigars as well? Rosalie sniffed the air. She thought she detected a whiff of smoke. Well, that was easily remedied. She'd throw open the windows and let some fresh air in while she dusted and cleaned.

The study outside the bedroom was just as much of a mess, with papers spilling out of the wastebasket—and even strewn around the floor by the desk. Good heavens, how hard was it to toss crumpled pieces of paper into a wastebasket?

And if His Imperial Highness missed the basket and couldn't bring himself to stoop down to pick up his rubbish, couldn't he get his valet to do it?

What exactly did the valet do to earn his keep, anyway?

She gathered the crumpled piece on the floor and the numerous sheets in the wastebasket and tossed them into her basket. At least there was quite a bit for Greta to sort through. Her friend liked to collect usable sheets of paper discarded by their betters for her sweetheart, Karl— who as court librettist was in constant need of supplies for his stories.

Quickly, she finished her work. Then, putting her basket, broom, and dustpan outside the room, Rosalie cast a quick glance around the suite.

She was about to step out, pulling the door shut as she withdrew, when Ulrike's cheerful voice startled her.

"Frau Heindl! There you are!"

Chapter Three

"Look at the heap of paper I was able to gather for Fräulein Schmidt."

Before Rosalie could say anything, Ulrike—a pert, young girl with the face and figure of a china doll—dumped the contents of her basket onto Rosalie's. But the exuberance with which she overturned her basket made Rosalie's topple over.

"Oh, no!" Ulrike's palm flew to her mouth, which had fallen open in dismay. "I'm so sorry Frau Heindl."

"It's all right, Ulrike." Rosalie lowered herself onto the carpeted floor. "Just help me pick these back up. They'll fit better in the basket if we smooth out the crumpled sheets," she added, unrolling loosely crushed balls of paper and pressing out the wrinkles.

Some of them had a few lines of writing on them; some had ink blots. Most were usable, Rosalie thought. But she'd let Greta sort through the pile and decide which ones were worth keeping.

Thank heavens, they were nearly done. Working quickly, she straightened out another lightly crushed sheet. The paper was thinner than the rest and her fingers nearly tore a hole in it.

"Be careful, Ulrike! Some of the sheets are thin—"

She'd been idly perusing the lines scrawled on the paper when the full import of what she was reading sank into her mind, and, unable to prevent herself, she uttered a loud gasp.

"Frau Heindl?" Rosalie was aware of Ulrike looking curiously up at her. "What is it?"

"Nothing," Rosalie hastily replied. "Nothing at all."

She raised her head, attempting a smile.

Dear God, who could've penned these vicious words? Had it come from among the papers Ulrike had collected? Or was it something she herself had picked up?

The note hadn't been tightly squashed into a ball; it had been lightly rumpled as though tossed in haste. It looked exactly like the scrap she'd found—not above a few minutes ago—lying by the Archduke's wastebasket.

Had this message—she couldn't bring herself to look down at it—been intended for His Imperial Highness?

"Are you sure?" Ulrike's voice broke into her troubled thoughts. "You look as white as a sheet, Frau Heindl!" The young maid's eyes dropped to the note in Rosalie's hand

Aware of Ulrike's avid gaze on her face, Rosalie crumpled the sheet back up and hastily stuffed it into her pocket.

"It's just that this paper is no good," she said. "It's too marked and splotched to be of any use to Karl."

But as she worked to clean up the mess, Rosalie's heart continued to beat rapidly and her fingers trembled. How could anything so horrible take place at the Esterházy Palace? It was unbelievable!

———◆◆◆———

By the time the opening bars of his wedding symphony filled the air, Haydn's good humor had been restored. He bent and dipped his body in time to its joyous strains—his bow sliding rapidly across his violin strings in unison with Luigi as the peasants clapped and cheered.

Luigi's hazel eyes crinkled and a smile broke out upon his face. "Look at that, Joseph! They love the music. What a joy that is to see!"

Haydn nodded, smiling as well, as he took in the villagers' response.

The Hungarian wedding dance he'd decided to incorporate into the first movement of the piece was having its desired effect. On the grassy banks surrounding the lake, colorful skirts twirled, feet tapped, and hips swayed. Spurred on by the onlookers, Narcissa had begun to wave her arms and dance as well.

Even Lucia, although she still clung to a nearby palm tree, was swaying her skirts.

But when the white, red, and gold barge carrying the bride and her father, Ercole III, Duke of Modena and Reggio, sailed into view, Haydn's gladness quickly evaporated.

Dressed in lacy white with a crown of pale pink flowers upon her dark bronze ringlets, Maria Beatrice D'Este stood stiffly upon the prow, clutching the golden handrail as though her life depended upon it.

No smile played upon her lips. She might have been a stone statue for all the effect the music had on her.

"She looks even more morose than the Archduke did when he arrived," Luigi whispered to Haydn.

"She might be at a funeral, listening to a dirge, she looks so solemn," Haydn agreed in dismay. It took an effort not to let his bow falter.

Was the music not to her taste? Haydn pursed his lips. It was too late to change that now. No one had bothered to acquaint him with the lady's predilections.

Or was it something else?

He discreetly craned his neck, trying to observe the atmosphere on the barge.

***

Her hunger forgotten, Rosalie bolted down the wide corridor that ran past the kitchen and the servants' hall. She wanted to speak with Greta, but her friend would be with the other servants. And the malicious note—it felt like a burning lump of coal in her apron pocket—wasn't something Rosalie could share with just anybody.

The door to the delivery room—right by the service entrance—caught her eye. She could go in there. It was a sunny room, little used by any of the other servants. Alone, she'd go over the monstrous note one more time and ponder the numerous questions buzzing through her mind.

She barged through the door, shut it firmly behind her, and leaned against it, her eyes closed. Her breath came in short, sharp gasps. She was beginning to calm down when a voice rang out close to her ear.

"Oh, there you are!"

Rosalie couldn't help herself; she uttered a little shriek as her eyes flew open.

"Greta!" she gasped, turning to where her friend sat at the far end of the long table. "Why didn't you say something? You gave me such a start."

Greta—a buxom girl with blond hair pulled neatly into double buns on either side of her head—grinned. "I didn't hear you come in, silly! It was only when I turned around that I saw you."

"You'll never bel—?" Rosalie began

But Greta, peering eagerly at the basket dangling from Rosalie's wrist, broke in, "That's a lot of paper. Is that all of it?" Her blue eyes moved toward the door. "Where are Ulrike and the others?"

"In the kitchen, I expect." Rosalie sighed. Was there no getting Greta's mind off any matter that didn't concern Karl? "I said they should have a bite to eat while they can."

Rosalie pulled herself away from the door. She'd also suggested the maids go out to the lake to catch a glimpse of the bride sailing in. But she knew it wasn't the whereabouts of the other maids that Greta was curious about.

"Don't worry. Ulrike gave me the papers she gathered." Rosalie set her basket on the table with a heavy thump. "And I have Frida's as well. There's plenty for Karl—some of it might be wrinkled or stained with ink."

"Oh, Karl doesn't mind," Greta assured her, poking through the basket. "He just needs scraps to scribble short notes about his characters or any idea he comes up with for a story."

Rosalie sighed. How was she to tell Greta about the note? Her friend seemed oblivious to everything else but the paper.

She watched as Greta withdrew some thick sheets, inspecting them carefully. "Such nice thick paper! Isn't it?" She glanced up at Rosalie, who stood frozen behind a chair. "Why don't you sit down? Are you hungry? I brought you some sweet rolls and coffee."

Greta pushed a tray with the food and a pot of coffee toward Rosalie.

Rosalie pulled out the chair next to Greta, but she wasn't in the mood for rolls or coffee. Greta was nattering on—something about the paper the musicians had discarded. It was all covered in staves—but maybe Karl could use it.

Finally, Rosalie couldn't bear it.

"Greta!" she said sharply. "There's something you need to see."

"Wha—?" Before Greta could finish her question, Rosalie pulled out the note and placed it before her friend.

Bending her glossy chestnut-colored hair next to Greta's blond head, Rosalie perused the note a second time. It sent a chill down her spine, the words were so venomous.

Do what needs to be done. Or your shameful secret will be exposed. Have you no thought for the child you've fathered—or the poor woman left to bear your sin as well as hers? Don't think you can get out of this without paying.

It must've had the same effect on Greta, for her friend looked up, her blue eyes as round as saucers.

"God have mercy! Who could've written that?"

———◆◆◆———

Haydn fixed his eyes on the barge, watching as His Serene Highness, Prince Nikolaus Esterházy, tried valiantly to engage the bride in conversation. But Maria D'Este, looking stonily out over the placid lake, barely opened her mouth. Her chin was thrust out at a stiff angle, and her mouth was compressed into an adamant line.

It seemed to get thinner every time she had occasion to glance at the voluptuous figure clinging to her father.

"Is that his mistress?" Luigi followed Haydn's gaze. "I can scarcely believe he brought her."

"It must be." Haydn eyed the woman. At least, she appeared to be enjoying his music. "Chiara," he said, recalling her name.

She was a famed opera singer, although her singing days were long behind her. She was better known now for being the Duke of Modena's constant companion—the woman with whom the Duke openly snubbed his wife, the Duchess of Massa.

There'd been quite the to-do both in the Esterházy Palace and the Habsburg court when it became known that the bride's father insisted upon bringing his mistress along to Eszterháza.

The situation had eventually been resolved when the Duchess of Massa, the bride's mother, hearing of the situation, had declined to come.

"She makes no effort to conform to decency, does she?" Luigi was gazing at the ageing beauty in open fascination. Her scarlet and black dress was entirely inappropriate to the occasion, revealing as it did every curve of her exquisite form and exposing a vast area of golden-brown bosom.

In every respect, Haydn reflected, she contrasted sharply with the bride's more modest garb and pale colors.

Oblivious to his surroundings, the Duke of Modena had his head bent low to his mistress's ear, his hand stroking her rump. And every so often Chiara burst into loud, gay laughter, drawing the bride's contemptuous gaze toward her.

"If the bride's eyes were daggers, the Duke's mistress would be dead a thousand times over," Luigi declared.

"One can hardly blame her. Her father behaves as though he were in his bedchamber." But what could be done, Haydn wondered, to amend the situation?

In her current mood, Maria Beatrice D'Este seemed determined to disapprove of everything. And that did not bode well for the Archduke's prospects—or his own, for that matter, should the marriage fail.

Haydn was beginning to have misgivings about his decision to have Narcissa sing the madrigals, but it was too late. The symphony had ended and the orchestra struck up the first madrigal.

The Archduke had just begun ascending the barge when Narcissa's voice —young, melodious, and clear—rang out. Haydn held his breath, watching the barge and its occupants closely.

To his surprise, Maria Beatrice raised her head and looked for the first time at the floating island. The song, sweet and lilting, seemed to please her. Her lips stretched into a soft smile, and she cordially accepted the bouquet of flowers the Archduke—by this time on board the barge—presented to her.

The Archduke was smiling as well, and the couple waved graciously as they slowly glided toward the floating island. Smiling more broadly—she was quite lovely when she deigned to smile, Haydn thought—Maria Beatrice tossed a pink rose from her bouquet at Narcissa, who deftly caught it.

Haydn sighed in relief. God be thanked, the gamble had played off.

"Bravo, Herr Haydn!" Maria Beatrice called happily. She seemed more relaxed now. The barge sailed past, and she tossed a few more roses at the orchestra—at Haydn, at Luigi, and the other musicians.

Chapter Four

ROSALIE regarded the thin sheet of creased paper between Greta's plump hands. Who had penned those angry words? Greta's question echoed in her mind.

"I've racked my brains," she said, her violet eyes wide with dismay. "I can't think of anyone who'd make such a harsh demand."

She stared at the paper. There was something about it that bothered her as well.

"Where did you find it?" Greta pored over the words again.

"I—" Rosalie's voice skidded to a stop. "I don't know."

Greta's head shot up. "You don't know?" She looked down at the note again, mystified, as though it might provide some explanation of what Rosalie meant.

"I-I mean, I'm not entirely sure," Rosalie faltered. She recounted how she'd come to find the note. "I only wish I'd thought to look more closely at the scrap I found in the Archduke's room. But I was in a hurry. . ." She shrugged.

But who could've imagined she'd turn up something like this? It was unbelievable.

"I doubt it was in one of the musicians' rooms, though." Of the three granted rooms in the palace, two were married, and chomping at the bit— like all their colleagues—to return to their wives in Eisenstadt.

"And Albert. . ." That was the Estates Director's nephew.

"Oh, he's too scared of Herr Rahier to put a foot out of place," Greta shook her head, dismissing the idea.

Then there was Jakob Friberth, the tenor newly hired from Vienna. He had no wife either. But he was in his forties, and Rosalie doubted anyone cared whether he kept a mistress or not.

Greta pensively cupped her chin in her hand. "It does make sense that it would be the Archduke."

His Imperial Highness was the only person with anything to lose.

Their employer's son, Prince Toni, was already married. As for Prince Antal, their employer's son-in-law, His Serene Highness would hardly call for his daughter's marriage to be annulled at this late stage.

The Grand Duke of Tuscany hadn't even brought his wife with him; there was little likelihood of His Grace being embarrassed.

But the Archduke's marriage was not a done thing.

"I hardly fancy his chances," Greta went on, "if this nasty tidbit were to come out."

It *was* nasty. Rosalie peered closer. "*Do what needs to be done,*" she murmured.

"All the lines and creases make it hard to read." Greta slid the paper closer to her. "And this paper is so thin!" She tried to smooth out the wrinkles in the paper but only succeeded in tearing it.

"Be careful," Rosalie began to say when the color and quality of the paper caught her eye.

It was thin, with a bluish tinge.

"It's nothing like the thick creamy paper His Serene Highness provides his guests," Greta remarked, wrinkling her nose. "It's as bad—dear God!" She looked up at Rosalie aghast. "Have you noticed—?"

Rosalie nodded. "It's exactly like the writing paper the maids use." And the musicians and other hired staff, but that was small consolation.

"Then it's one of us!" Greta gasped. "Someone who works here—a person we see every day and trust. Trying to extort money from a guest."

"Or worse." Rosalie stared at the paper grim-faced. She read the words again.

Do what needs to be done. Or your shameful secret will be exposed. Have you no thought for the child you've fathered—or the poor woman left to bear your sin as well as hers? Don't think you can get out of this without paying.

Could even a woman—seduced and cast aside—sound so bitter and unrelenting?

No, these were the words of someone who meant the Archduke harm; someone who would stop at nothing to avenge herself.

"I don't think the Archduke should've so casually tossed this note aside."

She turned to Greta. "What if he's in danger?"

Greta's jaw dropped open. "Whatever do you mean?"

"That whoever wrote this won't take too kindly to being ignored."

———•••———

"We'd better tell Herr Haydn." Greta peered at the wall clock.

Rosalie followed her gaze. The sun was glinting off the tiny face surrounded by colorful shepherdesses and flowers. She could barely see the numbers the gold hands pointed to, but their general position told her what she needed to know.

It would be hours before the Kapellmeister returned.

"We'll have to wait until he gets back." Sighing, she glanced down at the creased paper lying on the table between them. "What are we going to do until then?"

"Wait until who gets back?" a cheerful voice behind them boomed, giving both maids a start. Greta shrieked and even Rosalie, usually more contained than her friend, gasped and bit her tongue.

"Gerhard!" Rosalie squeaked, turning around to gape at the tall, muscular man who stood beaming in the doorway. "What are you doing here?"

She hadn't even heard the door to the service entrance open or the soft click of it being pulled closed. Nor had she heard her husband's sturdy boots ringing on the stone floor. She kept one hand behind her back, surreptitiously pushing the note toward Greta.

She hoped Greta would understand and stuff the paper into her pocket. If Gerhard suspected they might be looking into yet another crime, she might as well say goodbye to her job—or any freedom she enjoyed. He'd never let her out of his sight!

Gerhard fortunately seemed to notice nothing amiss. Holding aloft a bottle of wine, he stepped into the room. "It's for the opera tonight. Karl said Fiore would be by to pick it up. But—"

"The boy never showed up, I suppose." Greta sounded annoyed. Rosalie didn't blame her. Herr Haydn had agreed to hire Fiore, thinking the boy could help Herr Porta, the opera director, and Karl handle the technical aspects of the performance.

But, as now, somebody else usually found themselves saddled with Fiore's chores. More often than not, it was Greta's sweetheart, Karl.

"I have half a mind to tell Herr Porta." Greta's hands were on her hips. The note, Rosalie noticed, was fortunately not on the table.

"Now, now, there's no need to get all worked up over it. I had no great objection to bringing the bottle over myself." Gerhard's handsome features broke into a grin as he turned to Rosalie and pulled her into his arms. "How often do I get the opportunity to come by and steal a kiss?"

But it wasn't the first time Fiore had neglected his chores, and Rosalie said as much after her husband had soundly kissed her lips.

"Mark my words, he's out at the lake, enjoying the festivities while everyone else has their nose to the grindstone."

"No, no, lass!" Gerhard shook his head vehemently, his thick chestnut-colored hair falling over his forehead. He impatiently brushed it back with a quick swipe of his large palm. "Most likely the lad didn't want to show his face at the inn."

"Why?" It was Rosalie's turn to be annoyed. "It's not because he owes you money, is it?" It wouldn't be the first time, either. And why Gerhard stood for it, she didn't know.

She drew away from him.

"Now, now, lass!" Gerhard admonished her. "There's no need to worry your pretty little head over these things. I'll get paid, never fear."

How, she wanted to ask, staring at the floor and trying very hard not to pout. Gerhard rarely sought her advice—or took it—when it came to his business. Or any of his dealings, for that matter. He treated her more like a child than a wife!

She knew he often sold his wine on credit. But surely it was foolish to extend the favor to someone as unreliable as Fiore.

Even Greta agreed. "I wouldn't be too sure of getting paid, Gerhard. Not unless his uncle means to discharge his debts."

"Oh, Signor Pacelli won't do it." Gerhard shook his head. "Says he's had enough of the lad's shenanigans. But never fear"—he drew Rosalie back into his arms and gave her a reassuring squeeze—"he'll get the money."

"Ho—?" Greta began to ask when Gerhard went on:

"He'll get it out of the Archduke, I have no doubt."

"Get the Archduke to pay?" Rosalie and Greta yelped in unison. "How in the world is he going to do that?"

They glanced at each other.

How was Fiore planning to prevail upon the Archduke? By holding a scandalous secret over His Imperial Highness's head?

Gerhard sighed. "Well, if you must know, he does it by inflating the figures on His Imperial Highness's receipts."

"But that's dishonest!" Rosalie cried.

"Yes, I know, lass." Gerhard sighed heavily, clearly made uncomfortable by the situation. "I would say something. But His Imperial Highness seems only too willing to be duped. And since he can well afford it, I turn a blind eye to the whole affair. It was quite by chance that I found out about it."

Apparently the Archduke had paid Gerhard a larger sum than the wine merchant recalled charging him. But when Gerhard pointed that out, His Imperial Highness had brought out his receipt.

"There were numbers crossed out. New figures added. It wasn't in my hand, I can tell you that much. I tried to tell him so, but he had his nose in the air and said in his usual imperious fashion"—here Gerhard pitched his booming baritone into a high falsetto. It was nothing like the Archduke's voice, but it made both maids giggle—"*the numbers say what they say, my good man. Consider the entire thing settled.*"

"Well, it still doesn't seem right." Rosalie eyed Greta. Should the Kapellmeister be informed about Fiore's deceit?

Gerhard must have seen the glance they exchanged for he continued: "Now, don't go bothering your Herr Haydn about it. Fiore isn't the only one taking advantage of His Imperial Highness. Prince Toni does it as well.

"That's where Fiore got the notion from, I'll warrant."

"Prince Toni?" Rosalie wondered.

"He's deep in debt, didn't you know?"

Rosalie and Greta nodded. "Oh, we've heard His Serene Highness more than once," Greta said. "Yelling at Prince Toni, berating him. But who'd have thought he'd stoop so low?"

"Oh, he's a devious one, he is," Gerhard replied. "He's tried the same trick on Prince Antal, but his brother-in-law is sharp as a tack and won't stand for it."

Greta's blue eyes widened. "But he seems so nice. Always polite to the maids. Keeps his room clean, too, which is more than you can say for most young men." She shook her head. "He must be quite overcome with debt to do such a thing."

"So he must." Rosalie pursed her lips pensively. What else was Prince Toni willing to do for money? Would he go so far as to exploit a sordid secret, demanding money in return for his silence?

Her gaze drifted toward Greta's apron pocket and the tiny bit of paper peeking out of it.

Dear God, was it Prince Toni who'd penned it?

Chapter Five

T HE program over, swan-shaped boats guided the floating island back to the shore. It came to a gentle halt, bumping lightly against the grassy embankment just as Luigi played the final notes of his violin solo.

Oarsmen sprang out, and Haydn braced himself for the inevitable dipping and bobbing as they secured the platform to a post.

Luigi lowered his violin. "A two-hour respite should suffice, don't you think, Joseph?" he asked, leaning closer to Haydn.

The Kapellmeister nodded. "Any longer, and I fear we shall be in danger of running late."

The morning's entertainment had run long. He would've liked to grant his men a more extensive recess. But the opera buffa was scheduled to begin at six in the evening. And His Serene Highness would expect them to commence on time.

A final rehearsal was needed. Besides, the musicians were also required to change out of their Pierrot costumes into the new livery designed for the program. No, they could certainly not afford any more than two hours.

The musicians prepared to disembark. Haydn called out his instructions as they trooped past the cordoned-off area where he stood with Luigi, each carrying his instrument under his arm.

"Gentlemen, do not forget, we meet in the opera house in two hours. But for now, take yourselves to the Officers' Mess. The midday meal will be served there, as always."

To his surprise, Lucia, instead of waiting her turn, clattered by in her heels, rudely brushing past the men in her haste. Haydn couldn't see her face, but he had noticed she was the only performer without a rose.

An omission on the part of the bride? Or a deliberate snub? God forbid, Lucia should have taken it as such. He had barely time to consider these questions when Luigi nudged him in the ribs.

"The singers are to be fed in the coffeehouse, Joseph. Does Signora Pacelli know?"

Whether she did or not, Haydn knew not. But she would need to be told.

"Signora Pacelli!" he called her name, about to impart the directive to her.

But Lucia barely deigned to turn. "I am unwell, Herr Kapellmeister," she said, throwing him a quick glance over her shoulder. "Whatever it is, can't it wait?"

So saying she stepped onto the grassy shore and flounced away. Haydn could hardly contain his astonishment. What could've caused the singer to so forget herself? He was about to remark upon it, but Luigi appeared to have noticed nothing amiss.

"The constant swaying of our platform must have made her bilious," the Konzertmeister confided to him with a light shrug. "I saw her sipping at her wine earlier."

He was still speaking when redheaded Narcissa Leon approached, a graceful hand lifting the trailing silks of her gown. Coming to a halt beside Haydn, she regarded Lucia's fast departing back with a disparaging sniff.

"You might consider letting me play Vespina this evening, Herr Kapellmeister," she suggested. "Our Signora Pacelli is barely capable of performing the role. Besides"—she turned her lovely green eyes toward him—"His Imperial Highness seemed most pleased with my singing this morning. As did his bride. Did you notice?"

"How could anyone fail to do so?" he asked with a pointed glance at the two roses she held close to her bosom.

Having her sing the madrigals had been an inspired idea. But Lucia was still his most accomplished performer. He was not ready to relinquish the main role in the opera buffa to a lesser singer.

"Then I may have the role?" Narcissa reached out her palm, resting it on his silk sleeve.

"Ah, but Fräulein Leon"—Haydn forced himself to smile as he raised his eyes toward her face—"you are better suited to Sandrina." It was the role Narcissa had been assigned. "She must be played by a woman younger than Vespina. Younger and prettier!" He emphasized the last word.

Of course, it wasn't entirely true. At barely twenty, Narcissa was certainly younger. But prettier she was not. Lucia's beauty was incomparable—so stunning, it dazzled the beholder. It had dazzled him once; although that unfortunate phase —he shuddered in remembrance—was thankfully over.

Lucia was rather more aware than any woman should be of the effect her beauty had, and she tended to take for granted the extreme devotion it inspired.

Haydn resolutely shook off these thoughts, pleased to see the praise he'd tossed Narcissa was having its intended effect. Her lips, which had begun to curl petulantly, now stretched into a satisfied smile.

But she was not about to let go so easily. Cocking her head quizzically at him, she persisted: "But who will play Vespina, then? If Signora Pacelli cannot, that is to say," she explained hastily as his eyebrows rose.

"Why shouldn't she be able to perform the role?" Luigi interjected before Haydn could respond.

He laid his violin in its case and looked up. "Her queasiness will pass, I'm certain. Besides, if a replacement is needed, we have a third soprano in Miss Lidia." Smiling to soften his remarks, Luigi added, "She would not make as good a Sandrina as you do, Fräulein."

Narcissa snorted delicately but offered no further argument. Head held high, she proceeded to step off the island.

Haydn and Luigi were about to follow suit themselves when they found their way barred by Paolo Pacelli.

<hr>

"Hurry!" Rosalie gasped. She pushed the trolley weighed down with heavy platters of food. It rolled forward an inch. Dear God, at this rate they'd never get to the coffeehouse.

Behind her, Greta huffed loudly. "It works better," she panted, "if you stand in front of the dratted thing and pull." With a huge grunt, she heaved her cart forward.

Rosalie moved toward the front of her cart. They should never have loaded these down as much as they had. But it was too late to think of that now. She clutched the wooden rail in the front and tugged hard. The trolley did roll forward a little more easily. But it was still a struggle.

"I don't understand why the singers can't eat in the Officers' Mess," Greta grumbled. "Wouldn't it be easier for the performers to bring themselves to the meal than for us to take the entire meal to them?"

Rosalie tugged the rail again; the cart moved forward. She looked behind her. It was still a ways to the orange grove and the coffeehouse. Trees lined the entire path, dappling the gray flagstones with a lacy pattern of sun and shade. Beautiful though it was, it would've been nicer to simply go from the kitchen to the Officers' Mess.

"But at least, we don't have to carry the food one tray at a time," she consoled her friend. "It was good of Karl to build these carts for us." How the court librettist had ever found the time to do so, Rosalie didn't know.

"There's that," Greta conceded with a grimace. "But," she grunted, "it would be so much better with two more carts and several more hands. Not that His Serene Highness cares. I doubt we'll get any more maids to help us."

"No, we won't." Rosalie shook her head. They were nearly there. She craned her neck. It didn't look like the singers had arrived yet. She turned back to her friend. "Frau Schwann says the Princess is trying to prevail on His Serene Highness to hire some more maids. But you know how he gets."

Greta nodded. "Spends lavishly on one thing, and then tightens his belt when it comes to every other necessity." She stopped, taking a kerchief out to wipe the beads of perspiration glistening on her brow. The path was shaded, but the noonday sun was still hot.

"Meanwhile, here we are working ourselves to the bone. *Principal Maids to the Musicians,* indeed." Greta snorted, reciting their titles. "We're slaving harder than we did when we were ordinary maids!"

"It's only for a few more days." Rosalie smiled. Greta tended to get snippy when His Serene Highness went on one of his economizing sprees. But it never lasted long. Things would most likely be back to normal once the palace guests left.

Certainly the singers would be able to return to the Officers' Mess.

The opera singers had just started trooping into the coffeehouse when she and Greta finally wheeled the food in. Waiting footmen helped to carry the heavy platters of food from the cart onto the tables.

Standing by the cart, Rosalie took in her surroundings. She liked the coffeehouse. The walls were papered in blue. The round tables that were usually scattered around the checkered tile floor had been moved out of the way. But the fan-back chairs with yellow upholstered seats remained, lined on either side of long trestle tables.

Vases filled with yellow roses stood at intervals along each table.

She was just admiring the blue-and-gold porcelain stove by the marble countertop when Greta nudged her in the ribs.

"Look!" her friend hissed, pointing to a footman who stepped in bearing a huge bouquet in his arms. "Flowers for Signora Pacelli. She must've outdone herself this morning."

"I wonder where she is." Rosalie surveyed her surroundings.

"Still at the lake, I suppose," Greta replied. "Fräulein Leon isn't back, either."

"I see the Archduke still sees fit to console our prima donna," a male voice beside them remarked.

Startled, Rosalie's head pivoted in unison with Greta's to the right. Herr Trattner, the newspaperman from Vienna! She glanced at Greta, and they made wry faces at each other.

Herr Trattner looked like a little, bespectacled rat, and like a rat was always trolling for dirt. Rosalie wanted to ignore him, but Greta took the bait.

She poked her blond curls forward. "Why would Signora Pacelli need to be consoled?"

Herr Trattner's beady eyes turned their way, his head tilting to one side as he regarded them.

"She didn't sing a note this morning, didn't you know?"

"What? That's impossible!" Greta's eyes sought Rosalie's. "Everyone knows Signora Pacelli is the best singer Herr Haydn has. She was supposed to sing the madrigals."

"Ah!" Herr Trattner's head snapped up. "A sudden, inexplicable decision, then?"

He licked his lips, wrote something down in his little leather notebook, and then made his way toward the footman.

"What was he talking about?" Greta stared after the newspaperman, puzzled.

Rosalie shrugged. "He's probably just fishing for gossip." But curiosity led her to follow the man toward the footman. Greta trailed after her.

Chapter Six

THEY neared the footman just in time to hear him say, "The flowers are for Fräulein Leon."

"Aha!" Herr Trattner licked his lips again. "Her star seems to be on the rise. Inexplicably so, I would say."

Rosalie could hardly believe her ears. She looked at Greta who was gaping aghast at the footman.

"That doesn't make any sense. Are you sure?" Leaning close to Rosalie, she whispered, "For all one knows, the fellow can't read."

"I can most certainly read," the footman declared indignantly. He turned the bouquet around, revealing the small white, gold-fringed card attached to it. "See here! It's got Fräulein Leon's name written on it. His Imperial Highness distinctly asked that these flowers be delivered to her."

Rosalie and Greta stared at each other. That had never happened before. It was Signora Pacelli who received all the flowers and the compliments. She was the star singer. How had she come to lose her position of favor?

<hr>

"Herr Kapellmeister!" Paolo—with Miss Lidia at his side and Fiore behind him—shook his fist furiously at Haydn.

He nearly succeeded in punching Haydn in the nose. But the Kapellmeister managed to step adroitly back, and so avoided the blow.

He caught Luigi's eye. What had caused this unexpected outburst? It was loud enough to attract the curious gazes of the few villagers who still remained on the lake bank. The old violinist would have to be calmed down.

His English soprano was clearly incapable of containing the man. And Fiore—Paolo's nephew—lacked the presence of mind to do much. Why was Fiore even here?

Was he not needed in the opera house—to fetch and carry, see to props and sets, and the myriad other things expected of a stage assistant? But there would be time enough to admonish the boy later.

Paolo was without his cane, and the effort of gesticulating was making him totter. Miss Lidia tightened her hold on his arm in an attempt to steady him, but the old violinist shrugged her off irascibly.

"Tut, tut, woman! Quit your fussing. Have you no husband to attend to?"

It was a cruel remark, intentionally barbed, and the spasm of pain that flickered briefly across the plain Englishwoman's face was unmistakable. But Paolo neither saw nor cared.

"What were you thinking not letting Lucia sing her solos?" he continued his tirade. "Now she has gone off in a huff, and who can blame her."

The vexation on the old violinist's face intensified as he swiveled his head in search of his wife.

Haydn followed his gaze. Lucia was nowhere to be seen, but he was beginning to divine the cause of Paolo's frustration, and Miss Lidia confirmed it with her words.

"It's just that Lucia rushed away so quickly," she said, her voice breathless—from the strain of constraining Paolo—and apologetic. "Without so much as a glance or smile our way."

Haydn exchanged another glance with Luigi, who shrugged lightly and lifted his eyebrows. "Gold may procure you a wife," his Konzertmeister had once remarked about Paolo—a man whose treatises on music had earned him substantial royalties. "But winning her love is another matter."

With a sympathetic smile, Haydn turned back to the wizened, irate man glaring at him. "She meant no offense, Paolo. It was a sudden indisposition that caused her to hurry away."

"Indisposition!" Paolo seemed nonplussed as though Haydn had spoken in a foreign tongue. "What indisposition?"

"She has taken ill," Haydn said, aware he was merely repeating himself.

"It is nothing," Luigi hastened to add. Any murmur of illness would only sow further discontent among the musicians—already disenchanted with their overlong stay in Eszterháza. "The constant motion of our island made her uneasy. It will pass soon enough, I am sure."

But Paolo frowned. "Why should the motion of the platform cause her any uneasiness? She is long used to it. We have sailed along the Danube, and she's accustomed to standing and singing in the gondolas that travel along the canals of Venice. A platform on a little pond like this"—he gestured disparagingly at the Neuseidlersee—"why should it make her sick?"

"She didn't look particularly sick to me." Fiore now shoved his oar into the conversation. Haydn gazed at him in disfavor. "No doubt, she wanted to pursue the Archduke."

"And why would she wish to do that, young man?" Haydn was about to reiterate Lucia's own words before she bolted off, but was interrupted.

"Oh, be quiet, boy!" Paolo muttered irritably. "What do you know of the matter?"

But Fiore was deaf to his uncle's words. "Tante Lucia was hoping to win a position for herself in Milan with the Archduke."

The words bubbled out of the lad like water from a spring.

Paolo glared at his nephew, his lips tightening in displeasure. But Fiore's attention was on the Kapellmeister—his features bright and keen as though expecting a reward.

"Was she indeed?" Haydn's eyes narrowed, shifting toward the older man.

But Paolo refused to meet his gaze. Mortified, was he? Well, so he should be?

Haydn had fought hard for Lucia's contract—making sure both Paolo and Fiore were hired as well. And now she was looking to move on—at the slightest hint of a better opportunity? Although it was unlikely to be better; the Archduke—as Governor of Milan—could hardly command more wealth than His Serene Highness, one of the wealthiest noblemen in the Empire.

If nothing else, his parsimonious oldest brother would seek to curb any expenditure the Archduke wished to make on maintaining an orchestra and singing troupe. Haydn had enough experience with the Emperor to know His Imperial Majesty considered these things to be frivolities—neither essential nor useful in any royal court.

"The madrigals, had she been able to sing them, would've closed the deal. It's what we were hoping for, isn't that so, Onkel Paolo?" Fiore confided blithely.

"I see." Haydn stared grim-faced at Paolo. Lucia's ingratitude galled him. Small wonder, the Archduke's enthusiasm for her had waned. Her insistent begging must have put him off. "Why was I not informed of this matter?"

"She was not hoping for anything." Paolo's cheeks were red and he looked miffed. "But if an offer is made . . ." he allowed his voice to trail off.

"Then I trust the terms of her contract will be acceptable to whoever makes it," Luigi said with a smile. It would be nearly two years before Lucia's contract expired. To leave at this point would mean returning the generous salary paid to her as well as her husband for the time they'd been employed with the Esterházy family.

The sum owed—including as it did firewood, wine, and other provisions—was substantial enough for any potential employer to balk at making an offer.

Eager to leave, Haydn glanced pointedly at his timepiece. Luigi caught his drift.

"We have business to attend to, Paolo." He maneuvered himself onto the bank.

"And Fiore"—Luigi turned to the young man—"hadn't you best be getting back to your duties? I doubt either Karl or Herr Porta can spare you."

"You don't suppose it was Fräulein Leon who wrote that note you found, do you?" Greta whispered into Rosalie's ear as they returned to their position by the serving table.

"I suppose it could be." Rosalie looked over her shoulders. Herr Trattner was still quizzing the footman. The three sopranos were nowhere to be seen. "It would account for the sudden change in her fortunes."

Absentmindedly, she patted her apron pocket. The note was still there.

In the press of their duties, she'd all but forgotten it. And that afternoon when they'd seen the Archduke strolling back with his bride, head bent, listening intently to her words, it had seemed impossible that anything could shake His Imperial Highness's world. He'd looked so calm and untroubled.

Herr Trattner must've squeezed as much gossip as he could out of the footman, for he was looking around the coffeehouse eagerly. Rosalie could've sworn his nose was quivering as his eyes darted around. He looked like a bloodhound sniffing the air for prey.

His eyes alighted upon Master Johann who had just entered the room, and off he went.

Rosalie leaned toward Greta. "Didn't Karl's cousin—what's his name, the police guard?"

"Franz?" Greta offered.

Rosalie nodded. "Yes, Franz. Didn't he say something about newspapermen putting about false rumors in the hopes of extracting money from wealthy noblemen?"

"You think it was Herr Trattner threatening His Imperial Highness?" Greta's voice rose, her gaze weaving around the room toward the little man who—in his shirtsleeves now with his jacket slung over his shoulder—had just waylaid Master Johann. "I doubt he'd have the gumption to try any such thing. Not that I'd put it past him. But the Empress would skin him alive if she found out."

That was true enough.

"No," Greta continued, "if you ask me, it's more likely to be Fräulein Leon. I'll wager all I've got it was a woman writing the note."

⁂

The appetizing aroma of roasted pheasant stuffed with savory onions and raisins filled Haydn's nostrils as he and Luigi stepped into the Officers' Mess. The prospect of sitting down to the midday meal lifted his spirits.

He'd broken his fast so early and so hurriedly, his belly felt as empty as it had countless years ago when he'd been an impoverished lad scraping by in Vienna.

He and Luigi were headed toward the serving table laden with plates and chafing dishes when like a wily snake the Estates Director inserted himself in their path.

"A word, if you will, Herr Kapellmeister."

Luigi had stopped as well, his violin tucked under his arm.

"Can it not wait until the Kapellmeister has eaten?" he asked Rahier.

The Estates Director smiled icily. "I would not advise expecting His Serene Highness to wait." Turning to Haydn, he continued, "His Serene Highness ordered you be summoned into his presence immediately." Rahier's cold blue eyes glanced pointedly at the clock. "That was a full fifteen minutes ago, Herr Kapellmeister."

Haydn chose to ignore the not overly subtle insinuation that he was late to the midday meal. Rahier was a stickler for such things, never taking into account the numerous responsibilities that had to be discharged before Haydn himself could sit down to eat.

"It will be about the evening's performance, I suppose," he surmised, turning to Luigi. What else could it be? The morning's entertainment had gone well enough.

Rahier's smile widened.

"Ah, Herr Kapellmeister. I only wish it were as simple as that."

Haydn turned to him but deliberately kept his features blank. He had no intention of letting the man get a rise out of him. But Luigi, easily impatient, couldn't keep himself from reacting.

"It is about something else, then?" Luigi let his annoyance show. "And we are to believe that you know what it is?"

Rahier coolly inspected the gold cuff of his dark blue jacket, flicking an imaginary speck of dust off it.

"As a matter of fact, I do, Herr Tomasini." He raised his head, his lips twitching into a smirk. "The Grand Duke was present when His Serene Highness called for me. I found His Grace anxiously pacing the Prince's apartment. The Archduke's behavior is apparently no small cause for concern."

Haydn regarded the Estates Director suspiciously. Was Rahier lying? It would not be unlike him to put a malicious spin upon the truth. Nevertheless, a nervous coil of apprehension stirred in the pit of his stomach.

Rahier's gaze swiveled from Luigi's irate features toward Haydn. "Why the Emperor thought fit to put the young man under your care, I do not pretend to understand. But it would seem your feeble efforts to rein in His Imperial Highness have come to naught."

The stirring in the pit of Haydn's stomach intensified. Dear Lord, what had the Archduke done now? Had he already made his escape—barely hours after his bride's arrival? If he had—without Haydn so much as suspecting it . . .

The thought made Haydn shudder.

He faced Luigi grimly. "I had better see what the trouble is."

If it was truly about the Archduke, it did not bode well.

Chapter Seven

As Haydn followed the footman Rahier had hailed, the memory of the note that the Archduke had so carelessly dropped that morning surfaced into his mind.

He ought to have insisted upon inspecting it. Why hadn't he? The Emperor would surely take him to task over it—as would Empress Maria Theresa, the Emperor's co-regent and mother.

Haydn's gut twisted as his mind called up an image of the ageing Empress —a portly matron with a commanding presence, still beautiful despite her girth and still majestic. She had been gracious and warm toward Haydn, as though he were a close friend.

But for all that, Her Majesty expected nothing short of complete obedience. Not even a blind man could have missed the expectation, it had been made so plain.

Would she have to be informed of this latest turn of events? The Empress had tasked Haydn with keeping her informed of every aspect of the Archduke's meeting with his bride. It was unlikely anyone knew of his assignment.

"I require complete honesty, Haydn," Her Majesty had said. "But I also rely upon your utmost discretion." She had reached out to lightly touch his palm. "And I know I can count upon it, my dear Haydn."

Charged thus by Her Majesty, Haydn had barely hinted at the truth to Luigi and his younger brother, Johann. Certainly, there'd been no question of letting Maria Anna know. One might as well publish the news in the *Wienerisches Diarium*.

But Haydn had also received the distinct impression that Her Majesty wished to keep Prince Nikolaus in the dark as well. That meant he could expect no help—or advice—from His Serene Highness on this thorny situation. It was left to him to tackle it, unaided.

He gripped his hands tightly to his sides, willing himself not to be daunted by the prospect. If only there were a way of getting his hands on the letter the Archduke had discarded.

Briskly following the footman, he racked his brains.

———

The coffeehouse was fast filling up. Performers took their seats. Footman hurried by, bearing the huge platters of roast pheasant, gravy, and roasted vegetables the maids had carted in.

Rosalie waited until the throng moved away before responding to Greta's surmise about the note. Had a woman written the note?

"A woman wronged, maybe." She frowned pensively. "Fräulein Leon seems anything but."

The soprano swept into the room just then. A small smile played about her lips. It widened when Herr Trattner approached her, pen and notebook in hand.

"Oh, just look at her!" Greta muttered. "Did you ever see such a smug smile? She looks like the cat that got the cream. Well, she may have wrangled Signora Pacelli's madrigals from her, but she'd better not expect to get Vespina's part in the opera. It would ruin the performance completely." She shook her head. "Karl should put his foot down, if it comes to that."

"Put my foot down for what, my little dumpling?" A burly, red-haired man with a bushy beard pulled Greta into his arms and gave her a resounding kiss on her lips.

"Oh, nothing." Greta glanced over Karl's shoulder, shaking her head imperceptibly at Rosalie.

Standing behind Karl, Rosalie bobbed her head. Karl Elias Schulze, the court librettist, was burdened enough without needing any further worries heaped upon his head.

But Karl was not to be so easily dismissed. "But what were you talking about, my sweet?"

"Oh, it was the silliest thing," Greta said, still in Karl's arms, "Herr Trattner was saying Fräulein Leon sang so well this morning, she must expect to play the lead tonight?

"Why would she expect any such thing?" Pulling Greta closer to him, Karl's gaze scoured the room. "You two haven't seen Fiore anywhere, have you? I haven't seen hide nor hair of him since I sent him out to the inn."

Greta shook her head, exasperated. "He's never where he should be, is he? He didn't go to the inn, I can tell you that. Gerhard had to deliver the wine himself."

Karl nodded. "I know. Albert brought it back."

"At least Albert makes himself useful, for all that he's the Estates Director's nephew," Rosalie murmured. "It's more than you can say for Signora Pacelli's relatives."

"I don't see her either." Karl looked around, worried. "There's a final rehearsal at two. Without Fiore to handle the props and Signora Pacelli to play Vespina—" He shuddered.

"But, there's Miss Lidia." He tipped his head in the direction of the door. "Maybe, she'll know where they are."

With one last kiss and hug, Karl pulled away from Greta's arms.

⸻◦◦◦⸻

"Ah, there you are, Haydn." Prince Nikolaus gestured expansively, waving the Kapellmeister into the large covered terrace beyond the Sala Terrena. The English garden was visible through the open double glass doors —stretching into the distance in a glorious, lush vista.

Haydn trod slowly forward, careful not to allow his heels to clatter on the fine Carrara marble floor. The Grand Duke seemed to have no such concern, pacing back and forth—just as Rahier had reported. From time to time, His Grace poked his head into a tent-like contraption set up on the large coffee table in the middle of the room.

What His Grace saw in there and why it was causing him such consternation, Haydn couldn't fathom.

But not wishing to seem rude, he tore his gaze away, returning his attention to his employer.

"A matter of some urgency has come up, Haydn." His Serene Highness dismissed the footman who'd led Haydn in with a quick flick of his fingers. "It requires your immediate attention."

"Indeed." Haydn took the seat His Serene Highness offered him. "It concerns the Archduke, I gather," he said when he'd seated himself.

The Grand Duke immediately withdrew his head from the dark tent, his mouth opening, about to speak when the Prince cleared his throat and frowned. His Serene Highness's eyes, Haydn noted with some surprise, slid toward the corner of the terrace.

Haydn's own gaze followed, colliding unpleasantly with Fiore's slim figure draped against a pillar. The boy fortunately straightened up when he found himself the object of their scrutiny.

What was he doing here?

"Herr Kapellmeister." The lad smiled weakly at him, as though nothing were amiss.

Haydn allowed a single eyebrow to rise, quite fed up with the boy. How often did one have to issue the same instructions for the lad to obey?

"Shouldn't you be at the opera house?" he demanded.

"He is here at my express command, Haydn," the Prince informed him.

Haydn turned back toward his employer and bowed his head, acknowledging the remark. But why had Fiore been called? What did his presence here have to do with the Archduke? He was considering how best to ascertain these details when Fiore spoke up.

"His Serene Highness needed the camera obscura set up," he said, pointing toward the tent-like contraption.

"*Ach so!*" The boy did have considerable technical ability. It was one of the reasons Haydn had readily agreed to Lucia's stipulation that Fiore be hired in some capacity or other along with Paolo and herself. Fiore had been expected to take over the technical aspects of opera production, relieving Karl, a former stagehand, of those duties.

The problem, of course, was that the lad very rarely chose to apply himself.

"And a most excellent job you did of it, my man." The Grand Duke extended his arm, his fingers holding out a gold coin. "But you may leave us now." His Grace turned toward the Prince—who sat wide-legged, his form filling the capacious white-and-gold chair by the coffee table. "May he not, Esterházy?"

To Haydn's astonishment, the Prince had a gold gulden for Fiore as well. "A small gift for your observations."

Fiore's observations? What observations had the boy seen fit to make, Haydn wondered.

"Well, I knew everyone was looking for Tante Lucia," Fiore babbled. "How could I not utter a word when I saw her—just as I expected"—Fiore looked eagerly at Haydn—"with the Archduke?"

Dear Lord! The memory of their earlier conversation erupted uneasily into Haydn's mind—along with the startling claim Fiore had made about Lucia. Surely, the boy hadn't confided those details to the Prince as well.

"What else did you say?" The question was out of Haydn's mouth before he could stop himself.

"Only that Tante Lucia is frequently to be seen in the Archduke's company." Fiore regarded the Kapellmeister, his brown eyes staring, wide and innocent.

"And that was quite enough, Haydn," the Grand Duke said after he'd firmly ushered the lad out of the terrace. "It will not do. Her pursuit of him simply will not do."

Had the Archduke complained of Lucia's incessant demands for a position at his court? Haydn was still struggling to understand the situation when His Serene Highness hurled another firecracker his way.

"She must be dismissed, Haydn. Instantly."

"*Dismissed*?" Haydn faltered. "But what of the opera?"

It opened that very evening. And without Lucia, it would surely fail.

Chapter Eight

Haydn's mind was still reeling when he finally left the terrace. It was not Lucia's pursuit of a better position that had caused his employer and the Grand Duke such consternation. It was—what seemed to be—her romantic pursuit of the Archduke himself that was causing such uneasiness.

"See for yourself, Haydn." The Grand Duke had jabbed a finger in the direction of the camera obscura.

Haydn had dutifully poked his head through the black tent, scrutinizing the upside-down image that appeared upon the thin sheet of paper within. He had seen Lucia place her palm beseechingly upon the Archduke's sleeve.

The gesture was over-familiar, and although the Archduke had summarily rejected it, turning angrily away from her, Lucia's intimate gesture hinted at a friendship that was closer and warmer than was entirely appropriate.

What were they conversing about? All signs of Lucia's illness had dissipated. Had she feigned her sickness? Haydn withdrew his head only to meet his employer's disapproving features.

"Most unseemly. Distressingly so! What if the Duke of Modena had seen such behavior?" His Serene Highness asked.

It would be like the pot calling the kettle black, Haydn thought, but he refrained from pointing that out.

"Or the Duke's daughter," the Grand Duke had added grimly.

They had both apparently been invited to view the camera obscura. Fortunately, they had both declined, the Duke pleading exhaustion, his daughter wanting to attend to her devotions.

Haydn had managed to stay Lucia's dismissal, winning a temporary reprieve until the festivities were over and their guests had departed. Neither the Grand Duke nor Prince Nikolaus had asked for any further investigation into the matter.

"There's no reason to burden the Emperor with this information," they had both agreed, exchanging a glance. "It is a minor wrinkle and can easily be ironed out."

But Haydn himself was determined to get to the bottom of the affair. If nothing else, to determine if the Empress should be told.

And to that end, it would be expedient, he thought as he strode down the hallway, to retrieve the note His Imperial Highness had discarded that morning. Had it been not from Vienna, but from Lucia instead?

Fortunately, there was a way to find out. If only he'd thought of it sooner.

The low rumbling of his stomach reminded Haydn he had yet to eat. Passing a wall clock, he slowed, his head swiveling to take in the time. It was too late to return to the Officers' Mess. But he could have something sent up to the Music Room. It would give him the opportunity to gather the information he required.

A footman crossed the hallway, bearing a huge platter. Haydn hailed him.

"Be sure to find either Rosalie or Greta," he instructed. It mattered not which one of them was sent up; Haydn had found them both reliable. Years ago, his father, a neighbor of the Szabós in Rohrau, had sought his influence in obtaining a position for their young daughter.

Haydn had never had occasion to regret obtaining Rosalie her position. As for Greta, Rosalie trusted her implicitly, and Haydn saw no reason to question her judgment.

He rounded a corner, grabbed hold of the banisters, about to sprint upstairs, when he heard his name.

"Herr Haydn! A moment of your time, if you will."

His hand still upon the newel post, Haydn swiveled his head. A short, dark-haired man scurried up to him. Franz Trattner! God in heaven, what piece of gossip was the man seeking to peddle now?

Trattner, the publisher and editor of the rumor-mongering *Gazette de Vienna*, came to a halt below the stairs. Panting from his exertions, he gazed up at Haydn, his dark eyes glinting behind his round eyeglasses.

"You are just the man I wish to see, Herr Haydn. A little bird tells me—"

"What bird?" Haydn demanded, his patience wearing thin. Was it Fiore, he worried, broadcasting far and wide the scene they had all just witnessed through the accursed camera obscura?

Trattner bared his lips in an amused smile. His teeth were small and even, albeit yellow like a wolf's fangs.

"Does it matter which one? They all sing the same song."

"Of course they do," Haydn said sourly. Trattner was notoriously reticent about the sources he relied upon. "And what might that song be?"

Once again he wondered why the Empress had seen fit to allow Trattner access to the upcoming nuptials. Would it not have been better to have had the more discreet *Wienerisches Diarium* convey the news to the public?

"Well." Trattner cocked his head to one side, his eyes fixed on Haydn's features, ready to grasp at the slightest change in his expression. "It would appear Signora Pacelli has lost favor with the Archduke."

"What?" The word was out of Haydn's mouth before he could stop himself. It was hardly what he was expecting to hear.

"It is not true, then?" Trattner's head was still cocked. He looked like a cocky sparrow, small, insignificant, and annoying.

Before Haydn could respond, Trattner posed another question.

"In that case, what was behind the sudden decision to give her madrigals to Fräulein Leon?"

How had Trattner known the decision had been a spur-of-the-moment thing? Haydn was still grappling with the question when Trattner continued: "The good Signora was seen to walk off in a huff. And her husband—"

Ach so! Haydn rolled his eyes. Paolo had been airing his complaints, he supposed.

"My decision wasn't quite as mysterious as you suppose, Herr Trattner. Signora Pacelli was indisposed—"

"Too sick to sing the lead tonight?"

"Not at all. Now if you'll excuse me."

Eager to be away, Haydn darted up the stairs. Still, it was better for Trattner to think that Lucia had lost the Archduke's favor than to suppose that she was enjoying rather too much of it.

He couldn't help wondering, however, about the Archduke's reaction earlier that morning. Had His Imperial Highness been feigning his disenchantment with the singer? Or had Lucia's aggressive pursuit put him off?

What connection was there between the Archduke and his prima donna? That there was something had been all too plain.

⚬⚬⚬

The Music Room was at the other end of the wide carpeted landing. Haydn was about to enter it when he heard a commotion nearby. It appeared to be coming from the hallway that ran past the Music Room.

He cocked his head, straining his ears. Was that Lucia? Who was she screaming at?

He walked down the short corridor that led to the double doors of the library. Snatches of the altercation wafted toward his ears.

". . . running around with the Archduke . . . I am sick to death . . . vile accusations . . ."

It was unmistakably Lucia's voice, and judging by her words, it was Paolo who was the target of her wrath. The poor fellow must have discovered the unsavory truth and decided to confront his wife.

Haydn didn't blame the man; nevertheless the palace was no place for such wrangling. Determined to put a stop to their clanging, he strode toward the library and hammered his fist hard on the double doors.

"Signora Pacelli? It is I, Herr Haydn."

He had already tried the handle. The doors were locked.

He tried again, to no avail.

"Open the door, if you please."

The noise within immediately subsided. Haydn thought he heard a door banging shut. Then Lucia opened the door.

She brushed back her dark disheveled hair and smoothed down the flower-embroidered yellow skirt of her shepherdess's garb.

"All is well, I trust." Haydn entered the room, his eyes darting toward the door that led to the backstairs and out to the garden. He turned back to her. "Was Paolo in here?"

Lucia sighed. "It wasn't anything you need be troubled by, Joseph. I apologize for the noise." She laughed nervously. "We must have been making quite the racket for you to have heard us."

She reached out to touch his arm. Quietly, Haydn shook her hand off. He could not allow her to exert any influence over him.

"Signora Pacelli—?"

"Joseph," Lucia pleaded, resting her palm upon his chest, "there's no one here but the two of us. Surely, there's—"

"Your pursuit of the Archduke must stop. It is most unbecoming. The young man is about to be wed. To run after him like a deer panting—"

"Oh, for heaven's sake, Joseph, not you, too!" Lucia's eyes flashed dangerously, and she withdrew her hand from his breast. "I am tired of these idiotic insinuations, these insane jealousies." She stormed away to the window, her bosom heaving.

Haydn's own temper was swelling as well.

"Do you deny your pursuit of His Imperial Highness?" He followed her to the window, his nostrils flaring. Had he not seen her with his own eyes? Had not their employer and the Archduke's brother seen her as well?

He made a point of reciting these facts to her.

"Your behavior is causing such a scandal, His Serene Highness insists you be dismissed."

Lucia spun around at that.

"But Joseph—"

Haydn had borne enough. Had the woman no shame?

"You will address me as Herr Haydn or Herr Kapellmeister, if you please."

Lucia looked stunned. Her eyes widened and she drew back as though stung. "You can hardly deny what there is between us. It may be in the past, but—?"

Haydn held up his hand. "You are mistaken, Signora Pacelli. There was never anything between us."

Other than a near meeting of the lips, he thought wryly.

Fortunately, anything more had been prevented by Maria Anna unexpectedly barging in upon them at the Burgtheater.

The incident had served to quickly bring him back to his senses, although it had destroyed the delicate trust between himself and his wife. Since then, there'd been a coldness in Maria Anna's manner toward him that Haydn feared nothing would thaw.

Lucia laughed, a shrill sound that grated on Haydn's nerves.

"What are you afraid of, Herr Kapellmeister? Your wife?" Lucia swiveled her head all around, taking in the walls lined with bookshelves, the stove, and armchairs. "She isn't here."

"Does she need to be?" Haydn asked. For some reason, Maria Anna had fostered a close friendship with Lucia.

Why, he wondered yet again. What could his wife possibly want with Lucia?

He returned to the matter at hand. "Your pursuit of the Archduke must cease, Signora Pacelli. I care not whether it's because you're striving for a position in Milan—in breach of your contract, I might add—or whether you have developed feelings for the young man."

"Lucia held her head high. "Paolo is mistaken. I have no interest in leaving my position here. As for the Archduke, I may have flirted with His Imperial Highness. But I am certainly not in love with him." She sniffed. "The Archduke may be old enough to father a child, but he isn't old enough to satisfy a woman in her prime."

The Archduke may be old enough to father a child!

"How—?" Haydn stammered, but Lucia had already left the room.

The child the Archduke had fathered upon his paramour was a closely guarded secret. How had Lucia discovered it?

Chapter Nine

THAT evening, Haydn stood in the orchestra pit behind his harpsichord and tugged anxiously at his red jacket. The note Rosalie had given him was in his coat pocket. Feeling it rustle beneath his fingers, he cursed himself for not having the courage to dismiss his prima donna.

To think she'd been attempting to extort money from the Archduke—a guest at the palace, a member of the imperial household, no less. And under his very nose at that!

Clearly, Lucia's audacity knew no bounds.

He looked out over the auditorium, which—dazzling in its rich colors of red, gold, and green—was fast filling up. Paolo, Lucia's husband, wore the same livery of red and green as the rest of Haydn's musicians.

Seeing his thin figure rising proudly erect next to Maria Anna, Haydn's lips puckered in distaste. Was the aged violinist aware of his wife's disgraceful behavior? Had he put her up to it? Or was he merely content to turn a blind eye to her shenanigans?

God in heaven, Haydn thought, he ought to have dismissed Lucia the moment he'd heard the news.

He fingered the note again. Rosalie had delicately suggested Narcissa or even Trattner as its author. But Haydn had dismissed these possibilities. It was clear who had penned the note.

Who else could it be but Lucia? She was the only person who appeared to know the Archduke's carefully concealed secret.

"Brother!" Johann nudged him, startling Haydn out of his musings. "The orchestra awaits your signal," he whispered, pointing to where Luigi sat with his violin poised under his chin, looking expectantly back at them.

Obediently, Haydn struck the middle C on his harpsichord. It was followed immediately by the discordant clamor of violins, cellos, and basses striving to find the note he'd struck. Then the din faded, replaced by the muted sounds of machinery being wheeled onto the stage, concealed behind the vast red-and-gold curtain.

The sound of vocalists singing scales and warming up their voices could be heard as well, with Lucia's lovely soprano joining that of her colleagues.

"She sounds well enough, God be praised!" Johann murmured. Haydn had mentioned her sickness to his brother and his decision to let Narcissa sing the madrigals.

"I knew there was a good reason for your choice, brother," Johann had said. "But you should've heard the mountain Herr Trattner sought to fashion out of that particular molehill. And I fear Narcissa was all too happy to encourage the man."

The morning's events must've cured Lucia of any desire to feign a false illness, Haydn mused cynically. He would've gladly let Narcissa or Lidia take her role.

"And I doubt it would've been quite the unmitigated disaster we've feared," he muttered to himself. "Besides, it may come to that, in any case."

He must have spoken aloud, for Johann turned sharply toward him.

"What!" Johann's outburst caused the other orchestra members to look curiously their way. Aware of their gazes, he lowered his voice, "Why, brother? Why should Lucia need to be replaced?"

Haydn sighed. He had not mentioned His Serene Highness's demand that Lucia be dismissed—or his own conviction that she'd ceased to merit a position in the Esterházy opera troupe.

He succinctly explained the facts to his brother.

"Is it possible, you're mistaken?" Johann stared at him, his gray eyes wide with concern.

"How could I be? Her own words prove it. Not to mention the note Rosalie found in His Imperial Highness's bedchamber." Haydn shook his head gravely. "Why he chose not to confide the matter to me, I cannot understand."

"But"—Johann's brow furrowed—"how could she have gotten wind of the Archduke's peccadillo? The news is surely not freely broadcast in Vienna."

"I know not. I've wondered at the source of her information, myself. No doubt, His Imperial Highness foolishly took her into his confidence." While in his cups, most likely, Haydn added to himself.

"But, brother, if you dismiss her, you may give her further cause for mischief." Johann leaned closer. "Especially with Herr Trattner around. Not to mention, having to reveal her behavior to His Serene Highness?"

The words gave Haydn pause. He had not considered that aspect of the matter. His encounter with Trattner had made it all too apparent that the reporter, like an avaricious jackdaw, was on the hunt for juicy tidbits and would eagerly swallow any news Lucia fed him.

He had no desire to expose Lucia to the Prince, either. It would only highlight his own inability to properly appraise the character of those he chose to hire.

"But to allow her to stay—" he protested.

"Would let you keep a closer watch on her," his brother said firmly.

Haydn was about to reluctantly agree when Lucia herself emerged—stunningly beautiful in a gorgeous blue gown, but white-faced and clutching her stomach. She stumbled down toward the pit.

"Master Johann!" Ignoring Haydn, she plucked at Johann's sleeve, her large blue eyes wandering out into the auditorium. "Where is Frau Haydn? I find myself in need of her."

Much to his ire, Haydn saw Maria Anna rise to her feet and rush over.

"Lucia, my dear!" Maria Anna, a short, slender woman, bent anxiously toward the taller soprano. "Does your stomach bother you?"

Lucia smiled—a brave stretching of the lips that seemed more than ever like an act. "It's nothing that some of your tea won't heal, my dear Frau Haydn."

"How odd that your pains should come and go, willy-nilly," Haydn couldn't help remarking.

But Maria Anna responded before Lucia could. "Of course, they come and go, husband. That is the nature of her condition. I shall need hot water for the tea."

Why was she such a stalwart supporter of the woman who'd nearly become her rival? The question made Haydn uneasy. And why was Lucia so ready to turn to a woman whom she—Haydn was almost certain of this—clearly despised?

"There should be hot water in the coffeehouse." Johann jerked his head behind him. The place was conveniently situated across from the French garden, next to the marionette theater. "Should I escort you?"

"No!" The word came out more sharply than Haydn intended.

"Let Fiore do it," he amended hastily, seeing Maria Anna frown at him while Johann's eyes widened in surprise. "I need Johann with me."

Maria Anna nodded curtly and waited for the lad, her arm supporting Lucia's waist. That neither he himself nor Johann could be spared at this time—barely thirty minutes before the opening of the opera—fortunately needed no further explanation

"Dear Lord, she's taken ill again!" Greta's voice reflected the dismay Rosalie felt at the sight of Signora Pacelli clutching her stomach.

Like Greta, she craned her head forward, desperate to see what was going on.

Frau Haydn had her arms around the prima donna's waist. Shortly after, Fiore emerged from behind the stage curtain.

Standing on either side of Signora Pacelli, he and Frau Haydn helped her out of the auditorium.

"Oh, don't tell me they'll give Fräulein Leon the role now!" Greta turned anxiously toward her. "You did tell Herr Haydn she might've written that vile message, didn't you?"

"I did." Rosalie nodded. "But I'm not sure he believed me."

The Kapellmeister had looked thunderstruck as he cast his eye over the words scrawled on the thin, crumpled sheet of pale blue paper. He had turned it over, looking this way and that, when Rosalie had pointed out that the paper used was remarkably similar to the ones the maids and the musicians habitually used.

But when she'd mentioned the possibility of Fräulein Leon writing the note, he'd dismissed the suggestion.

"Narcissa's only fault is her overweening ambition." He'd shaken his head. "No, I doubt she had anything to do with this."

"He gives her too much credit," Greta now said. She glanced back at the stage. "I wouldn't put it past her to have slipped something into Signora Pacelli's coffee or wine."

Greta sat back, crossed her arms, and lifted her chin adamantly.

"That must be what's making her sick."

But Rosalie shook her head, convinced Greta was letting her imagination run away with her. Greta did tend to do that. But, stalwartly loyal, Rosalie would never say it out loud.

"It won't get her anywhere, if she has," she pointed out. "Herr Haydn says Miss Lidia will play the role, if it comes to that."

It was quite by chance, the Kapellmeister had said more to himself than to her, *that Fräulein Leon had sung the madrigals that morning*. Then he'd pored over the note, and had murmured the words she'd repeated to Greta. *If it comes to that, Lidia can play the role.*

"If Signora Pacelli falls sick again?" Rosalie had asked, mystified.

"Yes." The Kapellmeister had absently nodded, barely aware of her presence.

Greta snorted. "Well, you and I and Herr Haydn may know it won't get her anywhere. But does Fräulein Leon?" She shook her head. "Mark my words, she's behind this."

She leaned in toward Rosalie. "It's not the first time, Signora Pacelli has taken ill, mind you. Karl told me just this afternoon that she's talked about feeling queasy more than once. Almost always after a rehearsal."

Rosalie frowned. "I didn't know that." She turned to face Greta. "Has Karl spoken to Herr Haydn about this?"

Greta lifted her hands in a shrug. "It's happened more than once in Herr Haydn's presence. Of course, he may not have realized there could be foul play at work. Why, it only just occurred to me."

Rosalie's frown deepened. It had been bad enough that someone was trying to extort money from the Archduke. And now, it looked like Fräulein Leon was trying to get rid of her rival.

If Herr Haydn had to dismiss Fräulein Leon and if Signora Pacelli was too ill to perform, there'd be no opera. She almost voiced the thought out loud, but bit her tongue just in time.

She knew just how much the opera and its performance meant to both Karl and Greta. Would to God, nothing would spoil this moment.

Fortunately, Signora Pacelli returned just then, looking, Rosalie was glad to see, in much better spirits. She nudged her friend. "Look! She's back."

"Oh, thank heavens!" Greta's blue eyes brightened.

Moments later, the Prince and his guests entered the opera house and Herr Haydn raised his hand and struck the first note.

The opera had begun.

Chapter Ten

Haydn's fingers flew over the keyboard. The first act had gone remarkably well. That was no surprise given the energetic pace of the music and Karl's deft hand with comedy.

But it was Lucia's incomparable acting—Haydn was forced to grudgingly admit—that was taking Eszterháza by storm. A chorus of "Bravas!" greeted her every entrance—the loudest coming from Chiara, the Duke of Modena's mistress.

Haydn had feared Chiara's vociferous approbation might cause the bride to reserve her own approval. But even Maria D'Este's solemn features had softened at Lucia's performance, the telltale twitching at the corner of her mouth widening before long into a delighted smile.

That, Haydn supposed, was because Lucia played a jilted woman attempting to win her errant lover back. It was the sort of thing Maria D'Este— daughter of a woman cruelly forsaken—could surely sympathize with.

If only the soprano's morals were on par with her singing and acting talents, the Kapellmeister thought. Now more than ever, he was loath to dismiss Lucia. His Serene Highness would no doubt wish the opera to be performed again, and Lidia, though a capable singer, was hardly up to the task.

He threw a quick glance over his shoulder. Only the Archduke appeared to be unaffected by the prima donna, his warmest applause reserved for everyone but her.

Haydn sighed, looking back up at the stage where Lucia, disguised as an elderly woman, was attempting to sway the old peasant Filippo's opinion against the wealthy suitor he'd chosen for his daughter.

Haydn watched her closely. There was no sign of the ill-health she'd complained of earlier. Had she feigned her illness? To what end? To gain his sympathy?

Just then Lucia turned toward the audience, winking broadly as she sang her lies to Filippo. An uproarious cheer immediately greeted the action, reverberating from the farthest rafters of the roof. Naturally, the audience recognized her character, Vespina, despite her disguise.

That Filippo was oblivious to her true identity made the situation all the more hilarious.

But as Haydn observed her, Lucia clutched her stomach and groaned, still complaining about the wretched Nencio—Vespina's lover—who had supposedly abandoned her fictitious daughter.

Perplexed, Haydn felt his brow furrowing.

Had the pain that ailed her earlier in the evening returned? Or were the actions simply the antics of her character—disguised as an old crone, attempting to outwit a tyrannical old father standing in the way of young love?

Even the audience seemed not to know—unsure whether to laugh or not. Haydn hoped it was nothing more than Lucia exaggerating her role and exploiting its comic effect.

Nevertheless, his heart clenched in fear. Beads of perspiration had gathered like pearls on Lucia's forehead and her features seemed pale and clammy.

Dear God, this was no act. Lucia was clearly ill.

Would to God, she could persist until the curtain dropped.

⁂

"The second act is even better than the first." Greta leaned excitedly forward, her hands tightly clasped together. "Vespina has four disguises, and Signora Pacelli plays them all exceedingly well."

"Shhh!" hissed a woman behind them; she'd been humming along to the catchy tunes Herr Haydn had composed for the arias.

"Shhh yourself!" Greta hissed back, undeterred. She leaned over to Rosalie. "I don't think there's ever been a funnier buffa, do you?" Karl had regaled them with the plot. But it was something else to see the opera brought to life on the stage.

Rosalie smiled affectionately and reached out to squeeze her friend's plump palm. "It's the best we've seen. Gerhard thinks so as well, don't you sweet?" She turned to face her husband, who sat with his arm around her.

"It is!" Gerhard's blue eyes twinkled as he regarded them both. He grinned broadly as Signora Pacelli swaggered back onstage in male garb. "It's another one of her disguises, is it?"

Greta nodded, giggling. "She's pretending to be the German servant of an imaginary Marquis."

"And doing a remarkably good job of it, too," Rosalie said. "Small wonder Nencio doesn't recognize her." Signora Pacelli's Italian had taken on a distinct German overtone as her character, Vespina, interacted with Nencio, Vespina's former lover.

Nencio, much to Vespina's comic outrage, was now after Filippo's beautiful daughter, Sandrina.

"Your Signora Pacelli plays a good drunk as well." Gerhard's breath tickled Rosalie as he bent his head to whisper into her ear. "Unless she's had some help." He tipped his chin at the bottle in Signora Pacelli's hand.

It was half-empty, Rosalie noted in dismay, and some of the liquid sloshed out as the soprano lurched around onstage. The singer's voice seemed to be slurring as well.

"That's not the bottle you delivered just this morning, is it?" she whispered to her husband.

Gerhard glanced at the stage as Rosalie gazed anxiously up at him. "It had better not be," he said, his handsome features grim. "It's the last of its kind. If they need a bottle for any other scene, they'll have to look to His Serene Highness's cellars. I have no more."

The soprano's gestures were becoming wilder and more animated.

"I've seen roistering lads act more soberly than that." Gerhard's astonishment caused him to speak out loud, much to Rosalie's dismay. She glanced uneasily at her friend.

Greta was looking alarmed as well. "She must've drunk too much—and too quickly," she exclaimed. "Oh, why didn't Fiore think to fill the bottle with water or grape juice? He should know as well as the rest of us that Signora Pacelli is partial to wine."

"Did Karl think to tell him that?" Rosalie rolled her eyes and shook her head. Everyone knew Fiore did no more—and sometimes somewhat less —than what he was told. Whether that was due to lack of wit or idleness, she'd never been able to decide.

"She'd better not be too drunk to finish the opera!" Greta clutched the gilded backrest of the seat in front of her. "She has two more disguises."

Onstage, Signora Pacelli, disguised as a Marquis's servant, twirled around the tenor playing Nencio. Coming out from behind him, she took a wide step forward, stumbled, tripped, and then fell flat on her face. The bottle in her hand landed on the stage floor, spun halfway around, then shuddered to a stop.

"At least, there'll be wine enough to last the end of the opera," Gerhard blurted out.

But neither Rosalie nor Greta was paying him any mind. Greta rose half-out of her chair, prompting another irate "shhh!" from the woman behind them.

"But that's not part of the story!" she squealed, beside herself with worry.

⚬⚬⚬

In the pit, Haydn watched aghast as Lucia crashed gracelessly to the floor. For a brief moment, he wondered whether Karl had made a spur-of-the-moment change to the libretto. It was not unheard of for a librettist to do such a thing. But surely it was unwise to do it without consulting either the composer or opera director.

Almost simultaneously, another thought flitted through Haydn's mind. Had Lucia taken her role too far?

But all such considerations instantly fled when his gaze drifted up to Nencio's face. The panic-stricken expression plastered over the tenor's features and his wide, staring eyes told the entire tale. This was no spontaneous act. It had certainly not been intended.

Lucia was . . . Haydn's fingers felt stiff as they depressed, almost of their own accord, the keys of the harpsichord. Whatever afflicted his prima donna, she was clearly in no condition to continue.

Good God, what was to be done?

Raising his hand just high enough for the tenor to see, Haydn let it flutter through the air. A silent signal to Jakob Friberth—the tenor playing Nencio—to carry on as though nothing had happened.

What the man would do—or indeed could do—the Kapellmeister knew not. He could only pray for divine inspiration to fall upon his hapless tenor.

Fortunately, Jakob understood, nodding imperceptibly as he wiped the shock off his features. Deathly pale but smiling broadly, Jakob in his role of Nencio feigned glee at the situation.

"Ah, the drunken servant of a marquis!" Jakob gestured down at the prone Lucia. "If the servant is thus, can the master be any better?" Bending down, Jakob lifted the soprano's arms and began dragging her offstage.

He snickered at the audience. "What say you, we let that false villain, Filippo, think the marquis has changed his mind?"

Near the wings, Jakob dropped Lucia's arms to jab his forefinger at his chest. "Then Sandrina—beautiful Sandrina—can be Nencio's!" Still singing the last few words, Jakob, along with Lucia, disappeared behind the wings.

The loud burst of laughter that greeted the scene was satisfying evidence that the ploy had worked.

And fortunately the curtain fell just as Nencio and Lucia exited the stage. That was thanks to Johann's quick thinking, Haydn realized with immense gratitude, noticing his brother was no longer at his side.

Karl had written his libretto in two acts, but it did no harm to let the audience think a third was to follow.

Bouncing up from his seat, Haydn quickly turned and acknowledged the thunderous applause with a rushed bow. Then, leaving Luigi to conduct the orchestra as it played the music for the interlude, he hurried backstage— eager to discover what was amiss with his prima donna.

Lucia's body had been dragged into the area beyond the grooved slots in which the wings sat. It was crowded with a variety of props. But Jakob had managed to find a narrow space where she lay between cooking pots on one side and a large table on the other.

There Haydn found Johann bent over Lucia's still frame.

"What ails her?" the Kapellmeister asked anxiously. Against all hope, he continued, "Can she be revived?"

"I fear not, brother." Johann turned around, his features whiter than a meadow of edelweiss in the spring. "She is dead—God rest her soul!" He hastily crossed himself.

"Dead!" Haydn's eyes were drawn to Lucia's body, lying unnaturally still on the floorboards. At least she was face up. "B-b-but how?" Had she really been ill? Or—

Resolutely, he pushed the thought away from his mind. Best not to con- sider it an unnatural death.

Chapter Eleven

THE hurried clattering of wooden clogs on the floorboards told Haydn that Karl was approaching. He sensed rather than saw the court librettist—a burly man with bushy red hair and a coarse beard—come to a stop next to him.

There was a sharp intake of breath, then Karl crossed himself and averted his eyes.

"You'd best get a couple of the stagehands to carry her out, Karl." Johann still looked pale, but to his credit, he showed no other signs of discomposure.

He raised his head, his expression grave. "This is a matter for the barber-surgeon."

And possibly the Bürgermeister, Haydn thought, but he kept that notion to himself.

Karl nodded.

"Miss Lidia is ready to go on as Vespina," he continued in a low voice to Haydn. "I've made a few changes to the libretto, so her coming on in Signora Pacelli's stead won't take anyone by surprise."

Haydn nodded. "Have the singers been informed?"

Karl hesitated. "About the changes to the libretto, yes, but . . ." His voice trailed off as he took in Lucia's still form on the floor. "They think she is indisposed—"

"Sauced! Isn't that what you mean, Karl?" Narcissa sailed in through the open door. She sniffed disparagingly. "Didn't I tell you, Herr Kapellmeister, she was in no position to play the part?"

"So you did, Fräulein Leon," Haydn said evenly. "Just this morning. I wonder how you could've known?"

Johann's mouth dropped open and he gaped, first at Haydn, then at Narcissa. But the singer seemed unfazed by Haydn's insinuation.

She stared back at Haydn. "Lucia has only herself to blame for her predicament, Herr Kapellmeister."

Her cool impudence stunned Haydn. God in heaven, had the woman no conscience?

He barely registered the sound of footsteps behind him. They came to a halt and a breathless voice urgently called out: "Herr Kapellmeister!"

Haydn spun around, startled to see Gabriel Krause, the curly-haired young cellist standing there.

"The audience grows restive, Herr Kapellmeister," the young man said. "Master Luigi wishes to—" Gabriel must have just caught sight of Lucia's lifeless form, for his eyes grew round as saucers. White-faced, he staggered back.

"God have mercy, has she taken her life?"

Why had Gabriel drawn that conclusion? The question flitted briefly through Haydn's mind, but he had no time to consider it.

"No, she has not," Johann, still kneeling, calmly informed the cellist. He rose to his feet.

"Tell Luigi we'll be ready to continue in a few minutes." Johann turned to Karl. "Hannah"—the seamstress; Lucia had recommended her, Haydn recalled—"has made the alterations, I trust. And Miss Lidia is prepared to take Vespina's role, is she not?"

"She's not fit to take it," Narcissa burst out much to Haydn's annoyance. "I should play Vespina." She turned defiantly to him. "Herr Kapellmeister, after this morning's performance, I should be promoted to the lead."

"And who would play Sandrina?" Haydn asked, his voice tight with barely contained fury.

"Why can't Lidia?" Narcissa's chin jutted out stubbornly.

"Because"—Haydn clenched his fists, making an enormous effort to restrain his rising fury—"I wish you to play the role. Do not try me, Fräulein Leon. If I so much as hear another word of opposition on this point, I will not hesitate to dismiss you."

His chest swelling and his cheeks flushed with unaccustomed heat, he turned to Johann. "Call the barber-surgeon, if you please, Johann."

But yet another unsavory interruption awaited him at the door to the auditorium. Trattner had just stepped out, and the reporter's dark eyes blazed when he caught sight of the Kapellmeister.

Licking his lips, pen poised expectantly over his open notebook, Trattner blocked Haydn's way.

"Signora Pacelli, is she—?"

"Indisposed," Haydn said curtly, not wishing to reveal the truth yet. An untimely death—whether of natural causes or not—didn't bode well for the festivities. And he had no wish to let it cloud the celebrations.

"Sick?" Trattner's eyebrows rose. "Then the performers were right to fear for their—"

Haydn's lips tightened; he held up his hand.

"I see no reason why the delicate state of Signora Pacelli's should lead anyone in Eszterháza to fear for their health, Herr Trattner."

Although the mosquitoes and the swamp, Haydn had to admit, were certainly health hazards. But he'd have a mutiny on his hands if so much as a word about that got out.

Trattner, however, was not to be silenced.

"If the state of the good Signora's health was so delicate"—Trattner had cocked his head to one side, his eyebrows raised quizzically—"why was she allowed to go on tonight? Was that not irresponsible?"

Haydn rolled his eyes. Was there no getting around the infernal man?

"I have an opera to conduct, Herr Trattner," he said, and adroitly stepped around the man to re-enter the auditorium.

—◦◦◦—

Luigi was in the midst of playing an extended cadenza when Haydn returned to the orchestra pit. The Konzertmeister must have seen him out of the corner of his eyes, for he immediately turned to face Haydn, his eyebrows raised expectantly.

Haydn was hastening to Luigi's side, anxious to share the awful news, when to his dismay he saw Maria Anna and Paolo sitting at his harpsichord. What were they doing in the pit?

Paolo rose and, leaning heavily on his cane, hobbled toward Haydn. "Is Lucia well, Herr Kapellmeister?" His wizened face was wreathed in concern. "Such prancing around in her condition is hardly advisable."

Haydn found himself gaping at the old man, utterly at a loss for words. In her current state, Lucia was hardly capable of anything. But Paolo no doubt meant . . . He frowned. What did Paolo mean?

Before he could probe for answers, Maria Anna thrust herself into the conversation.

"To be sure it is not," she said. "And to make herself fall in such a fashion . . ." Maria Anna shook her head. "It was hardly wise. What could she have been thinking?"

"She did not make herself fall," Haydn replied firmly. God forbid, they should ask to go backstage to see his prima donna.

He caught Luigi's eye and made a circular motion with his forefinger—a signal to repeat the sinfonia that had opened the second act. A variation or two would make the piece seem sufficiently new to the audience's ears.

He'd hoped Maria Anna and Paolo would leave, but they remained standing before him; Maria Anna going so far as to grasp his wrist, shaking it impatiently. "How then did she fall, husband?"

"She must've been overcome with dizziness," Haydn said as Luigi gracefully transitioned from his cadenza to the opening bars of the sinfonia. "Or whatever it was that ailed her earlier this evening." But the explanation didn't suffice.

"Is she in need of any remedies?" Maria Anna asked at once, her voice rising to make itself heard over the swelling sound of the orchestra joining in with Luigi.

"Pshaw!" Paolo snorted before Haydn could think of a response. "Haven't your remedies done enough harm? It was most likely the brews you supplied her that caused her dizzy spell." He turned to Haydn. "Let the barber-surgeon be called. This is a matter for him."

"So, it is," Haydn readily agreed while Maria Anna openly bristled, but remained quiet all the same. "He is attending to her as we speak."

At least, he trusted that was the case by this time.

The slow rise of the curtain caught Haydn's eye. God be thanked, this conversation could be brought to an end.

"You'd best be seated," he urged, pointing at the stage. "The curtain begins to rise."

Under the guise of issuing further instructions to his Konzertmeister, Haydn moved to Luigi's side. Bending down, he quickly conveyed the news.

"Dead!" Luigi hissed, gripping his bow tightly. "How can that be? A young woman, untroubled by any serious maladies?"

Haydn shrugged, expressing his own doubts on the subject.

"Worse still, Narcissa insisted on being given her part, adamant that Lucia had brought her predicament upon herself."

Luigi's lips pursed, but he fortunately stopped himself mid-whistle. "You don't think she had . . .?" His voice trailed off as his hazel eyes searched Haydn's features.

"I know not what to think," Haydn responded grimly.

Although suspecting Narcissa of having a hand in Lucia's unfortunate demise was far preferable to entertaining suspicions of the only other culprit that came to mind.

He returned to his place, his gaze traveling toward the audience where the Archduke sat next to his bride.

Lucia had been carried belowstairs to the medium-sized room she'd used as a changing room. Johann ushered the barber-surgeon into the room, inwardly cringing at the prospect of having to enter the singer's private quarters.

It would've been bad enough had Lucia been a man. But to invade a woman's chamber—albeit one dead—was simply distasteful. Still, one's duty had to be done. Johann squelched his qualms, reminding himself it was for brother's sake—and poor Lucia's as well.

The room was cluttered. The costumes Lucia had worn—Vespina's peasant dress, the black garb of the old crone, the breeches and vest of the Marquis were piled on the floor.

Lucia must have thrown them upon the couch on which she now lay. The stagehands must subsequently have pushed them onto the floor, for some of the fabric remained on the edge of the couch, trapped under Lucia's form.

Someone—the seamstress, possibly—had shed Lucia of the male servant's garb as well, clothing her in a simple, loose-fitting dress. Johann was grateful for that. To let her remain in breeches and doublet would've been unseemly.

"The room, I fear, is in disarray," he said apologetically, gingerly skirting around the pile of clothes.

"It is no matter, Master Johann." Herr Hipfl had stopped before the heap of clothing and regarded the pile, amused. "I have seen far worse. The dead have no time to tidy up."

"The dead?" Johann repeated, surprised. Was Lucia's state that obvious? He'd been deliberately vague, not wanting to prejudice the barber-surgeon's judgment. Who knew, the woman might still have life in her. Stranger things had happened.

Suppressing his distaste, he stooped down to gather up the clothing, clearing the barber-surgeon's path.

Herr Hipfl stepped forward. His halo of unruly, gray-black hair fanned out from his smooth, unlined features as he turned toward Johann.

"Her chest would rise and fall, were she alive, Master Johann." He drew closer to the body and knelt down. "I should've thought you'd seen enough dead bodies to know that. But I suppose"—he took Lucia's wrist, feeling for a pulse, Johann surmised—"only a medical man would be aware of such a thing."

The barber-surgeon let Lucia's limp wrist drop and proceeded to delicately press upon her chest. "As I suspected. Long gone." He raised his eyes toward Johann. "I saw her clutch at her stomach just before she fell. Had she any ailments, you know of."

Johann shook his head. "Nothing so grave as to suggest she was on the point of death. She did complain of biliousness and a cramp in the stomach. But sister-in-law's teas always seemed to put her right."

The barber-surgeon nodded. "Then she must have been with child."

Chapter Twelve

"With child?" Johann's voice rose. "How—?"

Seeing Hipfl staring at him, he subsided. He had thought Paolo incapable of fathering a child. If Lucia was with child—Johann's horrorstruck gaze fell upon the dead woman—whose was it?

The Archduke's? From what brother had told him earlier that evening, it was entirely possible.

Feeling Hipfl's eyes upon him, Johann forced himself to respond. "I—er—I know not. If she was with child, she chose not to share that happy news with the rest of the troupe."

The barber-surgeon nodded again. "Her husband will know."

He resumed his examination. He was probing Lucia's stomach when a knock on the open door startled Johann.

"Master Johann?" Hannah, the seamstress, stood by the door. Her curious gaze was drawn briefly toward Lucia's form, but then returned to Johann's face. "Vespina's costumes are needed. May I take them?"

"Yes, yes, of course." Johann motioned her in. Recalling that Lucia had known her in Vienna, he decided to delicately sound her out about the singer's relationship with the Archduke.

"Is Signora Pacelli hurt?" Hannah asked, her arms laden with costumes. "Miss Lidia changed her clothes, but all she said was that Signora Pacelli couldn't go on with her performance."

Johann shook his head. "I fear she is no more, Hannah," he said gently.

"Oh!" Hannah gaped at him, then looked down at Lucia. "But she wasn't—" She frowned, blinking back tears and biting fiercely down upon her lip. "God have mercy!"

She mumbled the words over and over.

"She was well loved. Her loss will be keenly felt," Johann continued sympathetically. Taking a deep breath, he added, "Even the Archduke during his brief visit had come to appreciate her. She was close to His Imperial Highness, was she not?"

"She thought she was." Hannah's features had turned cold. "She should've kept to herself. No good ever came from flying too close to the sun."

Back rigid, she left the room.

No, it did not, Johann agreed. Dear God, how many children had the Archduke fathered out of wedlock?

⁓•••⁓

"What in the world is going on?" Greta peered at the stage in dismay.

Rosalie didn't know what to say. Signora Pacelli was clearly in no position to continue her performance. Miss Lidia had taken her place as Vespina.

"At least, they didn't give the role to Fräulein Leon," she whispered back.

The woman in front of them must have been equally startled, for she didn't bother to turn around to shush them as she'd done before.

"But the scene is different, too," Greta protested. "It wasn't in the original libretto."

Karl had inserted a scene with Vespina—disguised as a Marquis—and her brother, who was in the process of donning the garb of the Marquis's servant.

"It's just as well he included it, then," Gerhard said in a low rumble. "Miss Lidia looks nothing like Signora Pacelli. There's no fooling the audience about that."

That was true enough, Rosalie thought. Despite the snowy peruke with its masses of ringlets that covered Miss Lidia's hair and the embroidered jacket and satin breeches she wore, there was no mistaking that it was a different singer onstage.

Miss Lidia was tall and reed-thin with a long nose.

"No, there's not," Rosalie chimed in. "It was quick thinking on Karl's part." She squeezed Greta's hand, willing her friend to believe all would be well.

But it was equally clear the audience wasn't going to quietly accept the change.

"Who in the name of heaven is that? It's not Vespina, that's for sure," a chorus of voices called. "Where's Signora Pacelli? Call her back?"

The voices subsided when the Prince turned to glare at them and Herr Rahier, the Estates Director, sternly admonished them to be quiet.

But His Serene Highness's guests could not be so ordered.

"Where is the incomparable Lucia?" the Duke of Modena bellowed.

"She must be too sozzled to sing," his companion—what was her name? Chiara?—ventured, her bell-like voice filling the vast auditorium. "Isn't that so, Herr Haydn?"

"She is indisposed, madam," the Kapellmeister responded evenly, his fingers still flying over the keyboard.

Wondering how long Herr Hipfl's examination would take, Johann watched the barber-surgeon. Herr Hipfl had fortunately found nothing amiss yet. He was now inspecting the soprano's eyelids, lifting first one and then the other open.

"They have a yellowish cast," he commented.

"Death taking its toll?" Johann wondered.

"Perhaps." The barber-surgeon was non-committal. He moved his fingers down to the soprano's mouth, parted the lips open, and to Johann's eternal astonishment bent down toward the dead woman.

Barely a hair's breadth away from the singer's mouth he stopped. Whatever was the man doing? Johann craned his neck forward.

The barber-surgeon's nostrils wrinkled as they pulled several times on the air between his nose and her mouth.

"Musty sweet," he murmured, his gaze shifting around the room. "The wine bottle in her hand? Where is it? Was she drinking from it?"

Johann surveyed the room. "I know not. The scene did require her to quaff a small amount."

The bottle had been placed—corked—near her in the wings. Karl must've had the stagehands remove it.

He said as much.

"I shall need to see it," Hipfl said. "What was it flavored with?"

"Mint, I expect. She was partial to it."

"A tippler, was she?" Hipfl stared up at him.

"She may have been, I suppose." Now that Johann recalled, there'd been more than one occasion when Lucia had seemed disoriented and confused, lurching about on the stage as though she'd imbibed too heavily.

Had excessive drinking caused the trouble? Would to God, it were merely that.

But Herr Hipfl dashed his hopes.

"I doubt it," he tersely replied when Johann put the question to him.

He ran his forefinger inside Lucia's mouth. Then to Johann's horror, Herr Hipfl put the self-same finger—had it not just touched a corpse?—inside his mouth.

Feeling his stomach heave, Johann averted his gaze. Dear Lord, what did the barber-surgeon hope to accomplish with that?

"This was no natural death." The barber-surgeon rose to his feet, grim-featured. "Your prima donna, I fear, was poisoned, Master Johann."

***

Was Signora Pacelli really ill? Rosalie wondered. *Or too drunk to play her part?*

She'd certainly sustained a hard fall. It was a wonder she was still alive. Rosalie winced remembering the loud thud with which the soprano had fallen on the wooden floorboards of the stage.

The audience had just begun to enjoy the play—Miss Lidia wasn't doing a half-bad job, Rosalie thought, and even Greta agreed—when Master Johann entered the auditorium.

He looked paler than usual—a greenish tinge suffusing his features—and grim-faced as he headed toward Herr Haydn.

Whatever was the matter now?

***

"Poisoned?" Haydn missed a note in his astonishment. Fortunately, no one appeared to notice and the singers carried on uninterrupted. "How can Herr Hipfl possibly know that?"

"From the odor of her breath, the color of her eyes, and not least from the taste of her spittle," Johann responded.

"But she has not ingested anything except—" Haydn swallowed, glancing over his shoulder at where his wife sat. The last thing Lucia had swallowed was the concoction Maria Anna had brewed for her.

A strange unease filled the pit of his stomach. Had Maria Anna let her jealousy get the better of her?

Surely not.

But would Herr Hipfl and the Bürgermeister see the situation the same way? It would not be the first time his wife had been accused of poisoning a woman.

". . . the wine," Johann was saying.

"What wine?" Haydn asked.

"The bottle of wine she had with her onstage," Johann patiently replied. "Herr Hipfl surmises the poison was administered through the wine."

"She had imbibed some?" If it was the wine, then Maria Anna could not be held responsible. Neither—Haydn glanced over his shoulder again —could the Archduke, fortunately.

Unless—an unhappy thought occurred to him. Had the Archduke prevailed upon Narcissa to carry on his dirty business? Heaven knew, she would be only too willing to do it.

Moreover, Rosalie had informed him, His Imperial Highness had sent Narcissa flowers that afternoon. To what end?

Haydn shook his head. No, no that was unlikely.

"Karl says it was half-empty when she went onstage." Johann's words interrupted his thoughts.

"What was—?" Haydn stopped himself just in time. Johann was referring to the wine bottle, of course. He hurriedly changed his question.

"Where is the bottle? Has Herr Hipfl taken charge of it?"

Out of the corner of his eye, he saw his younger brother shake his head.

"Hannah carried the news of Lucia's demise to the stagehands, and Fiore, hearing that the wine might have been tainted, emptied out the bottle."

Dear Lord, had the boy no sense? Haydn couldn't prevent an exasperated huff escaping his lips.

"He meant well," Johann confided with a sigh. "He was worried lest someone else suffer the same fate. They've all apparently been chafing at the stricture to leave the wine alone."

"And all except Lucia abided by the stipulation, I suppose?" Haydn said. He had no desire to think ill of the dead, but his prima donna had clearly possessed an inflated sense of her own importance.

"I'm afraid so."

Haydn pursed his lips. Someone had known of Lucia's partiality for wine and taken advantage of it. The question was who?

Narcissa?

She was onstage now, her features never far from a pout because she'd not succeeded in her mission to take over Lucia's role.

Chapter Thirteen

HAYDN sat at the kitchen table, fingering the gold snuffbox the Duke of Modena had presented him. The opera had ended hours ago, and he had returned—along with Maria Anna and Johann—to the quarters His Serene Highness had assigned him.

As Kapellmeister, his quarters in Eszterháza, though cramped, included two bedchambers, a small parlor, and a tiny kitchen. The fireplace was large enough to make a pot of coffee, but any cooking or baking had to be done in the community kitchen below.

That incommodious fact had from the start been a thorn in Maria Anna's side, providing her ample fodder for her grumbling. Haydn had chafed at the inconvenience as well.

But tonight he found himself grateful for it.

Maria Anna was downstairs cooking, and Johann had offered to help her convey her pots and pans and all her ingredients up and down the stairs. Their absence gave the Kapellmeister the solitude he needed to sort through his thoughts.

He struck the snuffbox with his forefinger, watching it spin and come to a rattling stop. It was beautifully crafted. The lid was set with a white eagle fashioned out of mother-of-pearl. Gold-painted enamel formed the creature's talons and beak as well as the tiny gold crown atop its head.

But the Kapellmeister's mind was too troubled to appreciate its beauty. Who could've killed his prima donna? From the moment he'd learned of her demise, his suspicions had veered drunkenly from one person to another. But he was still no closer to an answer.

"It will have been someone in the orchestra or the troupe of singers, you can wager on it, Herr Haydn," the barber-surgeon had told him sagaciously.

Herr Groer, the Bürgermeister, had agreed with Herr Hipfl. "Find her enemy and you will have found her killer, mark my words."

Find her enemy? But Haydn could think of at least three.

"Two who would clearly gain from her death," he muttered to himself. "But then again, only one of these along with the third could've possessed either the means or the opportunity to poison her."

Dear God, what was to be done?

Just then the door was thrust open, and Johann entered bearing a platter of meat and another of vegetables. Maria Anna followed close upon his heels with a large bowl.

Seeing Haydn at the table, she turned sharply upon him. "Why are you just sitting there, husband?"

"What else was I supposed to do?" he retorted, irritated beyond measure. He had, it was true, been sitting for longer than was his wont. But how could Maria Anna have known that?

Her eyes lingered upon his head and then traveled down to his chest.

"You could take off your wig and hang up your jacket, husband. Or, is it too much trouble to expect you to lift your finger for such mundane tasks?"

Ach so! So that was how she'd found him out.

Haydn forced himself to stand up. He shrugged himself out of his gold jacket, slung it over his arm, and took off his wig.

Maria Anna had followed Johann to the stone countertop beneath the cabinets. Reaching up for some plates, she continued: "Sitting and moping over Lucia's death won't bring her back, husband."

"Moping?" Haydn lifted an eyebrow as he proceeded to hang up his coat and wig.

That was hardly an accurate description of his state of mind.

But Maria Anna's use of the word recalled Paolo's accusation earlier that evening. Lucia's husband had taken the news of her poisoning most ill.

"It will have been one of your evil concoctions," he'd said accusingly to Maria Anna the minute he heard.

"Nonsense!" Johann had protested. "Sister-in-law's brews helped relieve Signora Pacelli's symptoms."

"Besides, what reason could she have had to want Signora Pacelli dead?" Herr Hipfl, who'd been present, had asked.

"Jealousy, of course," Paolo, still glaring balefully at Maria Anna, had replied. "What else could it be?" Paolo's remark had caused the barber-surgeon to direct a curious look at Haydn from under his thick eyebrows.

The gaze, at once shrewd and knowing, had caused Haydn more than a little discomfiture.

Recalling the conversation, he wondered yet again if Paolo was right. Maria Anna knew more about herbs—which ones healed, and which ones were poisonous—than anybody besides the barber-surgeon himself.

Lucia willingly took her teas. As to Maria Anna's jealousy, Haydn was painfully aware they had never discussed the incident that might've aroused it.

Nothing further had ever taken place. Haydn had made sure of it. But whether Maria Anna was cognizant of that fact, Haydn didn't know.

He suppressed a sigh. Johann joined him at the table, giving Haydn an understanding smile as he slid into his seat.

"It isn't Signora Pacelli's unfortunate end, tragic though it is, that worries us," Johann turned to address Maria Anna. "I fear all the musicians as well as Signora Pacelli's colleagues come under suspicion as a result."

Maria Anna was spooning a rich dark gravy over the meat. At Johann's words, she stopped, her spoon suspended in mid-air, and turned to regard him with a frown.

"But Herr Hipfl can hardly suspect you or husband or Luigi of killing Lucia. And if it's one of the others, surely it's better to dismiss the man now than to harbor a killer."

"But in order to find out who it is, I must question them all," Haydn joined the conversation, grateful to his brother for diverting Maria Anna's suspicions elsewhere.

"Won't the Bürgermeister do it?" Maria Anna brought him his plate and returned to the countertop for Johann's.

"No," Haydn replied shortly. As always, Herr Groer had found a way to turn the case over to him. As though he had nothing better to do!

"They are your men, Herr Haydn," the Bürgermeister had begun apologetically. "It would be better for you to question them. You are well acquainted with their characters after all. Your questions would cause far less offense than mine. Surely, you agree?"

Haydn had done no such thing. But, unable to find a reason to disagree, he'd merely pursed his lips.

They were halfway through the meal when Maria Anna asked her next question.

"Had Lucia any enemies?"

Haydn nearly choked over his meat at her words. Why was Maria Anna —never particularly interested in either his music or his investigations— asking about such a thing?

Not wanting to divulge his suspicions, he found his gaze turning involuntarily toward Johann.

His brother fortunately took up the gauntlet. "None that we know of," he replied equably. "As far as we know, Signora Pacelli was well-liked."

"But someone wanted her dead?" Maria Anna persisted.

"So it seems." Johann nodded. He gently touched the snuffbox. "But for all that, the opera was well received, God be praised. Miss Lidia performed her part well, I thought."

"Truth to tell, it was Karl's quick thinking that made the difference," Haydn remarked. And Chiara's recognition of it, he added to himself.

The ageing beauty had sashayed up to him after the opera, full of praise for the opera and for the librettist's clever changes in light of their misfortune.

"I can think of few librettists who would've handled the situation quite so dexterously, my dear Herr Haydn. And few singers who could've adapted so well."

The Duke of Modena's generous gift had come at her urging. Karl had been presented with a snuffbox as well.

Maria Anna eyed the snuffbox now, letting out a disparaging sniff.

"It is pretty enough. And it was most gracious of the Duke to give it to you. But a purse of gold would've been more useful, in my opinion. I had hoped to make an offering to Saint Gerard."

An offering to Saint Gerard? Whatever for, Haydn wondered.

Surely, Maria Anna had long ceased to entertain any hopes of conceiving a child.

Although that wasn't the only reason for calling upon Saint Gerard. The recollection made Haydn sit up straighter. Anyone accused of a crime prayed to the good saint as well.

God have mercy, he thought. An involuntary shudder of agitation rippled through his body. *God have mercy!*

An hour later, Haydn was still troubled. Deep in thought, he pushed his fork through the soft layers of Maria Anna's *Erdbeerkuchen*.

Dinner over, he and Johann had retired to the tiny parlor for dessert and coffee. Now they sat in silence across from each other at the small coffee table.

Staring blankly at the harpsichord that stood by the window, Haydn brought the fork to his mouth. The strawberries were sweet, the cake moist and spongy, and the cream thick and sweet. But he was unable to savor his dessert.

How long would it be before the barber-surgeon accused Maria Anna of having a hand in Lucia's murder? How long before the Bürgermeister arrested her? And, knowing of her involvement, how was he to defend his wife?

"It is a difficult situation," Johann's voice, quiet and sympathetic, broke the silence.

"It is indeed," Haydn agreed, cutting into his slice of strawberry cake.

"It will require delicate handling," Johann ventured again. "Have you considered how best to deal with it?"

Haydn turned sharply to his brother. How could Johann have divined his thoughts? Were his suspicions so apparent?

"I was tempted to confide our fears to the barber-surgeon," Johann went on. The tines of his fork speared a small piece of cake, but he made no motion to lift it to his mouth. "But it would've meant divulging facts that should not be so carelessly tossed out to all and sundry."

Haydn frowned. What facts was Johann referring to?

"Maria Anna's remedies . . .?" His voice trailed off, unsure how to phrase the question.

Johann nodded. "That they worked so well to relieve Signora Pacelli's bouts of nausea could only mean one thing according to Herr Hipfl."

"Yes?" Haydn raised an eyebrow, still not comprehending. God forbid, the barber-surgeon should somehow have concluded from the situation an attempt to poison the woman.

Much to his alarm, Johann cast a surreptitious glance around the room, looking carefully at the door that separated the parlor from the kitchen. Then turning back to Haydn, he lowered his voice.

"Herr Hipfl suggested she might have been with child."

"With—" Haydn's voice rang out. It took him an effort of will to lower it. "With child?" he repeated, shocked. He pulled himself forward. "B-but whose . . .?"

Johann nodded. "I could hardly contain my surprise. I doubt Paolo possesses the ability to father a child." He paused, gripping his fork. His *kuchen* remained half-eaten on the dessert plate.

"After what you shared with me earlier this evening, I could not help but wonder . . ." Johann's voice trailed off.

Haydn's eyes widened as he felt for the note. It was in his coat pocket, he recalled, patting his vest. "I had better take it out of my coat before Maria Anna washes it," he murmured.

He turned to his brother, still trying to put his confused thoughts into some semblance of order.

"It would make more sense that His Imperial Highness might have—" He cut himself short, not wanting to broach the possibility out loud.

He swallowed, inhaling deeply. *The Archduke was old enough to father a child*, Lucia had said. Wasn't it more likely that she was referring to her own condition rather than to His Imperial Highness's escapades in Vienna?

"She could not possibly have discovered his doings in Vienna," he said, facing his brother.

"It is most unlikely," Johann agreed.

"Hannah's words seemed to confirm it as well," he added, repeating what the seamstress had told him.

Haydn sat back heavily. "His Imperial Highness seemed to know of her fondness for wine, too."

The barber-surgeon had speculated the poison had been administered in the wine. What better way to get Lucia to imbibe it?

"I was struck by that as well." Johann brought his piece of *kuchen* to his mouth, chewed, and swallowed.

Preoccupied with his anxiety about Maria Anna's role in Lucia's murder, Haydn had barely registered the Archduke's words. Now the memory of them struck an ominous chord in his mind.

Shortly after Chiara and the Duke of Modena had left the orchestra pit, Maria Beatrice had approached, followed by the Archduke. She had expressed concern for Lucia's well-being.

"You said she was indisposed, Herr Haydn," the bride had said, her blue eyes gazing wide-eyed up at him. "Has she recovered?"

Unable to lie, Haydn had shaken his head. "I fear not, my lady. There is no hope for her."

Archduke Ferdinand had snorted. "It doesn't surprise me. Imbibing too deeply will do that to a person. Had she shown more restraint, she might still be with us."

Maria Beatrice had looked sharply at the young man. "Your Imperial Highness seems far better acquainted with her habits—a common singer— than one would expect," she had commented waspishly.

The Archduke had shrugged. "It was common knowledge. Everyone knew how well she loved her wine."

Haydn pursed his lips. The armchair in which he sat seemed suddenly narrow and uncomfortably constricting. It had been bad enough when he'd suspected his wife of murdering Lucia. He had sworn before God to protect her. How could he turn her in?

But he had also sworn an oath to the Empress to guard her young son and to ensure the boy's marriage to the bride chosen for him. Would it do any good to inform Her Majesty of these latest tidings?

"I can hardly ignore the matter," he said unhappily.

"No." Johann pushed his empty plate aside. "And to involve Herr Hipfl and the Bürgermeister without informing His Serene Highness of the situation would be highly indelicate."

So it would. "But I scarcely know what to tell His Serene Highness." Haydn spread his hands wide, helplessly.

There was a moment's silence. Maria Anna's clattering in the kitchen sounded inordinately loud. Then Johann spoke.

"Show His Serene Highness the note," he suggested quietly. "Let him draw his own conclusions."

Chapter Fourteen

THE next morning, Haydn had no sooner entered the kitchen for his breakfast when Maria Anna made haste to chase him out the door.

"But I have yet to break my fast," the Kapellmeister protested, still standing by the kitchen door.

Maria Anna sighed. "Can't you eat at the tavern? Herr Hipfl wishes to meet you there."

Haydn's gaze followed her pointing finger to the folded piece of paper tucked under his coffee cup. Frowning, he approached the table, cautiously reaching out for the note as though it were a trap that might suddenly close upon his fingers.

What did the barber-surgeon want of him?

"Who can tell?" Maria Anna responded. "The boy he sent didn't see fit to supply a reason. All he said was that the barber-surgeon awaits you at the tavern."

Maria Anna glanced at the clock. "The sooner you go the better."

"Why?" Haydn raised his head, at once suspicious. Maria Anna, he noticed, had her bonnet on and was dressed to go out. A small purse hung from her wrist. The kitchen was clean, the table cleared of all dishes but for his coffee mug and a small plate with a roll on it.

Maria Anna exhaled heavily as though drained of her last reserve of patience. "I must go to the Heiligen Kreuzes." She glanced at the clock again. "Pfarrer Spalek leaves in an hour."

Haydn looked at her aghast. "And you wish to offer confession?" Whatever for, he wondered.

She was taking Lucia's demise remarkably well, he thought.

Maria Anna rolled her eyes. "Of course, not, husband. He has offered to join me at the altar of St. Gerard to pray with me."

The explanation did little to alleviate Haydn's anxiety. He glanced down at the note in his hands and slowly unfolded it.

Had the barber-surgeon already concluded his investigation and determined an arrest was necessary?

But the untidily scrawled words told him little more than he already knew.

Draining his lukewarm mug of coffee and grabbing the roll, he set out for the tavern. It was attached to the inn His Serene Highness had built a few miles west to house visiting performers.

Thoughtfully chewing his roll, Haydn walked under one of the ornate arcades, through the courtyard of the Music House where his quarters were located, and out onto the street.

What awful tidings awaited him now, he wondered.

Rosalie searched the coffeehouse as she and Greta wheeled their carts in. The atmosphere in the coffeehouse this morning was unusually subdued. Most of the performers were already seated at the trestle tables that ran down the room.

But Signora Pacelli was nowhere to be seen. Rosalie's heart sank. Was Herr Trattner correct in his surmise, then?

That would no doubt explain the singers' dampened spirits. The opera had been well received, but no one would know it from reading Herr Trattner's report.

"I don't see Signora Pacelli," she hissed to Greta. "Do you?"

Greta scanned the room as well before shaking her head. She pushed her cart to the serving table where footmen took charge of transferring the breakfast dishes to the chafing dishes.

"It doesn't mean a thing," she insisted stoutly. "Why, Herr Friberth isn't here either."

Rosalie had noticed his absence as well. But it was easily explained. He had most likely slept at the inn—with whatever woman he was currently taken with.

"And neither is Fiore."

That was not to be wondered at either. When was Fiore ever where he was supposed to be?

Signora Pacelli, on the other hand . . . Rosalie chewed uncertainly on her lower lip. The kitchen had been all in a tumult over the article Herr Trattner had published that morning. A copy of the paper had been on every surface within the palace.

There were copies stacked here on one of the tables as well, she noticed. Rosalie's gaze fell on the large headline.

Wine-Soaked Prima Donna Spoils Opera Premiere

It was not because she was indisposed, Herr Trattner had claimed, that Signora Pacelli had crashed to the floor in the middle of the opera. It was because she had imbibed too much wine.

The reporter had insinuated that Herr Haydn was to blame for Signora Pacelli's drunken state. The Kapellmeister's morals had been called into question on the strength of the mishap. Herr Trattner had even gone so far as to suggest the incident might have jeopardized the marriage alliance.

"Put it out of your mind," Greta whispered to her. "Why should what happened last evening put the bride off her marriage? If anything puts her off it'll be the news that the Archduke may have gotten someone here with child."

"But if what Herr Trattner says is true, Herr Haydn will be in grave trouble," she whispered back. Hadn't Frau Schwann told them Her Serene Highness had been furious at the news?

"You should've seen how her nostrils flared," Frau Schwann had informed Rosalie, her plump features agog with horror. "She threw down the paper in a temper. I'll warrant His Serene Highness is just as outraged."

Anger swelled in Rosalie's breast. How dare Herr Trattner write such a vile piece! What had the Kapellmeister ever done to deserve such behavior?

"He hasn't the courage to say so openly"—she leaned closer to Greta as she spoke—"but he may as well accuse the entire household of lacking morals. The Prince, the Princess, the musicians, and all the servants. It isn't just an attack on Herr Haydn and his musicians."

Greta frowned, apparently not having considered this aspect of the matter. "Then we need to find the truth," she said determinedly. "Where is Karl? He'll know."

Steered out of the opera house as soon as the curtain dropped, they'd not seen Karl again last evening. Pivoting their necks now and craning this way and that, they scoured the room.

But Karl wasn't in the coffeehouse.

A tall, slender, blond musician sauntered over to the serving table. It was Albert, the Estates Director's nephew.

"Pining after your Karl, eh?" He grinned at Greta as he piled rolls, thin slices of ham, and a large helping of cherry preserves onto his plate.

Greta rolled her eyes. "Of course not! We were wondering where Signora Pacelli is?"

Albert cast a searching glance around the room as though hoping to find the soprano somewhere within.

"She must still be ill," he said. He approached closer, lowering his voice. "Fiore tells me it was the wine that did her in."

"Did her in?" Greta yelped. "Is she dead?"

Albert looked shocked. "Fiore didn't say so and it's not the impression I got. I just meant to say the wine was bad." His gaze traveled toward Rosalie. "I fear Gerhard will have a lot to answer for. The barber-surgeon took the bottle of wine. No doubt, he suspects it was tainted."

"If it was, it had nothing to do with Gerhard," Rosalie snapped, annoyed beyond belief. Why should Gerhard's wine affect anyone? "Where is Fiore, in any case?"

Albert shrugged. "With his uncle, I suppose. I haven't seen him this morning. If his aunt is ill in bed, someone else will have to attend to old Paolo."

<hr>

The inn was a long, whitewashed structure with a gable roof and a stone wainscot that covered the lower third of the building. The tavern projected out from it in an L-shape.

It was too early for the tavern to be open, but the wooden door stood ajar. Eager to get the meeting over with, Haydn briskly sprinted up the two steps and pushed the door open, wincing as it creaked.

But neither Gerhard, who stood behind his stone counter, a rag in his hand, nor Herr Hipfl, who sat at a small stool before him, appeared to notice the sound.

"Are you quite sure, Gerhard?" the barber-surgeon was saying. "The leaves look like mint and they smell remarkably alike, too."

Gerhard stopped his scrubbing to stare at the barber-surgeon, an exasperated expression on his features. "I can tell the difference, Herr Hipfl.

My mother is a midwife, do not forget. I know a thing or two about herbs, never fear."

The explanation didn't appear to reassure the barber-surgeon, who exhaled heavily.

"Then there was nothing other than mint in the wine?"

Gerhard's deep blue eyes bore into the barber-surgeon's face. "I stay away from pennyroyal, Herr Hipfl. As does my mother. The little good it does far outweighs the harm."

Haydn stepped closer. "Pennyroyal?" He took a seat beside the barber-surgeon. "Is that what . . ." He hesitated, unsure whether to speak of the murder in Gerhard's presence. Even though it was unlikely the tavern-keeper would gossip.

Nevertheless, under the circumstances, it was best not to overly bandy about the word. Trattner was not the only reporter in the village. Even in a small backwater like Eszterháza, there was more than one anonymous broadsheet published, and the writers of such papers no doubt received their information from somewhere.

But Gerhard, certainly no fool, seemed to have already deduced the nature of his question.

"Herr Hipfl surmises it was pennyroyal that killed Signora Pacelli," the tavern-keeper informed him.

Chapter Fifteen

Frowning, Haydn turned toward the barber-surgeon. He knew very little about herbs, but even he was aware of the reputation of that particular herb. Was it not used to expel an unwanted child from the womb?

"I had my suspicions when I examined the body yesterday, Herr Haydn," the barber-surgeon replied. "But the wine bottle she carried with her onstage—"

"I thought it had been emptied."

Herr Hipfl nodded. "So it had. But there was a sufficient quantity left at the bottom for me to examine. The odor of pennyroyal was pungent. Wanting to be certain, I set what remained before a rat I'd caught for the purpose."

The barber-surgeon paused, his features solemn. "It took no more than a few drops to induce a deathly writhing in the poor creature."

"Then she was . . ." Again, Haydn struggled to form his question. Did the presence of pennyroyal in Lucia's system indicate an unwanted pregnancy? Or had she mistakenly dosed herself?

"The herb can be used to relieve stomach pains, can it not?"

"Yes, but there are better remedies by far."

The barber-surgeon rose, gesturing toward one of the wooden settles by the fireplace.

"Send the girl over with some ale, if you would, Gerhard?" he said, turning to the tavern-keeper.

Gerhard nodded, proceeding to take down two large glass mugs from a hook on the back wall as the barber-surgeon ushered Haydn toward the settle.

When they were both seated, he leaned across the wooden table between them and said in a low voice: "I am convinced Signora Pacelli was with child, Herr Haydn. The matter remains to be ascertained, of course. But if she was . . ."

The barber-surgeon's voice trailed off and he regarded Haydn for some minutes before bringing forth a small pouch of herbs.

"This was found in her changing room."

Haydn gripped the table, desperately trying to contain his shock. "Her room was searched?"

Herr Hipfl shook his thick mane of hair. "No, no. It was the seamstress who discovered it. She was gathering up Signora Pacelli's clothing at her husband's behest."

Haydn nodded, his eyes still on the pouch. Made of cream-colored muslin, it looked exactly like the bags in which Maria Anna dispensed her herbs.

But of course it was no secret that Maria Anna had given Lucia herbs. At the singer's own request. He said as much to Hipfl.

The barber-surgeon nodded sympathetically. "The question is was your wife aware of Signora Pacelli's pregnancy? If she was, she could be charged with illicitly aiding Signora Pacelli to rid herself of her child."

He cleared his throat. "Given what I've heard, I doubt it was Signor Pacelli who fathered the child. Although, of course, he will have to be informed his wife was with child when she died."

"Of course." Haydn reached out for the pouch, letting it twirl from his fingers as he examined it.

"It is a mixture of herbs. But the crushed pennyroyal leaves it contains are unmistakable."

Haydn was barely listening as he examined the pouch. Had Maria Anna ever given Lucia a bundle of herbs? He couldn't recall.

But she had given the Archduke a bundle of herbs to settle his stomach a few days ago. There was no way of telling whether this was the same bundle.

If it was, how had it found its way into Lucia's changing room?

He raised his head. "Maria Anna usually administered her remedies to Lucia in the form of teas." He paused, unsure how to communicate his conjectures.

"Lucia's symptoms came and went, so a tea made to remedy the particular situation was the best solution. She wasn't the only person who sought

Maria Anna's remedies, however. Archduke Ferdinand has a tendency to indigestion. The symptoms were always the same."

"This pouch you say was intended for the Archduke?" Herr Hipfl sounded skeptical.

"It may have been."

"How then did it find its way into your prima donna's changing room?"

Haydn remained silent, willing the barber-surgeon to draw the obvious conclusion. But it appeared not to have entered the man's head at all.

———◆◆◆———

It was Gerhard who brought their mugs of foaming ale to the table. He had no sooner set it down than the raucous cry of a rooster split the air. It was followed by five more—each equally loud and ear-splitting.

Then the first rooster sounded its call again.

"The girl is out collecting eggs," Gerhard explained when the noise had died away. "It sets the roosters off to see the eggs being taken away from the brood."

"Why keep them, then?" Haydn wondered aloud.

"How else would we get any eggs?"

Gerhard's reply caused Haydn to frown. It did not take a farmer to know that roosters weren't needed for hens to produce eggs. The hens laid them as a matter of course.

Why had Gerhard lied about so simple a matter?

Haydn glanced at the barber-surgeon, but Herr Hipfl was as oblivious to this lie as he was to the evidence pointing to the Archduke's involvement in Lucia's demise.

The barber-surgeon took a long draft of his ale. Haydn followed suit, strongly tempted to bring out the extortion note Lucia had sent to the Archduke.

But what good would it do to air the Archduke's misdoings in public?

"If it turns out Signora Pacelli is with child, we will have no choice but to question Frau Haydn," the barber-surgeon stated.

He took another sip of his ale, looking at Haydn over the thick glass rim of his mug.

"Of course, it may be that someone among your performers availed themselves of Frau Haydn's remedies."

83

Haydn shrugged. The only person who had availed himself of Maria Anna's herbs was the Archduke. And the barber-surgeon had shown himself disinclined to follow that line of reasoning.

"Most likely it was that," the barber-surgeon urged. He leaned forward, speaking in hushed tones.

"If you can question your performers, Herr Haydn, and ascertain who wanted your prima donna dead, we may put this matter to rest sooner rather than later." He fingered his mug. "I expect His Serene Highness will want the situation speedily resolved."

The barber-surgeon regarded him steadily as though expecting Haydn to cough up a name.

His suspicions about Narcissa notwithstanding, Haydn chose not to divulge her name. It was absurd to limit the list of suspects to his wife and his performers.

If Lucia were with child—and the child had been fathered by the Archduke, as seemed entirely possible—then the only plausible candidate for the murder was their imperial guest.

The Archduke had a far better reason to eliminate Lucia—and far more to lose if she remained alive.

"What makes you believe she was with child?" Haydn asked. He was not a medical man, but surely the signs of her pregnancy would've been visible. No one—not even her colleagues—had known of her condition.

She may, it was true, have confided her situation to Maria Anna, but his wife had made no mention of it.

"The symptoms your brother described to me yesterday strongly hinted at it," the barber-surgeon replied. "Then when I examined her, I noticed a pronounced distension of the belly. It seems highly likely, although a more thorough examination is needed to confirm it."

⎯⎯•••⎯⎯

"And was a more thorough examination formed?" Haydn asked.

A blush suffused the barber-surgeon's brown cheeks. "I could hardly do it myself, Herr Haydn. But rest assured, it is being done as we speak."

Before Haydn could ask who it was that had offered to perform this more thorough examination, the tavern door creaked open and a plump woman with a scarf over her head hurried over to where they sat.

"Mother!" Gerhard called, his jaw dropping open. "What are you doing here?"

The Widow Heindl lived, Haydn recalled, in Mörbish am See. He was as startled to see her as was her son.

"Herr Hipfl sent for me."

Gerhard looked from his mother to the barber-surgeon. Then his blue eyes widened as understanding slowly illumined his features. He crossed himself.

"A child has been killed as well?" he asked wonderingly.

When neither the barber-surgeon nor his mother contradicted him, his features hardened and his lips compressed into a thin line of disapproval.

"Whoever killed the poor woman should hang for his deed," he declared. "A child is a precious thing."

The Widow Heindl dragged a chair over to their table and sat at the shorter edge of it.

"You were right, Herr Hipfl," she began. "The poor woman was indeed with child."

"How can you be so certain?" Haydn wanted to know. Until the child quickened in the womb, how could anyone know? And the only person who could tell them the truth was dead.

The widow turned to him, not offended in the least by the question. "The mouth of the womb is high and soft when a woman has conceived," she explained.

"And hers was, I take it?" Haydn queried.

The widow nodded. "Besides that, the breasts were enlarged, the nipples swollen and dark, and the veins—"

Haydn held up his hand, the litany of horrid details making him bilious.

"That will do," he said. "I understand perfectly."

He climbed to his feet and drew his timepiece out of his pocket. Staring at it, he said, "I should go. My duties at the palace require my attendance."

"To be sure," the barber-surgeon replied. "You will endeavor to do as I recommended, will you not, Herr Haydn? The sooner this situation is laid to rest, the better for all concerned."

Haydn curtly dipped his chin and left.

———❖———

Deep in thought, Rosalie and Greta trudged slowly back to the palace. Back at the coffeehouse, Albert had suggested Signora Pacelli was merely out of sorts. But Karl, who'd come in some minutes later, had shaken his head at that.

"I fear she is no more," he'd said, his brown eyes worried. "Poisoned, if I understood the matter correctly."

"By the wine?" Rosalie had queried, anxious for Gerhard's sake. Although, how could it have been the wine?

Karl had nodded. "It would seem so. But I can't think who could've tainted it."

"I can." Greta leaned closer to her beau. "Fräulein Leon. Who else could it be? She's been itching to get Signora Pacelli's part."

Karl had smiled at this. "That she has, my sweet. But the cabinet where the wine is kept is locked. Fiore keeps the keys. Of course, that never deterred Signora Pacelli from getting at the wine. She never hesitated to pluck the keys off his belt, and Fiore lacked the courage to stay her."

"But wasn't it Albert who took charge of the wine yesterday?" Rosalie pointed out. Fiore, as usual, had been nowhere to be found. "He must've had the keys yesterday."

Karl's brow wrinkled. "I suppose he did. The wine was locked in the cabinet as it always is."

"Yes, but"—Greta shook her head—"Albert had no reason to befoul the wine."

But someone must have, Rosalie thought, as she pushed her cart laden with empty breakfast dishes. If it was the wine that had killed Signora Pacelli, someone had to have tampered with it.

Unless the prima donna had killed herself. But why would she do that?

"I can't believe she's gone," Greta muttered beside her. "She was alive and . . . well, mostly in good spirits just yesterday."

"And in the middle of the opera, too," Rosalie said. It had almost marred the performance, but Karl's quick thinking and Miss Lidia's performance had prevented that from happening.

Could someone, jealous of Karl's good fortune, have sought to do away with the prima donna?

But as soon as the thought occurred to Rosalie, she dismissed it. There were other ways to sabotage the opera. Killing the lead singer was surely too drastic a method even for someone burning with envy.

"You don't suppose the extortion note had anything to do with it, do you?" Greta wondered, scurrying to keep up with Rosalie.

Stunned by the question, Rosalie's feet abruptly ceased to move.

"She could hardly have written it," the maid said, her violet eyes shrouded in thought. "But"—she swiveled around to face Greta—"what if she knew who had?"

Greta bobbed her head. "Fräulein Leon. Mark my words, it's her. She may not have been able to prevail upon Fiore for the keys. But it was Albert who had them yesterday. And he's little more than a simpleton."

The more Rosalie considered the matter, the more sense it made. After all, the note seemed to have been written by someone who would brook no opposition.

"I think you may be right," she said to her friend. "Fräulein Leon isn't the sort of person to easily submit to being crossed. But"—her brow furrowed as an objection occurred to her—"that must mean she is with child."

"Hannah will know," Greta said, referring to the seamstress attached to the opera house.

Satisfied that they'd made sense of the situation, they hurried into the palace only to be met by Ulrike.

The girl stumbled into them.

"Oh, there you are, Frau Heindl, Fräulein Schmidt," she greeted them in turn.

"What is it?" Rosalie asked.

Ulrike glanced cautiously around the hallway, then bent closer to them. "You'll never believe what I've heard. It was all the talk in the Officer's Mess."

"What was?" Greta asked, her voice brusque with impatience.

Ulrike cast another glance around the empty hallway. "Signora Pacelli. She wasn't drunk at all. She's dead."

"Yes, we know," Rosalie said, as she began pushing her cart toward the kitchen. But Ulrike wasn't done.

"The musicians think she killed herself."

"*What!*" Rosalie spun around.

"Nonsense!" The denial flew out of Greta's mouth, drowning out Rosalie's exclamation. "Why would she kill herself?"

"They say she was with child."

Chapter Sixteen

DETERMINED to find the Archduke, Haydn hastened from the inn to the palace stables. If His Imperial Highness still had the pouch of herbs Maria Anna had given him, the Kapellmeister would concede his suspicions were unfounded.

If not . . . Haydn's feet ground to a halt. If not, the Archduke's guilt would be confirmed. And the prospect would place Haydn in an untenable situation.

Was he to establish the Archduke—a boy barely seventeen, about to be wed at that—as a murderer and cause him to be locked up? Or worse still, be sent to the gallows.

On the other hand—Haydn's eyes roved to the Music House which contained his apartment—was he to deliver up his wife to the same awful fate? If the bag of herbs hadn't come from the Archduke, who else could it have come from?

Fall was approaching, yet the day was unseasonably warm. The heat of the sun burned into Haydn's skin as he began slowly trudging toward the stables. His shoes beat a dreary rhythm upon the dusty cobblestones. He stared at the tufts of grass that pushed up between the stones paving the path and the few wildflowers that festooned his way.

Couldn't there be a third solution—one that involved neither the Archduke nor his wife?

He had agreed to take the young Archduke under his wing, to ensure the marriage alliance took place without a hitch. How would he answer to the Empress if it turned out that the Archduke had—under his care, as it were —committed a heinous crime?

A crime that both befouled the law of the land and blackened His Imperial Highness's soul.

He neared the palace and its gardens. The stables were located less than half a mile east of the Music House. Haydn was just about to turn onto the lime-tree-lined lane that led to the building when he caught sight of Jakob Friberth's tall form hurrying toward him from the direction of the Opera House.

"Herr Kapellmeister, there you are!" The tenor's sleeves were rolled up, revealing a pair of muscular, sun-browned arms. He carried a broadsheet in his hands.

"I don't believe it," Greta said as she and Rosalie stood side-by-side in the kitchen, washing and drying the breakfast dishes.

"Besides even if she was with child," Rosalie said, "what of it? She was a married woman."

Greta huffed noisily, scrubbing a silver coffeepot a little more vigorously than was warranted. "The musicians ought to be ashamed of themselves, spreading rumors like that. And she not even buried yet."

Rosalie nodded, but her gaze was on the silver. If Greta kept scrubbing it like that, she'd scratch the metal. "You'd best be careful with that pot," she warned. "It'll be a gulden or two out of our pay if you mar it."

Greta's soapsud-soaked hands paused in their task. She turned the coffeepot over, inspecting it. It had fortunately survived her scouring. She washed it and handed it to Rosalie to dry.

"Wouldn't Karl have told us if she'd killed herself?"

"To be sure he would," Rosalie agreed. "But there are so many rumors flying about. I wish we knew what really happened."

"Well, she didn't kill herself, that's for sure. It's just so much claptrap."

Nevertheless when Hannah, the seamstress, tromped into the kitchen, her arms laden with costumes, the maids couldn't help confronting her with the question.

Jakob Friberth paused to catch his breath while Haydn waited patiently, wondering what had occurred to cause the tenor such consternation. A middle-aged man in his forties, Friberth rarely allowed the vicissitudes of life to perturb him.

Yet here he stood before Haydn more agitated than the Kapellmeister had ever seen him.

"Did Herr Trattner criticize your performance, Jakob?" Haydn's eyes dropped to the broadsheet. He couldn't make out the headline, but it was clearly one of Trattner's publications. "I would not take it amiss. His opinion means nothing, I assure you."

Although even as he said this, Haydn's misgivings caused an uneasy flutter in his stomach. Trattner's words were the only account anyone would have to judge the performance. They could not be taken too lightly.

"That's not it, Herr Kapellmeister." Friberth unfolded the broadsheet and held it out to Haydn.

Accustomed though he was to the publisher's rumor-mongering, Haydn found himself staggered by Trattner's claims—that the opera had been brought to a halt by a drunken prima donna! It was outrageous.

"Basing his judgment on one person's lack of rectitude, Trattner sees fit to call into question the entire troupe's morals, Herr Kapellmeister. Is it true Lucia was in her cups? Narcissa claims Lucia was utterly sauced."

Friberth huffed out a breath. "Truth to tell, the way she was staggering around before she fell, I couldn't help wondering myself whether she'd indulged herself too freely."

Haydn, scanning the article's ridiculous claims, glanced up, his features grave. It was bad enough, Trattner should be spreading rumors. But that Lucia's colleagues should think so ill of her in death as well was not to be borne.

"Signora Pacelli is no more, Jakob. It was the effect of the poison she'd ingested that caused her to lurch and stumble onstage."

Jakob's eyes—a startling blue—widened. "Then it is true, she killed herself?"

It was the second time the Kapellmeister had heard such a claim. He frowned.

"There seems to be no reason to believe that she did," he began slowly. "But—" His frown deepened.

Could it, however, be true? If she had been with child—the conception the unfortunate result of an illicit relationship—might she not be tempted to take her own life? He decided to probe further.

"Why do you say Lucia killed herself, Jakob?" He searched the other's handsome features. "Had she any reason to?"

But the tenor shrugged. "It is what Gabriel Krause says." That was the young cellist, newly married, Haydn recalled, and forced to leave his bride in Eisenstadt. "No one knows the truth, and this"—Friberth shook the newspaper violently—"only generates consternation and confusion."

His large hands twisted and crushed the paper.

"I've also heard she was with child . . ." Friberth hesitated. "Paolo, I fear, was neither young enough nor man enough to . . . to . . . er satisfy her. And one can hardly blame her for seeking her pleasure elsewhere. But if . . ." His voice trailed off.

Haydn gaped at the man. The selfsame thought had occurred to him. And he was well aware of Lucia's propensities in that regard. But how had Friberth known? His eyes continued to bore into the tenor's blue orbs.

Friberth squirmed uneasily as though he were a butterfly pinned to a board.

"You asked if there was a reason for Lucia to take her life, Herr Kapellmeister. Might not this fact—if it's true—furnish a plausible one?"

Haydn slowly nodded. "Yes," he said. "Yes, it might well, indeed."

If that were the case, Lucia's death could certainly be laid at the Archduke's door—wasn't it his child, after all?—but at least no one could say His Imperial Highness had gone so far as to commit the deed.

Oblivious to the tenor's presence, the Kapellmeister pursed his lips. Still, the Empress would have to be informed of this unfortunate incident. He had hoped to avoid that.

But—Haydn's gaze drifted toward the crushed broadsheet in Friberth's hands—under the present circumstances, it would be best to supply Her Majesty with as detailed a set of facts possible to counter the appalling rumors Trattner had set afloat.

"What shall I tell the others?"

Friberth's voice, asking the question, intruded upon his consciousness.

"Herr Kapellmeister?"

Haydn raised his head.

"Tell them that Signora Pacelli is unfortunately no more. Poisoned, although how and why have yet to be determined. If anyone can shed any light on the matter, they are to come to me at once or go to Master Luigi or my brother."

"Signora Pacelli didn't kill herself, did she, Hannah?" Greta demanded.

If anyone knew, it would be Hannah. The seamstress had known Signora Pacelli in Vienna. It was the prima donna who'd recommended that Hannah be hired.

"Of course not. Wherever did you hear anything so silly?"

Hannah draped the garments over the back of a chair and plonked her heavy frame into another.

"The Archduke and his bride aren't ready to try on their costumes," she said. "When they will be, who knows? Although, I suppose it's for the best. I'm that thirsty."

Rosalie and Greta exchanged a quick glance. What a heaven-sent opportunity! They'd had questions for Hannah, and here she was.

"Have some lemonade, then," Greta quickly offered while Rosalie bustled about, taking down a glass from a shelf and pouring some lemonade from the pitcher on the windowsill.

When Hannah had taken a long draft from the glass, nearly emptying its contents, Greta said: "We'd heard she was with child."

She'd been about to say more, but Rosalie refilling Hannah's glass shook her head. It was best not to share the musicians' scandalous surmise.

Hannah didn't seem taken aback by the question. "Her nausea, coming and going as it did, made me think she might be. But her husband has never been capable of fathering a child. And now I'm quite sure it was the poison that was causing the trouble. What else could it be?"

Rosalie pondered this in silence. Had someone been dosing Signora Pacelli with poison on a daily basis? Who could it be but someone in the opera house? Someone like Fräulein Leon.

"We'd heard Fräulein Leon was with child as well. But that can't be true, can it?"

Hannah shook her head. "I doubt it. She's too clever, that one, to put herself in a situation like that. She'd lose her position"—Hannah shuddered —"her child, too, if it came to that. The world doesn't look too kindly upon fallen women."

"She seems quite friendly with the Archduke," Greta remarked.

Hannah shrugged. "Friendly enough, I suppose. But so was Signora Pacelli, and look where that got her."

Rosalie and Greta looked at each other. What was that supposed to mean?

"His Imperial Highness could hardly have saved her from getting killed," Rosalie said in a mild tone.

Hannah didn't respond, staring at the lemonade in her glass.

"We found a bag of herbs in her changing room last night," she said at last.

"A bag of herbs?" Greta and Rosalie chorused.

Hannah nodded. "Signor Pacelli is adamant it came from Frau Haydn. But he's mistaken. Frau Haydn never gave her any bundles of herbs like that."

She raised her eyes, staring steadily at them. Rosalie and Greta craned forward, waiting breathlessly for her to continue.

"But I did a see a bag of herbs just like it in the Archduke's study the other day."

"It was the Archduke's bag of herbs, then?" Greta cried. "But how would that get into Signora Pacelli's room?"

Hannah shrugged, as much at a loss as they were.

"Who can tell? But it's clear someone wanted to silence her."

"Why?" Rosalie wondered aloud.

"Because of what she knew, I suppose," Hannah replied. "What other reason is there?"

Rosalie was about to probe further, but the sudden sharp ringing of the Archduke's bell startled her out of her wits.

"I'd best be gone." Quickly, Hannah drained her glass of lemonade and rose. "Who knows what some will do to keep a secret hidden?" She shook her head.

Chapter Seventeen

LUIGI sat at Haydn's desk in the Music Room poring over the scores for the evening's performance. Years ago, the Duke of Modena had, on a visit to London, enjoyed a stupendous display of fireworks; it had been preceded by an equally remarkable musical performance by the great composer Handel.

His Serene Highness had wished not only to re-create the experience for his guest, but to rival it as well.

There would be a horse ballet that evening performed by the Archduke and his bride. This would be followed by a concert. After that, the evening would erupt in fireworks from the temple built by the Esterházy stables.

As the foremost soprano in the opera troupe, Lucia was supposed to sing many of the songs. But since the poor woman had met her maker, the songs would have to be edited to suit Miss Lidia's more limited range.

Preoccupied with his work, Luigi didn't hear the muted knock on the door nor the soft click of it opening. A loud clearing of the throat invaded his eardrums, startling him into shaking his pen. Streaks of black ink flew from the nib onto the paper.

He stared down at the sheet in dismay.

"Master Luigi!"

Recalled to the presence of someone in the room, he turned.

"Rosalie?" His eyebrows rose. "Is anything the matter?"

He searched her features. The girl looked distressed. What could possibly have occurred?

"Has Herr Haydn arrived?"

Frowning, Luigi turned his chair to face the maid. "The barber-surgeon sent for him this morning; there's no knowing how long he'll be. Is there anything I can help you with?"

The girl twisted her apron; she seemed quite unaware of what she was doing.

"We have some information—Greta and I—about . . ."

"Signora Pacelli's untimely demise?" Luigi ventured. He gestured toward a chair. "You have learned something, I take it," he began when she'd sat down.

Rosalie nodded. "It's about Signora Pacelli's sickness—the bouts of nausea she endured for the past few days. Hannah thinks it may have been the result of ingesting poison."

Luigi considered this. Johann had said something to him just that morning about Lucia carrying a child. The barber-surgeon had, in fact, considered the sickness to be a symptom of that.

He hesitated, wondering how much of this to share with her. But the girl had proven herself to be discreet—intelligent, too, come to think of it. And if her musings on the matter—and any gossip she was privy to—could help unearth the truth, what harm was there in sharing the facts of the case with her?

"Herr Hipfl is certain she has been poisoned. But that she suffered bouts of nausea led him to an entirely different conclusion."

Rosalie frowned. "What did he think had caused that?"

"He was certain she must've been with child."

"Oh!" The news seemed to take the girl by surprise. "But whose—?" She blushed, stopping herself just in time.

Luigi suppressed a smile. There was likely not a person in the palace who was unaware of Paolo's impotence. But that was neither here nor there.

"Did Hannah have any other reason for thinking Signora Pacelli had ingested poison regularly?" he asked instead.

"She's quite certain Signora Pacelli was killed because of what she knew."

The news caused Luigi to lean forward. "What *did* Signora Pacelli know, did Hannah say?"

"Hannah was called up by the Archduke and his bride before Greta and I could ask her about it. But we thought Herr Haydn should know."

Luigi nodded. "Yes, he should. But who could've done such a thing? And how was it even done?"

Rosalie had an answer for both questions and Luigi listened carefully as she outlined her thoughts.

"It must've been the wine. She sipped it constantly to settle her stomach. Everyone knew that. But"—the maid's nose wrinkled as a thought occurred to her—"Karl says the storeroom in which the wine is kept is habitually locked."

"I don't suppose it would take too much to convince Fiore to give up the keys," Luigi said wryly. "The boy will do anything for money."

"That could be how Fräulein Leon got hold of the keys, then," Rosalie mused. "She'd know as well as anybody else that Fiore has huge debts."

Luigi had no trouble believing that Narcissa wanted Lucia out of the way. Hadn't she been adamant about being given Lucia's role? But it was when Rosalie mentioned the attempt to extort money from the Archduke—he vaguely recalled Johann mentioning it to him—that he came to a startling conclusion.

Could Lucia have been carrying the Archduke's child? Surely, that was far worse than some peccadillo committed in Vienna? After all, what evidence was there of the Archduke's affair with a lowly maid and the consequences of that relationship?

She'd likely been banished to a secluded convent, her child taken away from her to be reared by peasants who would never know its parentage.

But Lucia—and the evidence of the Archduke's illicit relation with her—could hardly be dismissed.

Rosalie's next words only confirmed the dreadful truth.

"His Imperial Highness's herbs were found in her changing room?" Luigi could hardly believe it. It was as close to an admission of guilt as one could get.

Why should one suppose that Narcissa had stolen the herbs? Wasn't it easier to believe the Archduke had taken them to Lucia himself? After all, his motive for ridding the world of the soprano was far stronger than Narcissa's.

He recalled something else Rosalie had said. "Hannah said Lucia—Signora Pacelli, that's to say—knew something, didn't she? Some secret knowledge about someone that got her killed?"

Rosalie confirmed his suspicion with a nod.

God in heaven, it was the Archduke's secret Lucia had been carrying. In her womb, no less. And she'd been forced to take it to her grave. Luigi's gaze fell on his knuckles—pale and bloodless, they clutched the armrests on his chair.

God have mercy, how long had the Archduke been trying to kill Lucia?

No sooner had Rosalie left than Luigi propelled himself out of his chair and walked, and then sprinted toward the opera house. Finding Johann rehearsing with Miss Lidia, Luigi firmly clasped his friend's arm.

"Something urgent has come up. You will excuse us, won't you, Miss Lidia?"

Without waiting for a reply, Luigi dragged Johann out of the auditorium and into a secluded corner.

"I fear Joseph's suspicions about the Archduke were not unjustified," he began.

He enumerated the points he'd gleaned from Rosalie—Hannah's suspicions, the possible reason for Lucia's ongoing sickness, and—the most damning piece of evidence as far as Luigi was concerned—the bag of herbs found in her changing room.

Johann's features—habitually pale turned whiter still. "Brother will have to be told," he said. "And Hannah must be questioned."

He surveyed the tiny room they stood in and the hallway just behind him as though hoping to find the seamstress.

"She must still be with the Archduke and his bride," he said, turning back to Luigi. "But His Imperial Highness will need to be confronted."

"Joseph is the best person to do it. I hardly know what to do—whether to bring the matter to His Serene Highness's attention or . . ." Luigi's voice trailed uncertainly off.

"Brother will know what to do," Johann repeated.

That a bag of herbs had been discovered in Lucia's changing room was not news to Haydn.

He stood in the far corner of the enormous cobbled yard of the Esterházy stables, huddled with Luigi and Johann. The Archduke and his bride were to rehearse their performance for the evening, but neither had as yet made an appearance. However, Luigi and Johann had hurtled down the path, breathless and agitated, shortly after Haydn had arrived.

"Herr Hipfl showed me the pouch," the Kapellmeister now confessed. "And I fear it looks very much like the ones Maria Anna is wont to use."

His gaze traveled over his companions' shoulders toward the long, yellow ochre structure of the stable—richly decorated with wreaths and flowers for the occasion.

Stable hands bustled in and out of the vast double doors in the center of the building. Fortunately, no one took any notice of them, standing with their heads together, talking in low voices. The air contained the sweet scent of hay and the musty odor of horse flesh. The horses themselves—fine animals—poked their heads out of their stalls, whinnying curiously.

"He can hardly think sister-in-law had anything to do with the matter, can he?" Johann asked.

Haydn's eyes returned to his companions. "On the contrary, he insinuates that its presence suggests Maria Anna was helping Lucia get rid of the child."

Luigi snorted. "Only a nitwit would come to such a conclusion," he declared. "Besides, Hannah says as well the pouch must've come from the Archduke."

"That is the one saving grace," Haydn conceded. He had come to the selfsame conclusion. But Hannah's voice, seconding his opinion, lent it greater credibility. After all, she spent more time than he with the performers.

Moreover, Hannah was one of the few people who had occasion to go frequently in and out of every singer's changing room.

How curious, then, that Hannah had been unaware of Lucia's plight.

He must've spoken aloud for Johann responded to his question.

"Protecting her former mistress's reputation, no doubt," he quietly ventured.

Haydn nodded. It was possible. After all, Lucia had taken Hannah into her employ when the seamstress had lost her shop in Vienna. How could Hannah fail to be grateful?

He glanced over his shoulder at the path behind them. There was still no sign of the Archduke or his bride.

He turned back to the other two men. "I mean to question His Imperial Highness as soon as he arrives. There's no doubt in my mind that Lucia was carrying his child. And if he confesses to not having the herbs"—he exhaled heavily—"then he may as well confess to murder."

"Is it possible he could have been poisoning her this entire time?" Luigi asked.

"Everyone knew she drank wine to soothe her stomach," Johann added. "And if the poison were administered in the wine . . ."

Haydn considered the idea. "But her nausea could just as easily be explained by the fact of her being with child. Besides, how would His Imperial Highness get a hold of the wine in our store cupboards?"

"How hard is it to bribe a servant?" Luigi asked. "And we all know Narcissa would've gladly helped."

That was true enough. The wine had already been flavored with mint. Haydn had learned that much at the tavern. The addition of pennyroyal would not have altered its taste much at all.

"His Imperial Highness may simply have given her the herbs—ostensibly to soothe her stomach," Johann suggested. "That would mean she had willingly dosed herself with it, never realizing she was poisoning herself."

"Whatever the case, it does not negate the fact of His Imperial Highness having a hand in Lucia's death," Haydn said grimly. He was beginning to dismiss the idea that Lucia had killed herself. Why he'd ever considered it, he knew not.

"She was surely troubled by her situation," he now said. "After all, why would her colleagues believe she'd taken her life over it?"

"She did not kill herself, Joseph. I refuse to believe it." Luigi shook his head adamantly. "Nothing in the note she wrote His Imperial Highness or her pursuit of him indicates she was so lost to hope as to take her own life."

"Although . . ." Johann hesitated. "If she was anxious about Paolo's reception of the news, is it possible that . . ."

"That Paolo killed her?" Haydn's eyes widened, the possibility never having occurred to him.

They considered the notion in silence. Had Paolo killed his wife? He was too frail to lift a hand against her. Poison would be the way to do it. It was a woman's weapon—or that of a weak man's.

"Far better that it were Paolo than His Imperial Highness," Haydn said with a sigh. "But I fear the Archduke had greater reason to dispose of her."

He withdrew the note from his pocket. It had clearly been penned by a desperate woman. A woman who would stop at nothing to get justice.

Have you no thought for the child you've fathered—or the poor woman left to bear your sin as well as hers? Don't think you can get out of this without paying.

No, it was clear Lucia had been referring to her own predicament—not that of another. She had brought it on herself, yet Haydn felt a deep sympathy for her. She had not deserved to lose her life. And the sin she'd found herself in was not hers alone to bear.

Had the Archduke, lacking the courage to take responsibility for his conduct, sought to kill the one person who could bear witness against him?

Haydn raised his head. "If the Archduke and his bride arrive together, find some pretext to draw her away that I might have a few minutes alone with His Imperial Highness."

He had solemnly promised Her Majesty he would see her son married to his bride. But how could he, in all good conscience, allow an innocent young woman to be wed to a killer? Maria D'Este's future needed to be considered as well.

He would not—he simply could not—allow such a travesty. Young the Archduke might be, but he was old enough to know right from wrong.

Chapter Eighteen

"I wish to have a word with you, Herr Haydn." Maria Beatrice D'Este's solemn features were directed toward the Kapellmeister. Mounted upon a white horse, she towered over the three men.

Her blue eyes flickered toward Johann and Luigi and then found their way back to Haydn's face. "In private, if you please."

The Archduke and his bride had arrived a few minutes ago. Resplendent in the baggy satin trousers of a Turkish woman, wearing a richly embroidered long tunic of bright orange, with a crimson turban, the bride had ridden ahead of the groom. Her horse pawed at the ground, whinnying softly, as she gripped its reins tightly in her hands.

Haydn forbore to look at his companions. He had hoped for an opportunity to speak with the Archduke. But that would have to wait.

"Very well." Gesturing to Johann and Luigi to usher the Archduke toward the marriage arch constructed in front of the stable, Haydn led the bride's white horse to a secluded corner of the yard.

"The Empress speaks very highly of you, Herr Haydn," Maria Beatrice said as she gracefully dismounted her horse. She was an excellent horsewoman, Haydn noted.

She stood before him, a petite figure, her back perfectly straight—a force to contend with, for all that she was small. Her blue eyes regarded him steadfastly.

"Her Majesty directed me to you, Herr Haydn. She said you would answer my questions honestly."

"I will certainly endeavor to do so, Your Ladyship." He wasn't sure how to address her. She was an heiress to four states, but had no title in her own right. Her father, though a Duke, insisted upon being addressed as a Prince.

That had led to a frequent butchering of his title the previous evening as the footmen and other servants struggled to remember the right form of address. More than once, the Duke of Modena had been addressed as "Your Royal Grace!"

"Your Royal Highness, you dunce!" the Duke had angrily retorted each time. "I am to be addressed as Your Royal Highness. Not Your Grace. Or Your Royal Grace. But Your Royal Highness."

The memory would've been amusing, but for the situation Haydn currently found himself in.

"What questions did you have, Your Ladyship?" he probed gently, although from the way her eyes narrowed as they followed the Archduke, Haydn could guess at the object of her inquiry.

The bride's blue eyes returned toward him, fastening themselves upon Haydn's face. Her fingers were tightly clenched around her horse's reins.

"What was the nature of the relationship between your prima donna and His Imperial Highness?"

The bluntness of the question, voiced in an even, flat tone, took Haydn by surprise. He found his own head pivoting to where the Archduke stood talking with Luigi and Johann.

What was the relation between the Archduke and Lucia? He himself would dearly wish to know the answer to that question.

"His Imperial Highness," he began carefully, turning back to her, "appreciated Signora Pacelli's voice—as would any true connoisseur of music. He was most gracious and most generous in voicing that appreciation—as befits his status, of course."

The corners of Maria Beatrice's mouth turned down, as though Haydn had disappointed her.

"Were they intimate?" she asked, her voice hardening.

Once again, Haydn found his gaze roving toward the Archduke. How was he to answer that question? He turned back to the bride and her tight-lipped expression.

Instead of answering the question, he asked one of his own.

"Do you have misgivings about the wedding, Your Ladyship? Or the Archduke himself?"

Maria Beatrice bit her lip. Her eyes were on the Archduke's slim person —garbed in a gold-trimmed crimson robe worn over an orange tunic—as she responded. She gently nuzzled the horse.

"He seems amiable enough. I have no reason to question his devotion to God. But I fear he might be weak-willed, and . . ."

"If you choose to marry him, Your Ladyship, your fortitude may be the guiding force that gives him the direction he needs," Haydn pointed out. Her posture and attitude told him she was a woman of remarkable strength.

"But will he be faithful?" Maria Beatrice searched Haydn's features, her fingers stroking the horse's snow-white mane. "And loving? I will not tolerate the kind of marriage my mother endures."

Dear Lord, what could he say to that? Would to God, Johann were with him. His younger brother might have found the words to reassure this young woman.

"I know not, Your Ladyship," Haydn said honestly. "But I would recommend that you put before the Archduke your expectations of the marriage. See if his answers satisfy you. I will speak to His Imperial Highness as well and remind him of his duty to God, to the Empress, his mother, and to you."

She looked at him. Her hand had ceased to stroke her horse, who kept turning its head this way and that against her hand, urging her to continue.

"And if his answers do not satisfy me?"

"Then may God, your confessor, and your own conscience be your guide."

It was not an adequate response to her questions. But what else could Haydn say?

<hr>

Johann could not have been more dismayed than when Maria Beatrice D'Este announced she wished to speak with brother alone. Walking gravely beside Luigi, who was leading the Archduke's horse, Johann kept glancing over his shoulder at his brother.

How were they to determine whether the Archduke had supplied Lucia with the poison that had taken her life?

The rhythmic clip-clop of the horse's hooves on the cobbles beat against his mind, preventing him from divining a way to ask the question that needed to be asked.

Luigi was explaining the music and choreography to the Archduke as they walked toward the enormous arch erected in front of the stables. A figure of Psyche was carved upon one post. A figure of Eros, her lover upon the other. Upon the arch was a gold barque with a winged creature within it, Hymen, the Greek god of marriage.

It was only when His Imperial Highness dismounted his horse—a strong black stallion—wincing as he did so, that Johann found a way to broach the subject.

"Sister-in-law was asking after your health, Your Imperial Highness. I trust the herbs she gave you settled your stomach."

The Archduke made a face. "Yes, yes, they did the job. Please let Frau Haydn know I thank her for her solicitude."

"The herbs are to be taken in a tea twice every day, are they not, Johann?" Luigi, seeming to have divined Johann's purpose, asked. He turned from Johann to the Archduke.

"Every day until there's none left," Johann asserted with a nod. "Your Imperial Highness is following the instructions, I trust."

The Archduke's features darkened as though in irritation. "I fear I cannot follow those instructions—much as I would like to, of course," he said curtly. His tone indicated that he considered the matter closed.

"Does Frau Haydn need to make up another pouch?" Luigi said at once, ignoring the warning in the Archduke's voice. "She will be most happy to do it. Your Imperial Highness has only to ask."

But the Archduke was already shaking his head.

"No. No, that will not be necessary."

"But—" Johann frowned. "If the herbs affected a cure—"

"They did," the Archduke interrupted. "Most swiftly. And not having any further need for them, I discarded them. There's no need to trouble Frau Haydn. The job is done."

Luigi and Johann exchanged a glance. What job was the Archduke referring to? His own health?

Or Lucia's death?

It had not escaped Johann's attention that the Archduke had admitted to not having the herbs in his possession. If he had—in all innocence—supplied them to Lucia, why lie about the matter? Why claim that he'd discarded the pouch?

It was a most troubling lie.

"With child?" Greta repeated, aghast. "Signora Pacelli? Are you sure?"

The broom she'd taken out of the closet slipped through her fingers and clattered onto the stone floor.

"Yes, but be quiet," Rosalie hissed. She picked up the broom Greta had dropped and glanced quickly around the hallway. There was no one around. "We'd best go into the servants' hall," she whispered. "I don't want anyone to hear us."

Nodding in agreement, Greta picked up the bucket filled with dust cloths and the mops she'd left standing against the wall.

They were supposed to go to the opera house to clean the auditorium, but that chore was forgotten in the face of this stunning news.

"How does Master Luigi know?" she demanded once they were inside the servants' hall.

Rosalie closed the door and stood with her back resting against it.

"It's what the barber-surgeon says. And he should know."

"But . . ." Greta's forehead wrinkled. "But I thought Hannah said—"

"She did," Rosalie interrupted, her head bobbing up and down. "I nearly said it out loud when I first heard the news. That her husband is incapable of fathering a child. I stopped myself just in time."

She stifled a giggle, recalling how utterly unsurprised Master Luigi had seemed when she'd nearly blurted that out. "Although I'll bet it's no secret that he can't."

Greta still seemed puzzled. "But that would mean—" She patted her hair, pulled back as always into two blond buns. "You don't think . . . ?"

Her voice trailed off as she gazed wide-eyed at Rosalie.

Rosalie nodded, although she was finding it hard to believe as well.

"She must have written that letter herself."

"And His Imperial Highness killed her?" Greta's voice rose in wonder. "I suppose he'd have to, but . . ."

Rosalie stared at the yellow wall in front of her. That the Archduke had reason to kill Signora Pacelli was not in doubt. But would he do the deed himself? When could he have even done it?

"Wouldn't someone have noticed him if he'd gone into her changing room?" Greta asked her.

"His Imperial Highness would've stood out like a sore thumb," Rosalie agreed. Could he have been in disguise? It would have to be more than a change in clothing; his face and figure were so familiar to all the servants.

"Could he have had an accomplice?" Greta asked. "Fräulein Leon, perhaps?"

That was certainly a possibility, Rosalie thought. Still, something about the situation bothered her.

"Do you suppose he'd be foolish enough to leave his pouch of herbs behind—where anyone could recognize them and immediately point the finger at him?"

Greta tilted her head and regarded Rosalie.

"It may have dropped out of his pocket," she said at last. "That's the only explanation for it. He could hardly have tried to poison her with his medicaments."

"Unless. . ." Rosalie's brow furrowed. There was something her mother-in-law had told her, some herb she was to avoid at all costs. What was it now?

She racked her brains, but to no avail.

Could His Imperial Highness have given—or sent—Signora Pacelli his herbs in the hope of ridding her of her child? Had the herb then killed Signora Pacelli as well?

"It's very commonly found, this herb," she told Greta. "But it can kill a child you're carrying. And it can kill you as well."

Suddenly the name slipped into her mind.

Pennyroyal.

"Pennyroyal!" Greta gasped. Her hand flew to her mouth. "There's something you should see," she said. "I thought it was just so much rubbish, but . . ."

She pulled Rosalie deeper into the room.

Puzzled, Rosalie waited while Greta reached up, withdrawing a thick notebook from a shelf on the wall that contained several similar ledgers and notebooks.

Opening the notebook, Greta pulled out a folded broadsheet.

"I tucked it away here because I didn't want anyone to see it."

Chapter Nineteen

Gabor, the head groom, looked at the Archduke—who was struggling to get his stallion to execute a *piaffe*—and shook his grizzled head.

"Where can His Imperial Highness's mind be?" he asked no one in particular. "It's not on his horse, that much is clear."

Haydn made no reply, but he and Johann and Luigi exchanged a glance. Where the Archduke's mind was could easily be guessed. At least the lad had a conscience, Haydn thought to himself. The Kapellmeister hoped to be able to use it to extract a confession.

The rehearsal was coming to an end, but it had not gone well. The bride had performed her part gracefully, her horse executing its steps with precision and beauty.

As for the Archduke, his horse's walk during the mock joust between himself—a Knight of the Order of the Golden Fleece—and his bride-to-be—representing a Turkish warrior—had barely kept time with the music.

But now when the defeated Turk and the victorious Knight were to dance together, his horse ignored its master's commands, slamming its hock on the ground as soon as it raised it.

The Archduke's impatience was only making matters worse. He tugged at the reins and jabbed his knee into the stallion's side, making the creature ever more nervous. It was hard to watch, and Haydn found himself averting his eyes.

Finally, Gabor could stand it no longer. "No," he bawled, going to the middle of the yard and wildly gesticulating his arms. "No, Your Imperial Highness! Leave off the reins."

Haydn lifted his bow, ceasing to play.

"We have rehearsed long enough. It would be best to stop for the time being. Allow the horse to rest."

The Archduke, still sitting stiffly astride his horse, looked at Haydn, his face irate. "And what of the performance tonight? Am I to let the beast show me to be a perfect incompetent?"

"Of course, not," Haydn smoothly replied. "Gabor will help train the creature."

The Archduke's concern had supplied him with just the opportunity he needed to confront His Imperial Highness with his misdeeds.

"Without a rider would be best," Gabor interjected as he softly stroked the perspiring horse.

Haydn nodded his agreement. After the horse had perfected its *piaffe*—a collected trot in position—Gabor and the Archduke could rehearse the finale of the piece while he and Johann furnished the music.

"Luigi will escort Her Ladyship back to the palace," he finished.

"Very well," the Archduke agreed, although the sulky expression remained on his face.

Reluctantly, he dismounted his horse and bowed stiffly to Maria Beatrice D'Este, who was led away by Luigi.

Rosalie unfolded the broadsheet Greta had handed her.

The paper was large—about fifteen inches in length and eleven inches across. The publisher's name was missing and it was undated, but the black ink and the smudges left on it when Greta had folded it suggested it had been freshly printed.

"Poison Takes Prima Donna's Life!" ornate letters proclaimed the news.

A picture in the middle of the article showed a woman lying face down on the stage, surrounded by other singers.

Rosalie raised her head. "Where did you get this?" she asked her friend.

"Karl had it with him when he came here to ask us to clean the auditorium," Greta replied. "He caught Fiore reading it instead of attending to his chores."

"Fiore must've got it from the tavern," Rosalie surmised. Small though Eszterháza was, it had its share of printers. The publications were typically left at the tavern for villagers and palace servants to read. For a few pfennig, one could even bring back a copy.

She turned back to the article, scanning the opening paragraph.

A fine opera performance was marred yesterday by the sudden death of the opera's lead singer, Lucia Pacelli. Although initial rumors suggested Signora Pacelli was drunk, we now know the poor woman to have been poisoned.

Greta peeked over Rosalie's shoulder. "That was not the part that bothered me," she said. "It was this"—she pointed to the next paragraph.

Tragic as the situation is. It is made far worse by the fact that the poison took not one but two lives. We have been made aware that the unfortunate Signora Pacelli was with child.

"After what Hannah told us," Greta said, "I didn't think anyone needed to read that."

"No," Rosalie agreed. "Especially since they insinuate the child was illegitimate."

The conception of the child must have been no small miracle, the article read, *for the prima donna's husband is said to be remarkably deficient in that regard. That makes the nature of the poison that took her life even more telling. For, dear reader, we hear it was pennyroyal.*

"There!" Greta jabbed at the mention of the herb. "It's the same herb Gerhard's mother told you to avoid."

Rosalie re-read the words. Was the writer of the article trying to say the soprano had taken her own life—in a misguided effort to rid herself of an unwanted child?

But when she shared that supposition with her friend, Greta shook her head vehemently.

"Oh, no, that's not it. Look!" Greta pointed a pudgy forefinger at the final paragraphs of the broadsheet.

"No further clues are available save this one—that a bundle of herbs said to belong to His Imperial Highness, Archduke Ferdinand Karl, was found in the dead soprano's changing room."

"How could they have heard about that?" Rosalie wondered. "That the herbs belonged to the Archduke."

"From the same place they heard the rest of it," Greta said. "Hannah must have been gossiping. Or they overheard the barber-surgeon. Didn't you say he was at the tavern with Herr Haydn?"

"Yes, but—?" Rosalie's eyes narrowed as she considered the matter. Unable to put her finger on what was wrong, she bent her head to continue reading.

"Of course, we cannot say with any certainty that the two circumstances are related. We, therefore, implore the reader not to give in to any speculations based on the sparse facts available so far."

Greta snorted. "We urge the reader not to speculate, they say. Not speculate, indeed. How could anyone avoid it after reading this?"

The question caused an icy chill to run down Rosalie's spine.

Did someone want them to believe the Archduke was responsible for Signora Pacelli's murder?

"But why?" Greta asked, puzzled when Rosalie voiced the notion aloud.

"Out of spite, I suppose," Rosalie said. "To make sure the marriage doesn't take place."

Although when she said it out loud, the thought seemed outlandish. Why should any of the servants or the performers care whom the Archduke married? Or even whether he did so or not?

Yet Rosalie was quite sure she was right. And now she remembered why.

"Didn't Hannah say Signor Pacelli thought the herbs had come from Frau Haydn?" she asked.

Greta's blue eyes narrowed, attempting to recall what the seamstress had said.

"So she did," she said at last. "What of it? Everyone knows it's Frau Haydn who dispenses medicaments in small muslin pouches."

Rosalie turned to face her friend. "Then why doesn't the article mention Frau Haydn's name? Why go straight to the Archduke?"

For some moments, Haydn and Johann stood on either side of the Archduke, silently watching Gabor calm the stallion down. The long, rhythmic strokes of the head groom's arm along the horse's glossy black flank seemed to ease the irritation out of the Archduke's being as well.

"My brother tells me, Your Imperial Highness, that you find your constitution much improved," Haydn eased into the conversation.

"I do, indeed," the Archduke replied, looking on as Gabor urged his stallion into a walk.

"You have discarded the herbs, I hear," Haydn continued.

The words were like a whiplash, causing the Archduke's head to snap around to face the Kapellmeister.

"So I did. What of it?" His blue orbs stared coldly into Haydn's brown eyes.

"The herbs seem to have made their way into Signora Pacelli's hands," Johann quietly responded. "Brother was wondering how? And why?"

A furrow appeared on the Archduke's brow and he began to turn toward Johann. But before he could say a word, Haydn took up the thread.

"The barber-surgeon discovered your bundle of herbs. It turns out they include the very substance that proved so fatal to Signora Pacelli and caused her demise."

"I d-d—?" The Archduke's head pivoted from Haydn to Johann and back again. He swallowed once, twice, then emitted a harsh laugh. "If that is true, Herr Haydn, surely your wife is to blame. I didn't make up that vile concoction. It was your wife's doing."

<hr>

Haydn's eyes blazed. The Archduke's utter lack of remorse was galling. To kill a woman and then to lay the blame at another's door was so coldly callous, the audacity of it took Haydn's breath away.

"My wife would never have administered pennyroyal to a woman in Signora Pacelli's condition."

"Her condition?" The Archduke repeated. A nonplussed frown appeared on his brow that exasperated Haydn no end.

"She was with child," he said. "But I am sure you were aware of that."

He withdrew Lucia's note from his pocket and handed it to the Archduke. The nobleman's white features, rigid and expressionless, told Haydn all he needed to know.

"This was discovered in your study. It is the note you discarded yesterday, is it not?"

The Archduke raised his horrified eyes from the crushed piece of paper toward Haydn.

"I thought Lucia had written it, but—" He paused, his eyes searching the stable yard.

Was he feigning bewilderment, Haydn wondered. His eyes sought Johann's.

"But what, Your Imperial Highness?" Johann gently probed.

The Archduke turned slowly toward Johann. "But when I confronted her with the fact—and offered her money in exchange for her silence—she was most offended."

"As any woman in her condition surely would be," Haydn said.

"No." The Archduke scratched his head. "It seemed to me she was offended that I should suspect her of stooping so low."

Haydn didn't know what to make of this. "But you don't deny the child was yours," he pressed.

The Archduke looked up, dazed. "I had no notion she was with child. She never mentioned it."

Haydn stifled a sigh. The Archduke's brains seemed to be addled. His responses made no sense. The Kapellmeister resisted the urge to drag his hands through his wig. God grant him patience. At this rate, they would never get to the bottom of the affair.

But Johann, fortunately, was undeterred in the face of the Archduke's obduracy.

"If you had no notion of her condition," Johann said, "why was Your Imperial Highness so convinced it was Signora Pacelli who was attempting to extort money from you?"

"Well, who else would it be?" The Archduke stared blankly at them both.

Chapter Twenty

For the first time, Haydn found himself longing for the days when he was a starving choirboy in Vienna. His belly had been perpetually empty, but at least he'd possessed the freedom to clobber anyone who tried his patience.

Mindful of his position, he quelled the urge.

"And the reasons for her demands?" Johann persevered.

"Well . . ." For the first time, the Archduke looked bashful. A faint pink tinged his pale cheeks as he lowered his head. "She was taking up on behalf of . . ." his voice trailed off again.

But Haydn had finally understood what the Archduke was referring to.

"It was the incident in Vienna, I suppose." How had Lucia known about that, he wondered.

"I offered at the time to . . . to do the right thing," the Archduke stammered, his eyes on the cobblestones. He glanced up at Haydn. "It was not my decision to send her to a convent. Or to take away her child. I did not even know such a thing had happened."

Haydn frowned. Then how had Lucia known?

"She wished you to reverse the poor girl's fate?" he asked.

The Archduke nodded. "Mother will not hear a word I have to say on the matter. There's no talking to the Emperor, either." He sighed heavily. "It must be the first time they are in agreement on anything." He spread his hands wide. "There's nothing I can do. It was in vain that I tried to explain it to her."

"And Signora Pacelli's child?" Haydn persisted. "You deny it is yours?"

"I am old enough to know how a child is fathered, Herr Haydn," the Archduke replied stiffly. "I assure you I had no opportunity to beget one with your soprano. She had no interest in me."

Whose child was it then? Jakob's? Haydn recalled his conversation with the tenor.

"And the herbs?" Johann asked.

"I have already told you about the herbs. I asked my valet to get rid of them. I couldn't stand the taste of them and had no intentions of taking a second dose."

Haydn searched the young man's face. Was he telling the truth? The herbs had clearly not been disposed of.

How had they found their way to Lucia's changing room? Had she consumed them by mistake? Or had someone murdered her?

⚬

The Prince and his guests had just sat down to their midday meal when Luigi returned to the palace. Escorting Maria Beatrice D'Este to the Sala Terrena where the meal was being served, the Konzertmeister headed back to the entrance hall.

He was about to make his way to the Officers' Mess for his own meal when a folded sheet of paper placed on a low console table caught his eye. Curious to see what it was, Luigi made his way toward the hand-carved mahogany piece.

It was a broadsheet—one of the many anonymous publications put out in Hungary. The news—as was to be expected—was about Lucia's demise.

Luigi tilted his head to read the headline: *"Poison Takes Prima Donna's Life!"*

Well, that was more accurate and more honest than the miserable report Trattner had put out. In his effort to paint Joseph as either immoral or incompetent, or both, the nitwit Trattner had only succeeded in showing himself to be an inept purveyor of news.

Pursing his lips at the memory, Luigi unfolded the broadsheet and casually perused the article. He had not expected to find more than the broad facts of the case.

But what he read made his heart sink.

It was bad enough that the writer was aware of Lucia's illicit relationship and its fatal consequence—the child she carried in her womb. But the insinuation—however subtle—that the Archduke had fathered the child and had, therefore, silenced its mother was far more troubling.

That they themselves suspected it, was one thing. Whether it was the truth was quite another.

Luigi gripped the paper, nearly crushing it. Was the entire village privy to the sordid tale? He knew too that no matter what they suspected, there was a chance—albeit a very small one—that the Archduke was innocent of the charges. That had happened in more than one case. It was best to be cautious.

That the Archduke's pouch of herbs had been discovered in the dead soprano's changing room could hardly be denied. But His Imperial Highness had claimed to have discarded the herbs. What if his valet had failed to carry out his instructions?

What if Lucia's child had been fathered by someone else? It could just as easily have been Friberth or one of her other colleagues, couldn't it?

Although if that were the case, it hardly made sense for Lucia to attempt to extort money from the Archduke, did it?

Unless—the thought made Luigi pause. He stared out the open entrance doors, his hazel eyes crinkling as he considered the matter.

Had Lucia preferred to let Paolo believe it was the Archduke who'd fathered her child? It would be more palatable than letting poor Paolo think his rival was one of the other musicians.

His hazel eyes—shrouded in anxiety—returned to the broadsheet in his hands.

The Archduke's marriage was not a sure thing. These rumors could hardly be allowed to circulate unchecked. Not until they'd been proven one way or another.

He glanced at the clock. He would've preferred to wait until Joseph returned. But there was no time for that.

The Archduke's story would have to be confirmed.

"If he did throw away the herbs," Luigi muttered to himself, "then we can be sure someone else was responsible for taking the pouch to Lucia."

Who and why were questions that could be dealt with later. For now, something had to be done—and quickly at that—to determine the truth and nip the gossip in the bud. If not, rampant speculation would be taken for the truth.

"If anyone knows what happened to those herbs, it'll be His Imperial Highness's valet," Luigi mouthed the thought at the broadsheet in his hands. "The question is will the conceited knave deign to answer my questions."

He shook his head. It was unlikely that the valet, intent on saving his own skin, would do anything but lie. The maids, on the other hand, might have an easier time getting the truth out of the high-handed rascal. It would be best to let them handle the task.

His decision made, Luigi waved a passing footman over.

"Send one of the maids up to the Music Room, will you?" he ordered.

Maria Anna was in the kitchen when Haydn returned home.

Hearing his footsteps cross the threshold, she whipped around, exasperated.

"What brings you home, husband?" She glanced at the clock on the wall. "At this hour, no less. I have nothing for you to eat."

Haydn followed her gaze to the clock. *Ach so!* It was well past the hour for the midday meal. And now that Maria Anna mentioned it, he was hungry.

"A few slices of bread, some of your cheese, and some pickle will suffice," he assured her, catching sight of the items on the kitchen countertop.

Maria Anna let out a long-suffering sigh. "Very well, then. I still don't understand why you brought yourself home. Isn't there food to be had at the palace?"

Haydn ignored her grumbling. He seated himself at the kitchen table. He was wondering how to put his questions about Lucia to her when Maria Anna broached the subject herself.

"Did the barber-surgeon have anything of interest to report to you?" she asked, not bothering to turn around. Her knife clacked loudly against the wooden cutting board.

"He confirms Lucia was with child," Haydn began only to be interrupted by a loud snort.

"Any fool could've told you that, husband." Maria Anna carried a plate of bread, cheese, and pickles over to the table, setting it in front of him.

Haydn's head jerked up. "You knew of her condition?" Lucia had not bothered to confide in anyone else. Even Hannah, the seamstress, a long-time friend of the soprano's had been unaware of the fact.

"Why wouldn't I? Why else do you think she needed medicaments?"

Haydn stared at her. "Why did she need medicaments?" he asked warily, not sure he wished to know the answer. God have mercy, had his wife been supplying Lucia with the means to rid herself of her child?

"To settle her stomach, of course." Maria Anna rolled her eyes. "Your ignorance never fails to astonish me, husband. When a woman is in the delicate condition Lucia found herself in, it takes very little to make her queasy. Has no one bothered to tell you that?"

Haydn chewed his bread thoughtfully, digesting the information his wife had provided. If Lucia had sought remedies for her nausea, then surely she had no desire to rid herself of her child.

"Herr Hipfl wondered if she'd sought to expel the child from her womb," he said at last, swallowing the piece of bread.

"Why in the name of heaven would she do that?" Maria Anna's voice rose in astonishment. "The candles she so diligently lit at St. Gerard's altar and her prayers had finally borne fruit. Why would she rid herself of the very thing she wanted?"

It was true Lucia had desperately wanted a child. But if the child had been fathered by a man other than Paolo, would she have been quite as eager to give birth to it?

Haydn glanced at his wife. She had answered the question he had lacked the courage to voice openly. Yet he couldn't help but probe further.

"It was Paolo's child, then?" he inquired.

Maria Anna sniffed. "Whose did you suppose it to have been? Yours?" Her blue eyes held his, challenging him to respond.

Made uneasy by her stony gaze, Haydn averted his eyes, turning his attention to the half-eaten bread on his plate.

A few minutes later, he resumed the discussion. "Those who know Paolo are quite certain he could not have fathered a child. I am told he had none by his first wife, either." How he had heard this, Haydn didn't know, but he was certain someone had mentioned it.

It may have been Lucia herself in the early days of their acquaintance.

"It was St. Gerard who helped them, husband." Maria Anna leaned forward eagerly. "I realize you are a man of little faith. But constant prayer to the saints can overcome any obstacle. Lucia proved it to be the case."

Haydn suppressed a sigh. He had as much faith as the next man. But prayer, he had come to see, was futile in their case. No prayer and no saint could cure Maria Anna of her barrenness. But it would be a cruelty to point that out to her.

Lucia had clearly exploited his wife's weakness. Haydn's nostrils pinched together in cold fury at the realization. Worse still, she'd encouraged Maria Anna in her delusions with her lies. Why else had his wife taken to lighting candles at St. Gerard's altar?

Haydn was willing to wager an entire year's income Lucia had neither lit any candles herself nor offered any prayers. No, there was a more rational explanation for her condition.

"You may tell the barber-surgeon she had no desire to rid herself of her child," Maria Anna's voice broke into his thoughts. "She eagerly awaited its arrival."

"I will let him know," Haydn agreed quietly. He would discreetly make inquiries at the church as well. *If Lucia's conception turned out to be a miracle,* he said to himself cynically, *he'd willingly give up music.*

He sliced off a large piece from the hunk of cheese on his plate. "Did the Archduke's mixture of herbs contain pennyroyal?" he asked.

"They help settle the stomach," Maria Anna replied. She had risen from her chair, turning to go toward the counter. Now she glanced over her shoulder. "Why, is he in need of any more?"

Haydn shook his head. "Apparently, he discarded them, having no further need of the medicaments. But the pouch found its way to Lucia's changing room, and Herr Hipfl fears she may have ingested some of the mixture."

"It would've been best not to, but I doubt the herbs would have done her any harm," Maria Anna said, returning with a few more slices of bread. She set the plate and a dish of butter before him. "There is some *Apfelkuchen* left, if you want it," she offered.

The news cheered Haydn. The small repast had failed to satisfy him. A slice of dessert with, hopefully, some of Maria Anna's sweet cream would go a long way toward filling his stomach.

He eagerly plucked a freshly cut slice of bread and bit into it. The Archduke's herbs could not have killed Lucia. The information did much to ease his anxiety. But—

He frowned as another thought occurred to him.

He set down his bread. "I thought pennyroyal was to be avoided at all costs by women in Lucia's condition. Herr Hipfl is certain it was what killed her."

"It's the oil that kills. Not the leaves, husband."

"The oil?" Haydn repeated, not understanding.

"Yes, the oil, husband. Isn't that what I said? I have some in my kitchen," she informed him, pointing toward one of her cabinets. "There's no better way to get rid of pests. But only a fool would use it as a medicinal remedy."

Haydn gazed at the cabinet. "But you are sure the leaves do no harm?" he persisted.

"As certain as I am that you sit before me, husband, asking foolish questions," Maria Anna responded curtly.

"Then the Archduke's herbs—" Haydn began.

"Would not have killed Lucia," Maria Anna said firmly. "And I see no reason why she should've stolen them, either. She had only to ask if she found herself in need of any remedies."

Haydn scratched his chin. Who had placed the herbs in Lucia's changing room, then? And to what purpose? From what he'd discovered, it was unlikely to have been the Archduke.

He must've spoken aloud for Maria Anna said: "Someone must want us to believe it was His Imperial Highness who was responsible for her death. They must think you'd let the matter go if you considered the Archduke responsible for it."

Haydn nodded. His wife's surmise made sense.

"I would not have let it go even had that been the case," he said. "But I don't suppose her killer was in a position to know that."

But he wondered if there was not a more nefarious reason for shifting the blame onto the Archduke. Was someone attempting to prevent His Imperial Highness's union with Maria Beatrice?

Who stood to benefit from that unfortunate situation if it ever came to pass?

The only person Haydn could think of was confined to a convent in Vienna.

Chapter Twenty-One

Luigi was pacing back and forth on the carpeted floor of the Music Room when he heard the knock on the door. He turned as the door began to open. But to his dismay it was neither Rosalie nor Greta who entered the room.

A dark-haired girl with a pert nose and the general appearance of a china doll stood before him.

"You called, Master Luigi?"

He raked his fingers through his hair.

"Is Rosalie down there?" he asked. "Or Greta?"

The girl—what was her name now? Ulrike, was it?—shook her head.

"They're at the opera house, Master Luigi. But I'm quite capable," she added proudly. "Frau Heindl frequently says so. And Fräulein Schmidt agrees."

Her blue eyes gazed at him, eager to take on whatever task he had in mind.

But Luigi wasn't sure at all of the propriety of entrusting their concerns to her. He resumed his pacing, the sound of his heels muted by the thick carpet on the parquet floor.

He turned to gaze at the maid, still expectantly waiting. Could she be trusted to be discreet? Or would she gossip?

He paced toward the window and stared at the beautiful gardens outside. Had the girl the intelligence to draw out the truth from a suspect? Was it possible she might put herself in danger?

He gripped the windowsill. On the other hand, here she was.

He turned to face her.

"It is a delicate task. I wish you to speak with the Archduke's valet."

The girl nodded eagerly. "Of course. What am I to say to him?"

Luigi hesitated, still unsure of the wisdom of his decision. Then, suppressing a sigh, he filled her in.

"A few days ago, Frau Haydn prepared a packet of herbs for His Imperial Highness," he began. "The Archduke has unfortunately misplaced the pouch."

Far better to couch it that way, Luigi thought, than to tell her what he suspected. He was about to continue when he realized Ulrike had cocked her head to the side and was regarding him quizzically.

"Misplaced his herbs? But he asked that they be thrown away." Her hand flew to her mouth. "Oh dear, was the valet mistaken, then?"

Luigi stared at her. She might as well have been speaking Greek for all that he understood.

"His Imperial Highness wished to get rid of his herbs?" Luigi uttered the words as slowly as an untrained musician performing a piece at sight.

"Yes." Ulrike bobbed her head. "Well, so his valet said. He dropped the pouch into my hands and asked me to dispose of them."

"When?"

"Why it must've been yesterday."

"And you got rid of them?" Luigi asked again.

"Wasn't I supposed to?" Ulrike wanted to know. "The valet said his master had no desire to take any more of it, it was that vile. I didn't think His Imperial Highness would want it again so soon after . . ." She shrugged.

"No, no, of course not. But . . ." Luigi's eyes darted toward the broadsheet he'd left on the fortepiano. If the herbs had been disposed of, how had they found their way to Lucia's room?

"It can't be true, can it?" Ulrike's voice roused Luigi. He returned his gaze to her. She was pointing to the broadsheet. "I thought it was just so much gossip."

She picked up the sheet and studied the words.

"There was a pouch discovered in Signora Pacelli's changing room," Luigi admitted. "If it was the Archduke's—" He exhaled heavily. "I fear it may have contained a substance fatal to her in her condition. The barber-surgeon suspects it may have been the cause of her—"

He was interrupted by an audible gasp. Ulrike's blue eyes were wide. Her jaw had dropped open and a slim hand covered her mouth.

"Did you throw the pouch away yourself?" he asked, wishing to reassure himself of the fact. If she'd asked someone else to do it, it was possible the task hadn't been attended to.

Ulrike swallowed. "Yes, yes, of course. Just as he asked me to—the valet, I mean."

Then the Archduke had been telling the truth. If he hadn't sought to kill Lucia, was it possible the child was not his either? Noticing the maid gazing at him, Luigi ceased his musings.

"Very well, then," he said to her. "Since you've cleared up the question, there's nothing further to do."

The girl bobbed her head, nervously wringing her hands on her apron. Poor child, she must think she was being taken to task for misconstruing her instructions.

Forcing his concerns away, Luigi smiled reassuringly at the girl.

"It matters not I'm sure. If the Archduke has any further need of herbs, Frau Haydn can mix up some more."

⁕

Ulrike was troubled. She'd told Master Luigi she'd disposed of the Archduke's herbs. It wasn't exactly a lie. But she'd omitted an important detail.

Had Master Luigi asked her to tell him where she'd thrown the herbs, the truth would've come out. As it stood, he'd taken her word for it that she'd taken care of the task herself.

But she hadn't.

She'd meant to, of course. But when Frau Heindl had suggested she and Katya and the others go out to enjoy the festivities yesterday, she'd completely forgotten about the herbs. And by the time she remembered—

Ulrike twisted her apron. It wasn't as though she'd neglected her duty. She'd asked her friend to take care of the job. She hurried along the flagstone paths laid in the midst of the gardens.

She'd better find out if the task had been attended to.

No one would believe His Imperial Highness had a hand in killing Signora Pacelli. When the details emerged—as they surely would—Ulrike would be the one blamed for her death.

God have mercy, how had the herbs found their way to the poor woman? Who knew a harmless bundle of herbs could contain something so fatal to her? Oh, if only she'd taken care of disposing of it herself.

But she'd trusted her friend to see to it . . . Would that serve as an adequate excuse?

Would she have to make confession? The thought stopped her in her tracks. If she did, would Pfarrer Spalek understand, letting her off with an extra rosary or two? Or was this what the priest called a mortal sin— something utterly unforgivable?

Ulrike's heart seemed to shrivel up inside of her.

Worse still, she'd compounded her neglect with the lie she'd told Master Luigi.

The warm sun poured down upon her—feeling not like a blessing but like the searing heat of accusation.

Brushing away her tears, Ulrike hurried on. Maybe it was all just a mishap. Her friend would know.

She was breathless by the time she arrived.

"What brings you here?" Her friend looked up, surprised. A pile of trinkets lay on the table beside an ornate jewelry case. Dresses needed to be hung up.

Ulrike glanced at the floor. It stood in need of a good sweeping.

Picking up the broom, she set to work.

"Those herbs that I gave you yesterday—the Archduke's herbs," she began, briskly sweeping the floor. "You did throw them away, didn't you?"

"Of course. Would I have offered to, if I hadn't meant to do it? You didn't have to bring yourself all the way here to ask."

The offended tone and the frown made Ulrike falter. She hadn't meant to sound ungrateful—or even distrustful. It was just that . . .

"They say the herbs were in Signora Pacelli's hands," she explained. "It may have been what caused her . . ."

Her friend snorted. "It's her own fault, if it did. She was forever after what didn't belong to her, our prima donna, and what she couldn't have."

"B-but she could have hardly taken the herbs out of a rubbish bin," Ulrike persisted. "You did throw them away, didn't you?"

Desperate, she searched her friend's features—the blazing eyes, the flared nostrils, the lips pinched into a thin, white line.

"They'll lay her death at my door if they find out I didn't . . ." She expelled a deep breath. "You'll be blamed as well."

"She must've stolen them, then," her friend snapped. "You know she was a thief. Never happier than when taking someone else's lover, cavorting with someone else's husband, stealing money, wine."

That was true enough, Ulrike thought. But would the soprano pluck something out of the rubbish heap? That hardly seemed likely.

"But where did she steal the herbs from?"

Her friend gathered up a necklace, lovingly setting it into the velvet-covered jewelry box.

"I suppose she must've seen the pouch sitting on top of the cabinet. I remember setting it down there—just for a minute, of course. It wasn't there when I returned. I thought I'd tossed it. But if what you say is true, I must've been mistaken."

Her friend glanced up at her.

"There's no need to look so stricken. No one will blame you. Why should they? Here"—Ulrike watched as her friend's fingers closed around the stem of a wine glass—"have a sip of wine. Now that our beloved prima donna is gone, at least the rest of us can savor some of this *kékoportó*."

Ulrike sank down onto the bench in front of the dressing table. The wine was sweet, strongly flavored with mint. She could see why Signora Pacelli enjoyed it so much.

She smiled at her friend. Her friend was right. She did feel better. She gulped down some more of the liquor—it slid smoothly down her throat.

Then a sudden, sharp pain shot through her stomach. Ulrike clutched her stomach. The pain stabbed her again. And again. Her stomach heaved.

She'd never felt such agony.

"What is this?" she cried. "What . . . *Oh!*"

The glass fell from her hands, shattering to the floor.

Ulrike's friend gazed upon her—the cold, dispassionate stare of a barber-surgeon watching a rat writhe in pain.

Chapter Twenty-Two

"Refused to marry His Imperial Highness?" Haydn clutched the gold-trimmed edge of his chair, the news having nearly propelled him out of it. "B-but that is impossible."

His gaze veered wildly from Leopold, Grand Duke of Tuscany, to His Serene Highness.

The Prince inclined his head a fraction of an inch, a curt acknowledgment of the bitter, unexpected truth. Maria Beatrice D'Este had suddenly, inexplicably declared herself unable to give herself in marriage to Archduke Ferdinand.

The news had caused both the Prince and the Grand Duke of Tuscany no small degree of consternation, and Haydn had found himself summoned into their presence as soon as he set foot inside the palace.

"On what grounds?" Haydn expostulated, the words bursting out of his mouth before he could consider their impropriety.

The Grand Duke of Tuscany paused in his hectic perambulation of the room.

"She has refused to explain herself," His Grace spoke through clenched teeth. "And Ferdinand won't confide in me either. A more stubborn, hard-headed lad I've yet to see." Resentment and bitterness sharpened his tongue. "I dearly wish the Emperor hadn't saddled me with his welfare."

"It does little good to complain of that now," the Prince reminded his guest. "What's done is done. All we can do is remedy the situation."

He turned his attention to the Kapellmeister.

"What precisely occurred at the rehearsal, Haydn?"

Sunlight poured in through the window bathing His Serene Highness in a warm glow. He leaned forward now, moving out of its reach, and kept his gaze firmly upon his employee.

"He did something to offend the poor woman, I suppose." The Grand Duke paced frenetically from the writing table at one end of the room to the porcelain stove at the other. "He must have. Why else would she reject him now?"

He spun around to face Haydn as he spoke.

Feeling like a butterfly pinned in place by the twin pairs of eyes piercing his being, Haydn struggled to collect his thoughts.

"Nothing happened, I assure you, Your Grace. The last time we met, she was quite prepared to take His Imperial Highness as a husband." He felt his brow wrinkling. "I'm at a loss to understand what can have caused her to change her mind."

"Nothing happened? You're quite sure of that?" The Grand Duke of Tuscany's pale blue eyes bore into Haydn's face.

"Nothing out of the ordinary," Haydn faltered, casting around in his mind for an explanation. "His Imperial Highness was having trouble getting his horse to execute a *piaffe*—"

"That's it, then." His Grace's lips curled in contempt. "Ferdinand's horsemanship has always left much to be desired. What man can be expected to take the reins of government when he can barely control his horse? It's in vain that we've impressed upon him the importance of excelling in that area. One can hardly blame the bride for shying away."

"But she left the stables agreeable to the marriage," Haydn felt obliged to protest. It was certainly true—as far as he was aware.

But a twinge of uncertainty flickered through his being. There were unsavory rumors floating about the Archduke; had the bride been made aware of them? He thrust the question out of his mind, intent on reassuring His Grace.

"As to the *piaffe*—with Gabor's help, thanks be to God, the matter has been corrected."

He looked to his employer, but there was no support to be had from that quarter.

"It is your prima donna's disgraceful conduct on the stage, then, Haydn. You should've dismissed her as I instructed you to. You demurred, and now we pay the price."

"Her conduct?" Was His Serene Highness referring to Trattner's scurrilous report that morning? "Surely, it is hardly her fault that she is dead. Poisoned, according to the barber-surgeon."

The Prince glanced at the folded newspaper on the side table. "Her shenanigans were the result of poison?"

Haydn nodded. "Her Ladyship was well aware of the fact that Signora Pacelli had tragically met her demise in the middle of the performance last evening." He tipped his chin to indicate the paper. "Herr Trattner seems to have chosen not to inform himself of the true particulars."

"The man should lose his license," His Grace muttered. "But if it's not his vile report, what is it?"

Haydn hesitated. He had an idea of where the trouble lay, but he was not sure how to bring up the matter. It would mean revealing Lucia's attempt at extortion. His own silence on the matter could also not be easily explained.

He rapped his fingers on the frame of his seat, casting around in his mind for the appropriate words to communicate the news.

"It appears that word of His Imperial Highness's escapade in Vienna has got out. I have only recently learned of it and was hoping to get to the bottom of the matter before mentioning it. But with Signora Pacelli dead, there is no way to determine how she heard the news."

The Grand Duke wheeled around, shocked. "She was attempting to extort money from him. Is that what her pursuit of him was all about?"

Unwilling to lie, Haydn gave an imperceptible shake of the head.

"Money doesn't seem to have been the object of her demand." At least, it hadn't seemed to be the only object. "It appears that she merely wished His Imperial Highness to reverse the poor girl's fortunes. To get the girl out of the convent she finds herself confined in and to return her child to her."

His Serene Highness's eyes narrowed. "Why would she concern herself with the fortunes—or misfortunes—of a stranger?"

"I know not. Clearly, the girl was connected in some way with Signora Pacelli. I would've preferred to question her directly. But now that she is no more—to question her husband or her nephew too openly only risks making the matter public."

"That must be avoided at all costs," the Grand Duke declared firmly.

"I cannot think of anyone who could have been privy to the news," Haydn continued. "Anyone with connections in Vienna who might've heard so much as a word of the affair."

But as he spoke, a possible answer drifted into his mind. His gaze traveled to the table where the newspaper lay.

"Herr Trattner has connections in court, does he not?"

"You think he could be the source of the rumors?" His Serene Highness asked. "I don't see what he could possibly gain by it." He turned toward His Grace. "The maid couldn't have been connected to him in any way, could she?"

The Grand Duke of Tuscany, standing pensively by the porcelain stove, shook his head. "I'm quite sure she was no relative of his. No, if Trattner's involved, it's because he's being well paid to act as someone's instrument."

"Yes, but to what end?" His Serene Highness demanded again, somewhat impatiently.

The Grand Duke straightened up. "Why to prevent the marriage, of course. I would wager half of Tuscany—all of it, in fact—that Frederick of Prussia is behind the entire affair. The King knows as well as the rest of the world that Austria is well positioned to control Italy almost in its entirety should the marriage take place. With Antoine's marriage to the Dauphin, our alliance with the Bourbons has also been consolidated."

"Good grief!" The Prince's heavy features deflated as suddenly as a bubble pierced by a child's probing finger. "I had not considered that aspect of the matter."

"Mark my words," the Grand Duke declared darkly, "the King means to marry Maria Beatrice D'Este to his younger brother. Henry is still unmarried."

"And likely to remain so, if he has anything to say about it," Haydn blurted out. His visit to Prussia a year or two ago had taught him that Prince Henry and his eldest brother, the Prussian King, shared the same unnatural proclivities.

"His preferences veer in the same direction as the King's," he explained, aware of the Grand Duke's questioning gaze on him.

His Grace straightened up. "Then Maria Beatrice D'Este must be saved from that unfortunate alliance," he said firmly.

"And Trattner must be—" the Prince began only to have his Kapellmeister interrupt him.

"If he is involved, it would be best not to show our hand by having him dismissed. The King, I fear, is wily enough to bribe someone else into taking his place."

The Prince and the Grand Duke exchanged a glance.

"Very well," His Serene Highness agreed. "But make sure not a word of our current troubles reaches his ears. And if there's so much as a breath of gossip, cut it off immediately."

⸻ ⬥ ⸻

Rosalie leaned against the door to the opera box that Prince Toni and Prince Antal had shared the evening before. Her back was sore from hunching over the vast auditorium floor. She and Greta had swept and mopped the entire space until the floors gleamed.

Then they'd climbed the short flight of stairs in the foyer to the Prince's oval box at the back of the theater. His Serene Highness hadn't used it yesterday, preferring to sit with his guests directly in front of the stage.

From what they'd heard, the opera singer who'd accompanied the Duke of Modena was far too short-sighted to view the performance from one of the boxes in the gallery above.

"Is it true, she's His Royal Grace's mistress?" Greta had hissed in her ear when they'd seen the woman in her outrageous gown the previous evening. "I can't believe he brought her here. What a hussy she looks!"

The memory made Rosalie giggle. Greta knew full well how the Duke wished to be addressed. But she'd insisted on getting it wrong.

Now Greta stood her broom against the gallery railing and propped her elbows upon it to survey the auditorium below.

"What a mess His Serene Highness and his guests left for us to clean, to be sure!"

There'd been food crumbs on the floor under their seats and puddles of wine where the beverage had sloshed out of the wine glasses.

"Why, the area where the servants were seated was cleaner than the front of the auditorium. Who'd believe it?"

"It's because we know there's no one to pick up after us." Rosalie turned around and gave her friend a rueful grin. She gestured toward the oval box behind them.

"At least Her Serene Highness didn't leave her box in shambles."

"Most likely, Frau Schwann cleaned up after her," Greta said with a knowing look. "Although she did forget the Princess's handkerchief." She patted her pocket. "I found it on the floor."

Rosalie sighed wearily, then stepped back from the door of Prince Toni's box. "I suppose we'd better get this over with. Thank heavens, it's the last box we have to clean."

But when she opened the door, she staggered back, wrinkling her nose in disgust. Wine glasses lay shattered on the floor. The wine had already stained the floor. Empty bottles rolled in the dust and bits of food were scattered all around.

A flash of white caught her eye. It darted toward the door.

"E-E-eeek!" She and Greta screamed in unison, jumping up as a soft, furry object brushed against their ankles. Their screech sounded unnaturally loud even to Rosalie's ears, and she quickly subsided.

"Oh, Lord, a rat!" Greta's plump fingers dug into Rosalie's arms.

"I'm not surprised with the rubbish they've left behind," Rosalie said. She tried to sound calm, but she couldn't suppress the shudder that rattled through her being.

"I'm not going in there." Greta still clung to her. She peered over her shoulder. "Did you see where that thing went?"

Rosalie shook her head. There was doubtless a hole somewhere that the rat had disappeared into. Most likely, it wouldn't return. Not when there were people around. But—she shuddered again.

She was about to suggest they call for Karl when the redheaded librettist rushed into the gallery.

"What is it?" he called, alarmed. "I was just coming up to see you when I heard you two shrieking." He peered over their shoulders.

"It was a rat," Rosalie confessed, feeling foolish. "It was in there." She pointed back toward the box.

The corners of Karl's mouth twitched, but to his credit he maintained a sober face.

"And it startled you two, did it? Did you see where it went?"

"Somewhere there." Greta pointed in the direction from which he'd come.

Karl dutifully turned around, but there was no sign of the pesky rodent. He turned back toward them.

"Never fear, we'll set a trap for it."

He led the way to the stairs back down to the foyer.

"There should be a trap and some pennyroyal oil in the supply closet under the stage," he said.

"Pennyroyal oil?" Rosalie stopped short.

Karl glanced over his shoulder. "Yes, it's remarkably effective against rats and other such pests." He continued down the stairs. "You wouldn't think the oil of an ordinary plant could be so deadly. But so it is."

Greta looked at Rosalie. "We'd heard the entire plant was deadly," she said. She lowered her voice to a whisper. "It turns out Signora Pacelli ingested some of the leaves and that's what killed her."

"Nonsense!" Karl shook his bushy mane of red hair. "The leaves do one no harm. It's the oil." He looked over his shoulder again. "One of the singers in Milan consumed some, that's how I know."

"Whatever for?" Rosalie wanted to know.

"She was with child. Her lover—a nobleman—had abandoned her. And she thought to rid herself of the baby."

"And she died?" Greta was aghast.

Karl nodded somberly. "A most painful death. At first we thought she was drunk, the way she was staggering around. Then she clutched her stomach and moaned and crashed to the floor."

Just like Sigora Pacelli, Rosalie thought. The same thought must've occurred to Greta, for her friend exchanged a brief glance with her.

"And there's pennyroyal oil in the opera house?" Greta asked.

Karl shrugged. "How else would you have us deal with the rats? There's not much point catching them only to let them go. They just come back. Might as well kill them. And tainting the bait is much the best way to do it."

He opened a door discreetly placed in the rear of the foyer. It led to a stairway that took them to the basement.

"The supply closet is right here at the bottom of the stairs. It's a small, dark bottle."

But when Karl pulled open the closet door, there was no bottle to be found. Rosalie could see mops, brooms, and countless other items. But no bottle of pennyroyal oil.

"Where could it be?" Karl muttered, frowning. He shifted a few items around, pulling things off the shelves. "I've told Fiore often enough not to leave it lying around. The lad pays me no mind."

He banged the door shut. "We'd better go find him and ask him what he's done with it."

Karl sounded annoyed.

Chapter Twenty-Three

IT was in a singularly agitated mood that Haydn left the Prince's study. He'd been instructed to find Maria Beatrice D'Este and to persuade Her Ladyship to change her mind. But he couldn't bring himself to do it. Not yet, at any event.

Not until he had stilled the turmoil in his mind.

The realization that someone was deliberately working to prevent the Archduke's marriage had shaken the Kapellmeister to the core. He had never suspected there might be vast forces stacked against him. And yet such seemed to be the case.

It was imperative he come to some understanding of the obstacles he was pitted against, and the best way to counter them. Otherwise, his efforts would come to naught yet again.

To that end, he slowly made his way up to the Music Room. Johann was at the opera house, too busy with his responsibilities to be called away. But Haydn hoped Luigi was available.

His Konzertmeister had a pragmatic mind and the ability to penetrate the foggiest situation and discern the hidden motives that influenced it.

To his relief, Luigi was in the Music Room. Seated at the writing desk, he turned around the moment Haydn opened the door and greeted him with a smile.

"Ah, there you are Joseph! I've gone over every score for the carousel this evening, making all the changes needed. All that's needed is for the copyist to write out the individual parts, and—" Abruptly he broke off.

"You seem more than a little perturbed. What is the matter?" Thrusting his chair back, Luigi hastily rose as Haydn strode into the room.

Fiore was in the prop room, organizing the flats for the opera.

"The bottle of pennyroyal oil?" he repeated, his brow furrowed. He stood the flat he was carrying against the wall. "It should be in the supply closet. Isn't it there?"

"No," Karl growled. "When did you last use it? Haven't I told you to always put it back?"

Fiore's frown deepened. He scratched his head.

"Ah!" Suddenly his face cleared. "Fräulein Leon asked for it." He turned toward them, his eyes widening in relief. "I remember now. She said there was a rat in her changing room that needed to be dispensed with."

"Then it's in her changing room?" Karl asked.

"It must be," Fiore replied.

"Next time do the job yourself instead of trusting the singers to do it." Visibly irritated, Karl turned on his heels.

They followed him down the hallway, which curved around to the changing rooms and the stairs that led up to the stage.

Fräulein Leon's room was next door to Signora Pacelli's. A small crescent-shaped mahogany table stood against the wall between the doors. Karl was about to knock on the soprano's door when he stopped abruptly by the table.

"Here it is!" He plucked the small bottle that Fräulein Leon must've left standing by the enormous vase.

He looked up, relieved. "We'd better go in and check on the trap," he said, knocking on the door. "She won't relish the sight of a dead rat in her changing room."

He rapped on the door a second time.

"I'm surprised she undertook to deal with it herself. She's not one to lift a finger if she can help it."

"She must not be in," Rosalie said when his third knock failed to produce a response.

"I suppose not," Karl agreed. Hesitantly, he turned the handle and slowly opened the door. Warily, he peered around the edge of the doorway. "She's not here," he said, opening the door wider.

But he'd barely stepped over the threshold when he stumbled back again, crossing himself over and over again.

"What is it?" Greta asked, peeking curiously over his shoulder.

"It's—" Karl gulped and swallowed several times. "It looks like Ulrike." His gaze dropped to the bottle of poison in his hands. "She's . . . she's . . ."

"No!" Greta cried aghast as Rosalie's hand flew to her mouth.

It couldn't be! Dear God, was it possible that Ulrike was the "rat" Fräulein Leon had needed to get rid of?

Karl recovered himself sufficiently to firmly shut the door. "We'd best send for the barber-surgeon," he said. "This is a matter for him."

***

"It is the bride," Haydn said without preamble, stopping by the fortepiano. "She refuses to marry His Imperial Highness."

Luigi's mouth dropped open. "Why?" His gaze flickered to a point on Haydn's left but veered quickly back again. "She cannot have—?"

Unable to contain himself, Haydn spoke over his friend.

"I fear rumors of the Archduke's fling in Vienna may have reached her ears," he burst out. He recounted the details. "How Lucia knew, I can only surmise. I suspect it was Trattner who was her source. He may well be the man manipulating our perception of her murder."

Luigi considered this, whatever he'd wanted to say forgotten in the light of these tidings.

"If the Archduke had no reason to kill Lucia, and it seems he made no attempt to do so, then—"

"Precisely," Haydn agreed, moving toward the group of chairs by the writing desk. He sank down into one. "Someone wishes us to believe His Imperial Highness was in her changing room. But the herbs would not have killed her. Could not, in fact. Maria Anna was quite clear on that point."

Luigi joined him, taking a seat across Haydn in the carpeted area by the window.

"I was going to say that it may be that our Lucia did not pen the blackmail note either."

Haydn felt his eyes widen. "I must confess the thought hadn't occurred to me. Yet"—he paused before continuing slowly—"yet the conclusion is straightforward enough."

Luigi nodded. "Why pen an anonymous note when she was willing to confront him in person?"

"Quite so." Haydn found himself nodding enthusiastically in agreement. Luigi had already shed considerable light on the matter.

"Trattner, then," he said. "Who else would know about the affair in Vienna? He is the only person with connections in court."

"If the letter-writer was referring to what occurred in Vienna," Luigi pointed out, much to Haydn's bewilderment.

"But what else could—?" he began.

"I'm afraid we're not the only ones to have suspected a liaison between His Imperial Highness and Lucia," Luigi interjected. He got to his feet and made his way to the fortepiano, plucking up the newspaper neatly folded upon it. "The rumors have spread to the purveyors of Hungarian news as well."

Haydn cast his eye over the paper. He had considered Trattner's report bad enough. But this was far worse. The insinuation was subtle but unmistakable.

"It is all lies," he said, raising his head despairingly toward Luigi, "but who would believe it? God forbid, Her Ladyship should've seen this."

He threw the paper upon the low table before him.

———◆◆◆———

The barn at the back of the tavern grounds was always pleasantly cool. But today it felt like an ice box, Rosalie thought. She sat on one of the three-legged stools Gerhard had brought out for her and Greta, blankly watching the barber-surgeon conclude his examination of Ulrike's body.

"Death has stiffened her," he said to no one in particular as he walked around the long table that held Ulrike's curled-up form. "But it's clear she died in pain. Look, how her neck is arched back, her features contorted."

Rosalie pressed her eyelids shut. She couldn't watch, much less listen.

Ulrike was dead. Such a pretty young thing, not much younger than Rosalie herself. Gerhard's strong arms were around Rosalie, his warm cheeks pressed against her face. Even so, she found herself shivering, nearly close to tears.

"How cold you are, lass!" Gerhard said softly. He glanced at Greta as he spoke. The plump girl sat white-faced as well, clutching Karl's arms. "Let me bring you both some mulled wine. It will do you good."

The thought of ingesting anything made Rosalie's stomach turn. But she knew Gerhard was right. A hot drink would go a long way toward driving away the numbness that had seized hold of her. She was no good to anyone in her current state.

She opened her eyes, trying to murmur a response, but her lips were too frozen to utter the words.

"A blanket or two wouldn't be amiss either," Karl suggested. "They haven't stopped shivering since we arrived."

The barber-surgeon paused, turning toward Gerhard before he could leave. "Is the Widow Heindl within? I have need of her services again."

The question stopped Gerhard in his tracks. He exchanged a stunned glance with Karl. Rosalie saw his reaction, but found herself unable to understand it.

"You cannot think," Gerhard began. His gaze dropped toward Ulrike's still form, then flickered quickly away. He swallowed, unable to continue.

Herr Hipfl regarded him impassively. "There's only one reason to ingest the oil of pennyroyal. To ingest it willingly, that is to say. I can think of no other way to tell whether she administered the poison to herself or was forced to drink it."

It took a while for his words to make sense. Gerhard had already left by the time Rosalie understood what the barber-surgeon was getting at.

"She wasn't with child," she began to say, but her voice came out in a hoarse croak that even she could hardly hear. She cleared her throat and tried again. "She was not with child."

"Who, Ulrike?" Greta seemed to come out of her frozen state as well. "No, of course, she wasn't. Who would suggest such a thing?"

"Shhh," Karl said soothingly. "Calm yourself, my dumpling. Let the barber-surgeon do his job."

But Greta ignored his remonstrance, struggling out of his arms to make herself heard.

"She was killed, mark my words."

Her shrill tone caught the barber-surgeon's attention. Startled, he raised his eyes, peering at them from under his thick eyebrows.

"What did you say? She was killed, you say?" He walked toward them, looking sternly at both girls. "What do you know of this matter, then?"

"She was killed for what she knew," Rosalie replied flatly. It was as clear as day to her, although whether she'd be able to articulate her thoughts, she didn't know.

Greta's blond head bobbed. "I'll wager she knew who killed Signora Pacelli, and why they were trying to make it seem His Imperial Highness had a hand in the murder."

⸺•••⸺

Luigi returned from the fortepiano to resume his seat across from Haydn.

"I can think of very few beyond our immediate circle, Joseph, who thought the Archduke had fathered Lucia's child."

He had dismissed Haydn's concern about the rumors circulating in the broadsheet. They could easily be countered with the facts at their disposal.

Still trying to summon those facts into his mind, Haydn stared at the Konzertmeister. Whatever was Luigi trying to say?

Luigi leaned forward. "Only consider, who had cause to suspect the Archduke? The only reason you did, Joseph, was because of what you observed yesterday. That and the extortion note. No one else perceived anything untoward in their relationship. Now, her lover, assuming she'd confided in him, might've been aware of the situation—and seen the potential for misconstruing the circumstances."

Haydn pondered the notion. It did make sense. Lucia's lover certainly had reason to throw suspicion elsewhere—and the Archduke made as good a scapegoat as any. A better scapegoat, if truth be told. Most would consider His Imperial Highness to be immune from the consequences of his behavior.

"Her lover would have reason to kill her as well, wouldn't he? Although so would Paolo, I suppose—if he'd discovered the truth."

"True enough," Luigi conceded. "Paolo might well have surmised the Archduke to be responsible. Lucia spent enough time in His Imperial Highness's presence to give rise to that suspicion. And I expect Paolo, jealous as he is, would've noticed."

"On the other hand"—Haydn regarded the broadsheet speculatively—"what purpose does it serve for either man to bandy about these canards? To throw suspicion off himself?"

He fingered the broadsheet.

"If there's a more nefarious motive to these scandalous whispers, I'll warrant it's Trattner who's behind them." He sighed. "I suppose we'll only know more when we can find out who the publisher of that rag is and discover the source of his information."

But how were they to do that? It seemed an impossible task. Almost anyone in the vicinity of Eszterháza could've written the publication.

He was about to say so when Luigi picked up the broadsheet. "Gerhard will know who the publisher is, I am sure, Joseph. I expect the man gets most of his scandal from the tavern."

He raised his head. "Although someone must have fed him this other information—someone misinformed about the truth. Or inclined to take advantage of the situation."

"Trattner," Haydn repeated grimly.

He was about to launch himself to his feet when a knock on the door sounded. A footman, his expression harassed and work-worn, entered the room.

Chapter Twenty-Four

"THERE is an urgent summons from Herr Hipfl," the man announced. "He wishes to see you at once in the tavern."

"Whatever for?" Haydn demanded.

The footman shook his head. "I cannot tell. The boy who came was most inarticulate. Something about a second death and the opera house—"

"Dear God!" Haydn crossed himself as did Luigi. "I had best go at once," he said to his Konzertmeister, quickly getting to his feet as he did so.

"Th-there is more," the footman stammered.

Haydn looked at him, barely able to contain his impatience. What else could there be?

"Her Ladyship, Maria Beatrice D'Este, wishes to see you at once as well."

The Kapellmeister hesitated. If Her Ladyship had summoned him, he could not ignore her request. On the other hand, if another of his performers had fallen victim . . .

"Let me go," Luigi offered. "I will see what Herr Hipfl has to say—and see what I can find out from Gerhard as well." He tipped his chin discreetly at the broadsheet Haydn that lay on the table between them.

Haydn inclined his head. He would have preferred to go himself, but that was not to be.

"Very well."

⁂

The Widow Heindl had confirmed Rosalie and Greta's suspicion. Ulrike had no reason to kill herself.

Slipping her broad, brown wrist out from under Ulrike's skirt, Rosalie's mother-in-law had gazed at the barber-surgeon.

"She's not with child, Herr Hipfl. The girl is a virgin."

The barber-surgeon had wanted to question Rosalie and Greta more closely, but Gerhard and Karl had stayed him. The Widow Heindl had agreed.

"Look at them! They're in no state to consider what happened, much less why," she'd said. "Let them drink their wine and warm up before they tell you what they know." Her shrewd, blue eyes regarded them skeptically. "If they know anything, that's to say."

Rosalie flushed. Her mother-in-law disapproved of her involvement in Herr Haydn's cases, she knew. But how could she stay silent—or uninvolved?

She wrapped her cold hands around the hot glass of mulled wine and slowly sipped, savoring the heat flowing into her icy limbs.

Where was she to begin? If only they'd had an opportunity to speak with Herr Haydn or Master Luigi first. How was she to tell the barber-surgeon about Signora Pacelli's attempt to extort money from the Archduke?

She glanced at Greta, who was gazing at her imploringly. Dear God, Rosalie thought. It was up to her to decide how to approach this matter, what to reveal and how much.

She took a deep breath and swallowed.

"Hannah, the seamstress, said Signora Pacelli may have died because of what she knew."

"What did she know?" the barber-surgeon asked her. His unruly hair stood around his unlined face like a gray halo.

Rosalie considered this. When Hannah had first made her remarks, she and Greta had both thought Signora Pacelli knew who the extortionist was. But what if Signora Pacelli herself was the blackmailer?

Her eyes drifted toward the bench standing against the wall on the other side of the barn. A sheet-covered form lay on it. It was Signora Pacelli, no doubt. What had she known?

"Hannah didn't say," she said carefully. "But Greta and I both thought it might be something to do with His Imperial Highness."

The barber-surgeon's bushy eyebrows rose. "Are you saying His Imperial Highness killed your soprano, girl?"

"No." Rosalie shook her head, wishing Greta would speak up, too. But her friend seemed inclined to let her do the talking.

Marshaling her thoughts, she continued: "His Imperial Highness couldn't have killed anyone."

Herr Hipfl, who'd been staring at her in a challenging manner, now appeared puzzled.

"How can you be so sure of that?"

"The broadsheet publications all but say he has," Gerhard muttered.

"Yes, well, they're wrong. Everyone knows Frau Haydn dispenses herbs in muslin pouches. Why should anyone assume the herbs found with Signora Pacelli belonged to the Archduke?"

Gerhard seemed about to say something, but Rosalie spoke over him, determined to go on.

"Besides, His Imperial Highness couldn't have entered the opera house without someone noticing him. And he certainly wouldn't have left his pouch there himself."

"Or asked someone else to take it and leave it there, announcing his presence," Greta chimed in.

"That's true enough," Gerhard muttered in a low, wondering tone.

Karl frowned. "You mean someone wishes to harm His Imperial Highness or besmirch his name?"

Rosalie nodded. "It may be that Signora Pacelli knew who it was—"

"And most likely Ulrike knew as well," Greta added.

"Or—" Rosalie frowned as another thought occurred to her. The enormity of the notion struck her with sudden force, and she straightened up.

She looked at Greta.

"Remember, we thought someone might've taken the Archduke's herbs to Signora Pacelli's changing room. What if it was Ulrike?"

Greta's jaw dropped. "You mean—?"

Rosalie nodded, but questions swarmed through her mind. Had Ulrike stolen the herbs? Or had she taken them at the Archduke's behest?

No, no, it couldn't have been the Archduke. No, it must've been someone in the opera house who was responsible for the herbs ending up where they had.

After all, it was someone at the opera house—Fräulein Leon from the looks of it—who'd killed Ulrike. The Archduke had been nowhere near the place.

"The girl must have been working for someone," Rosalie said softly.

"Who, Ulrike?" Karl wanted to know.

Rosalie nodded.

———•••———

Maria Beatrice D'Este was waiting for Haydn in the winter garden of the Esterházy Palace. Haydn strode through the tile-covered length of the room to the round table where she sat, stiffly staring at the pomegranate, myrtle, and bay trees in front of her.

The table was set with a tray bearing a silver pot of coffee, a sugar bowl, and creamer. Her Ladyship clasped a porcelain cup in her hands; a second cup was on the tray next to the coffee pot.

Haydn was aware of his footsteps ringing on the tiled floor. Yet Her Ladyship did not so much as glance at him when he approached, curtly gesturing for him to be seated instead.

"Your Ladyship wished to see me?" Despite his best efforts, the legs of the chair scraped noisily against the floor.

Watching her carefully tilt the spout of the coffee pot into the second cup, Haydn wondered why she'd sent for him. Surely, it was not merely to reiterate her decision to call off the marriage.

Could it be she was having second thoughts? Hope stirred in his breast. But her words and the sheet of paper she slid toward him along with the coffee cup caused his expectations to shrivel.

"I found this on the floor of my room after lunch," she said, her voice low and tight.

It was the selfsame broadsheet Luigi had shown him some minutes ago.

"Pushed under the door, I suppose," Haydn said, glancing down at the broadsheet and its bold headline. The thought made him uneasy, confirming as it did his earlier suspicion.

Someone was working to thwart the alliance.

Her Ladyship turned to face him for the first time. "Is any of it true?" Her eyes glittered with unshed tears. "Consider carefully before you answer, Herr Haydn. I will brook no lies."

Haydn made no reply. Instead, he cast his eye slowly over the article, pretending to peruse it. Someone had gone to considerable trouble to ensure that Maria Beatrice D'Este read the unsubstantiated and wholly venomous conjectures voiced here.

The question was: who? That it was an intentional, carefully considered act was plain to see.

Clearly, it was someone who wished to frustrate the Empress's hopes of seeing the Archduke married to Her Ladyship.

Trattner? Who else could it be?

Haydn could see no reason why either Paolo or Lucia's lover—whoever that might be—would wish to prevent the marriage from taking place. But was it Trattner who had slipped the broadsheet under Her Ladyship's door? Or had he made use of one of the maids?

At least the rumors could be countered, the Kapellmeister thought, looking from under his eyelids at the flowering plants, pineapple, and peach saplings that were artfully arranged in colorful pots on the floor.

He raised his head, meeting Her Ladyship's cold blue stare squarely.

"These are vile rumors. Completely unfounded, I assure you."

"His Imperial Highness's herbs were not discovered in your prima donna's changing room?" she asked.

"That was not of his doing." Haydn leaned forward in his eagerness to convince her of the truth. "His Imperial Highness asked that the bundle of herbs be discarded. The maid who undertook to do it has of her own accord confirmed that this is so. Who retrieved the bundle to take to Signora Pacelli and for what reason, I fear I cannot say."

Haydn was about to suggest calling for Ulrike that Her Ladyship might satisfy herself on that point, but Maria Beatrice had already moved on to a different, more thorny issue.

"And the supposed relationship between the Archduke and your prima donna?"

Chapter Twenty-Five

THE barn door was ajar when Luigi arrived at the tavern. No one seemed to be around, although the low hum of voices emanated from the tavern beyond. Where was Herr Hipfl?

Casting an uncertain glance around him, the Konzertmeister stepped into the barn. A form lay huddled on the table in the center of the space. A woman, he surmised judging by the slightness of the figure.

Luigi hurried across the floor, his feet sinking into the soft straw, to see who it was. God forbid it should be Narcissa. They were already short one soprano. To make do without another would be very nearly impossible.

He paused by the table, shifting the soft linen that covered the still figure upon it—and froze.

God have mercy, it was Ulrike! He'd spoken with her no more than a few hours ago. How had she come to die?

"Poisoned. Just like Signora Pacelli." The barber-surgeon's low, grim voice startled Luigi. The cloth he was holding up dropped from his nerveless fingers. Arm still outstretched, he slowly swiveled his neck.

"B-but why?" he stammered. "Why would anyone wish to kill her?"

"That's what I would like to know." Herr Hipfl glared at him fiercely through his eyeglasses. He rarely wore them.

The effect they had on Luigi was unnerving. His arm slumped down to his side.

"Herr Haydn has not been entirely forthright with me," the barber-surgeon continued sternly. "And I wish to know why."

"Not been forthright with you?" Luigi repeated, wondering what exactly Joseph had said to cause the barber-surgeon such displeasure.

"I've asked him repeatedly to consider who amongst the performers might wish Signora Lucia dead. Rather than answer the question, he pointed the finger at His Imperial Highness. And now this girl"—Herr Hipfl's features softened as he regarded the maid—"is dead."

Luigi glanced down as well. Why would anyone have killed the girl? What had she to do with anything?

"Killed by the same hand"—Herr Hipfl continued—"as that which took Signora Pacelli's life. I'm convinced of it."

"What?" Luigi's head snapped up. But something about Ulrike's manner when she'd last spoken with him returned to his mind.

"She must've known something," he muttered.

"So the other two maids—Rosalie and Greta—tell me," Herr Hipfl said. "I've had to hear it from them that Fräulein Leon had reason to kill her colleague."

"She bore Signora Pacelli a great degree of jealousy, it is true. But neither Joseph nor I considered that strong enough reason to kill. What else did Rosalie and Greta say?" he added, suddenly anxious. God forbid, they should have spoken of the extortion note.

The barber-surgeon stared coldly at him.

"It turns out someone has been attempting to cast the Archduke as a murderer." Herr Hipfl's lips tightened. "Herr Haydn was not above throwing blame on His Imperial Highness either. I suppose it was to drive suspicion away from his wife and her herbs. But the attempt nonetheless was despicable."

Luigi's cold fingers gripped the table. How was he to assuage the barber-surgeon's outrage without reference to the more delicate matter of the extortion note?

No. He shook his head, staring at the wooden floorboards visible through the thick layer of straw. No, there was nothing for it, but to tell the truth. As much of it as could be revealed.

He raised his eyes.

"It is not Joseph's fault," he said. "We had all come to the same conclusion."

The relationship between the Archduke and Lucia? Haydn suppressed a sigh, casting around for a suitable explanation.

It was with an effort of will that he allowed his eyes to remain on Maria Beatrice's features; they seemed to be pulled toward the small tables that stood at various intervals on the floor, displaying miniature orange and cherry trees from Japan.

"There was none, Your Ladyship. It was a misunderstanding—albeit un-understandable," he said at last. "I myself labored under that misapprehension. But when I confronted Signora Pacelli, she strongly denied having any such relationship with His Imperial Highness. She merely sought a favor from him."

It was as close to the truth as Haydn could manage.

"What kind of favor?" Maria Beatrice D'Este's blue eyes narrowed suspiciously.

"It was for a friend in Vienna," Haydn replied. "One that His Imperial Highness did not feel himself to be in a position to comply with."

"A favor for a friend?" Her Ladyship repeated thoughtfully. "I expect it will have been a singer."

He inclined his head, allowing her to think that was so.

"I suppose she wanted to secure a position for her friend in the court of Milan."

"That is a possibility," Haydn conceded. He did not wish to openly encourage her belief in the lie. On the other hand, it was certainly more innocuous than the truth.

Besides, the Archduke's youthful affair with the maid in Vienna was over. His Imperial Highness seemed to have ceased pining for her. There was surely no need for anxiety on the subject.

The thought did little to assuage Haydn's guilt, however. It would be best for the Archduke to make a clean breast of it, confess the tale and ask for forgiveness, and an opportunity to prove himself a good husband. After all, in His Imperial Highness's favor, he'd been willing to marry the girl.

He was pondering how best to persuade the Archduke to that course of action when Her Ladyship's voice, more cheerful now, intruded upon his consciousness.

"I must say I am pleasantly surprised and most pleased that His Imperial Highness demurred in making any kind of promises to your prima donna. Most men would have considered the marriage all but done, and have presumed to make decisions on the basis of it."

Haydn nodded. "I would imagine that when it comes to the hiring or dismissal of artists, His Imperial Highness is aware that Your Ladyship's wishes must be consulted as well."

Certainly, the Empress had been at pains to assure Haydn that the Archduke had been carefully instructed to take his spouse's wishes into account at all times.

"She is the older of the two, Haydn," Her Majesty had said. "And it would be wise for Ferdinand to allow her to take charge. It will make for a more harmonious relationship."

But the true reason for the directive, Haydn suspected, was because Her Ladyship was the more likely of the two to allow herself to be led by the Empress. Her Majesty had made it clear the Archduke and his spouse were to regard themselves as no more than regents in Milan, ruling on behalf of the Habsburgs.

He turned now to Maria Beatrice D'Este.

"It would be well if Your Ladyship were to inform His Imperial Highness that the marriage is to take place after all," he said gently. "The sudden break has made him most despondent."

Whether it had or not, Haydn knew not. But his brother the Grand Duke of Tuscany's bitter reproaches on the subject surely had.

<hr>

Luigi swallowed as the barber-surgeon stared at him, his gray eyes cold and stony. He had never seen such disbelief in anyone's eyes. He could hardly blame the man; their suspicions seemed utterly incredulous now.

He forced himself to continue

"It was but yesterday that His Serene Highness took Joseph to task. The Prince and the Grand Duke of Tuscany both feared Lucia was attempting to seduce His Imperial Highness. Joseph saw the couple himself in the garden. Later, a note surfaced. Joseph believed it to have been penned by Lucia."

He paused, but Herr Hipfl said nothing, merely gesturing for him to continue.

"Your surmise that she was with child made us believe. . ." Luigi's voice trailed off.

The barber-surgeon frowned. "You thought the Archduke had gotten her with child and had then chosen to kill her?"

Luigi shrugged. "There is a lot riding on the marriage alliance. If it fails to go through, His Imperial Highness has been threatened with Holy Orders."

The barber-surgeon continued to regard him skeptically. "And what does the good Kapellmeister think now? Has he concluded he was in error?"

Luigi nodded. "There was nothing between the two. Lucia merely sought a favor—on behalf of a friend." It was one way to describe the situation, he supposed.

"And the letter?"

"An anonymous note," Luigi explained. "Not addressed to anyone. It was found discarded on the floor . . ." he shrugged again, hoping the barber-surgeon would let the matter go.

"It has become very clear to Joseph," Luigi continued more forcefully, "that someone has gone to great lengths to force us to the conclusion that the Archduke is guilty of murder. The merest rumor of such a thing would be disastrous."

The barber-surgeon snorted. "Yet, Herr Haydn saw fit to spread it himself this morning."

Abruptly he changed the subject. "What do you suppose the poor girl knew?" he asked, tipping his chin to indicate the dead maid on the table.

Luigi cast his mind back. Now that he thought about it, she'd seemed uneasy when he'd questioned her. The thought that the Archduke's herbs might have caused Lucia's death acting like a bolt of lightning on her.

"I wonder if she knew who it was trying to sully the Archduke's reputation," he said.

If it was Trattner, would the man have gone so far as to kill her?

But Ulrike had believed—as he and Joseph had at the time—that it was the leaves of pennyroyal in the Archduke's herbs that had poisoned Lucia. Would Trattner have killed Lucia? Merely to point the finger at the Archduke and to prevent his marriage?

That hardly seemed possible.

Could it be that Ulrike had possessed some inkling of who might have killed Lucia? Wasn't that more likely?

He must've voiced the thought aloud for Herr Hipfl immediately said: "I am glad to see that you agree with me, Herr Tomasini."

"What?" Luigi glanced down at the man; the barber-surgeon was short, and Luigi, a good nine inches taller, towered over him.

"If Herr Haydn had seen fit to be straightforward with me this morning, we could have brought this unfortunate case to a close far sooner. And without this poor child losing her life, at that."

The barber-surgeon sighed. "But what's done is done. I have sent word to the Bürgermeister. Herr Groer is making the arrest as we speak, I expect."

Luigi was flabbergasted. "But whom could he possibly be arresting?"

As far as he could see, Ulrike's murder had only complicated matters. What light could it possibly have shed for the barber-surgeon and the Bürgermeister?

It was Herr Hipfl's turn to look bewildered.

"Why, Fräulein Leon, of course. Who else would have reason to kill both Signora Pacelli and this unfortunate girl?"

Chapter Twenty-Six

HAYDN could hardly believe the barber-surgeon had decided to have Narcissa arrested.

"A more self-absorbed woman I have yet to see," he said to Luigi and Johann. "I don't say she is incapable of murder, but . . ." His voice trailed off.

After the initial shock of the news, Haydn had offered very little in the way of protest. The facts spoke strongly against his soprano. Ulrike's dead body—God rest her soul—had been discovered in Narcissa's changing room; the pennyroyal oil but a few paces away outside the room.

Moreover, Narcissa's intense jealousy of Lucia certainly supplied her with sufficient reason to kill her rival.

But something about the situation didn't sit right with him.

"When could she even have had the time to do it?" Johann wondered. "She and Miss Lidia were with me most of the morning, rehearsing the songs for the evening's performance."

The three men were sitting in a quiet corner of the tavern. Haydn had come out as soon as he'd heard the news, and Johann had followed the Bürgermeister, who'd led Narcissa away in shackles.

Both Herr Hipfl and Herr Groer, the Bürgermeister, had been extremely pleased with themselves.

"It's not always that we're able to decipher problems of this nature before you, eh, Herr Kapellmeister?" The Bürgermeister had given Haydn a playful jab in the ribs. "But you may rest assured justice has been done. Your performers are safe, and the festivities can carry on as usual."

"I can only trust Meninger's soprano can learn her parts in time for the concert," Haydn said bitterly. The unexpected arrest had put him in an impossible situation. He could hardly call off the entertainment at the eleventh hour!

"Meninger assures me she can read and perform at sight," Luigi assured him now. "It's fortuitous he was able to spare her at such short notice."

Friedrich Meninger managed a traveling troupe of opera singers. They performed in various cities throughout Europe, and Meninger's boast was that his troupe could put on any opera after no more than an hour or two of rehearsal. It was for just this reason that the Prince had engaged his company for the duration of the festivities in Eszterháza.

What a blessing that had turned out to be, Haydn thought. Who'd have believed that in the course of no more than a day, he'd lose not one but two of his sopranos? If only Herr Groer had waited a day or two before arresting Narcissa.

He chided himself for the thought as soon as it entered his mind. If Narcissa was the killer, she deserved to be behind bars. But was she?

"I can't fault Herr Hipfl for his logic," he said slowly, his fingers gripping the mug of foaming ale Gerhard had provided.

The tavern-keeper had also supplied them with a plate of sausages and a dish of pickled cabbage along with some bread. The food was nearly untouched, none of the three having much appetite for it.

"Clearly the same hand killed both women."

Luigi nodded vehemently. "I'm inclined to agree. The poor girl was most nervous when I explained that the herbs might've been fatal to Lucia. I wish I'd paid more attention to her behavior and questioned her more closely at the time. She must've known who was responsible for depositing the herbs in Lucia's changing room. But I thought . . ."

He shrugged his regrets away, but Haydn knew his Konzertmeister couldn't help blaming himself for Ulrike's death.

"What I cannot fathom," Johann suddenly broke the silence, "is why Narcissa would've wanted to involve the Archduke in the matter."

Haydn frowned. "What . . .?" he began to ask when his brow cleared. The niggling doubt that had been plaguing him sharpened into focus.

"That's it." He turned to his brother, his eyes widening in shocked realization. "She had no reason to cast suspicion on the Archduke. You're absolutely right. Why not throw suspicion anywhere else? At her other colleagues, for instance?"

"Could she not have been hired by the King of Prussia?" Luigi asked, his hazel eyes veiled in uncertainty. "She has performed in Potsdam. Remember, she told us the King commended her for her performance."

"Yes, but that was as part of Meninger's troupe." Impressed by Narcissa's singing, Haydn had offered her a permanent position with the Esterházy troupe. Were it not for her constant need to be the center of attraction, he thought regretfully, she would've worked out quite well. "I doubt she was there long enough to sufficiently earn His Majesty's trust to be engaged as a spy."

Johann fingered the broadsheet. It was the same newspaper that had been pushed under Maria Beatrice D'Este's door. Haydn had been carrying it with him when he strode into the tavern.

"If Narcissa is the spy we're looking for, it must have been she who supplied the publisher of this broadsheet with these disreputable tidbits." Johann raised his eyes. "But when would she have had the opportunity to slip the paper under Her Ladyship's door?"

"Perhaps she was working with someone else," Luigi ventured.

"It's possible," Haydn agreed.

"But it's more likely that the two things are unrelated, isn't that so, brother?" Johann turned to him.

Haydn considered the question. Was the murder unrelated to the blackmail? He wasn't inclined to think so.

"I know not." He expelled a heavy breath. "But it might be best to proceed as though it were." He could think of no way to prove Narcissa innocent. That she had no reason to scapegoat the Archduke would not suffice.

He glanced down at the broadsheet. "We'd better get to the bottom of this affair. Her Ladyship has agreed to the marriage once more, but until the nuptials take place, our position is precarious." And who knew, changing tack to track down the extortionist might serve to reveal the killer as well.

Johann unfolded the broadsheet and scanned it once more.

"Do you suppose the only motive behind these obviously scandalous rumors was to purchase the Archduke's silence?"

"The man would need to ensure the Archduke laid eyes on his publication," Haydn pointed out. "No, I'm more inclined to believe that whoever provided him the news was trying to thwart the marriage." Why else would anyone bother to make sure Her Ladyship saw the publication?

He turned to face Luigi, but his Konzertmeister looked at him ruefully before he could continue.

"I have yet to ask Gerhard who the publisher is. What with one thing and another, I fear it completely escaped my mind."

Haydn nodded. "It is no matter. We will do so now."

Peering around the high backrest of his seat, he caught Gerhard's eyes and beckoned him toward them.

⸺·❈·⸺

The palace was abuzz with gossip by the time Rosalie and Greta—having sufficiently recovered from the shock of finding Ulrike's dead body—returned from the tavern. The news of Ulrike's murder and Fräulein Leon's arrest had spread.

"Is it true?" Katya and Frida, Ulrike's fellow servants, had demanded the minute they caught sight of Rosalie and Greta in the courtyard.

The maids had fended off the questions as best they could and then had fled to the delivery room by the service entrance.

"I still can't believe it," Greta said. "I'm not surprised, mind you. But I can't believe it."

"I'm glad it's over," Rosalie replied. A mirror hung on the wall facing her. She saw her features—white and pinched—within it. The barber-surgeon and the Bürgermeister, usually slow to react, had been most decisive in this case. "I'm glad Fräulein Leon is behind bars."

"So am I," Greta agreed devoutly. "And to think it was her own laziness that caused her downfall."

"What do you mean?" Rosalie turned to face her friend.

"Well"—Greta shrugged—"if she'd thought to put the pennyroyal oil back where it belonged no one would have been any the wiser. At least, not for a very long time."

"That's true enough." But why, Rosalie wondered, had Fräulein Leon been so careless? "It's almost as though she wanted to get caught."

"It would've happened eventually," Greta said, popping a *Zitronenkeks* —a lemon-flavored biscuit—into her mouth. "Who but a fool would kill someone in their own room and then leave the body lying there?"

But wasn't it possible that someone else had killed Ulrike and left her dead in the soprano's changing room? Rosalie was just about to mention this when a soft voice interrupted them.

"Is it true Fräulein Leon killed Signora Pacelli?"

"Hannah!" Rosalie and Greta greeted the seamstress in unison.

Gerhard perused the broadsheet Haydn had handed him.

"Markos might know," he remarked, raising his eyes. "He's the only one in the village with a printing press."

"His brother works in the palace stables, does he not?" Luigi asked.

"Yes, Gabor." Gerhard nodded. That was the head groom, Haydn recalled. A good source of gossip, he supposed. Was it Gabor who had provided this tripe?

"Although I wouldn't be surprised," Gerhard went on, "if it's Markos himself who puts these out. He's a quiet fellow, but he asks a lot of questions. Sits with his mouth open, too, just like a fish whenever there's any kind of talk. He was here only this morning. Shortly after you left, Herr Kapellmeister."

"Asking questions?" Haydn wanted to know.

"He rushed in and collared Herr Hipfl just as he was about to leave. Not a word about the money he owes me, mind you. He had no time for that. No, all he could think about was whether Signora Pacelli had been poisoned. Was it true, he asked. When the barber-surgeon said it was, Markos asked about the medicaments found in her possession. Were they to help her conceive a child?"

"What did Herr Hipfl say to that?" Haydn asked.

"That he knew not whether she had trouble conceiving. She was already with child."

"You've heard the news, then?" Greta waved the seamstress in and gestured toward a chair.

"I was there when the Bürgermeister came for her." Hannah pulled out a chair and sank into it. She looked from Greta to Rosalie. "But why would she kill Signora Pacelli?"

"So that she could take the lead in the opera, of course," Greta said. "Why else would she kill her? She killed Ulrike as well."

Hannah looked doubtful. "But singers are always jealous of one another," she objected. "That's hardly a reason to kill someone. They might stab each

other in the back, of course. But it's as far as they'd go. And as for Ulrike
—"

"Ulrike was found in Fräulein Leon's changing room, Hannah," Greta pointed out, somewhat tartly. "The pennyroyal oil that poisoned the poor girl was just outside the room."

Hannah looked troubled. "I don't like Fräulein Leon any more than most other people. She's too proud for her own good. And I've never seen anyone more thoughtless. But she's no murderess. Besides, she was with Master Johann most of the morning. She had a fitting with me later."

She stared up at them, her chin jutting out. "And why would she kill Ulrike of all people?"

"Because Ulrike knew she'd killed Signora Lucia," Rosalie said quietly, "and was trying to lay the blame at the Archduke's door."

Hannah's jaw dropped. "H-how can you be so sure of this? Has the Bürgermeister extracted a confession already? She was screaming her innocence for all to hear when he and his men came for her."

"His Imperial Highness had gotten rid of the herbs Frau Haydn gave him, Hannah," Greta said. "Ulrike told Master Luigi so. That his valet gave her the herbs to throw away."

"And you think Ulrike gave them . . . to Fräulein Leon instead? So that Fräulein Leon could point the finger at His Imperial Highness? But what had she against him?"

"That I don't know," Rosalie confessed. The question had been nagging at her as well. She looked at Greta. "It's not like she's with child." At Herr Hipfl's behest, her mother-in-law had examined the prisoner as well.

Fräulein Leon wasn't carrying the Archduke's child—or anyone else's, for that matter.

"The only one with child was Signora Pacelli." Greta turned to Hannah. "And from what you told us, I don't suppose her husband fathered it."

"I don't suppose he did," Hannah replied. "But what does that have to do with anything?"

Rosalie's gaze veered toward Greta's. They hadn't told anyone—other than Herr Haydn and Master Luigi—about the extortion note. They hadn't mentioned it to the barber-surgeon or the Bürgermeister either.

Would it be wise to share the news with Hannah?

On the other hand, it was Hannah who'd surmised that Signora Pacelli had died because of what she knew. Besides, Hannah had once owned a store in Vienna catering to fashionable ladies. If anyone could be trusted to keep her mouth shut, it was her.

Rosalie glanced quickly over her shoulder. The door to the delivery room was ajar, but no one seemed to be in the corridor outside.

She turned back. Leaning closer to Hannah, she spoke in a low whisper.

"We discovered a note in the Archduke's study yesterday. Someone is trying to extort money from him?"

Hannah gaped. "You looked through his correspondence?"

"No, of course not. He'd read the note and tossed it. I found it on the floor when I was cleaning his study. It wasn't signed, but it must've been from a woman. She claimed to be with child."

"Oh?" Hannah sat back, her arms folded.

Rosalie stared at her. Couldn't Hannah see what she was trying to say?

"Don't you see? When you said this morning that Signora Pacelli had been killed for what she knew—we immediately thought she must've known who it was that was blackmailing His Imperial Highness."

"Oh," Hannah said again. Her features cleared. "Oh, I see. But there's no one here who's with child."

"Other than Signora Pacelli herself," Greta said. Her head swiveled from Rosalie to Hannah. "Do you think she was carrying the Archduke's child? And that she was blackmailing him?"

"She would never do such a thing," Hannah burst out immediately. "I don't say she was faithful. But she wasn't carrying on with the Archduke either. She had no interest in him, I'm certain of it."

"What did she know, then?" Rosalie asked.

The question seemed to leave Hannah stumped. She subsided. "She only wished him to do the right thing. She didn't give me all the details. All I know is that it had something to do with Vienna."

Rosalie looked at Greta. "I wonder if Fräulein Leon had got wind of it as well, whatever it was. Maybe she was trying to blackmail the Archduke."

"I don't think she knows anything," Hannah said firmly. "Signora Pacelli wasn't one to blab."

"Herr Trattner, then?" Greta suggested. "Although, if it's him, Fräulein Leon must be innocent."

Hannah frowned. "But why would Herr Trattner kill Signora Pacelli? Simply to point the finger at the Archduke? I can't say I much like him; he's a weasel. Still, it makes no sense."

She got up to go, shaking her head.

"I'd be surprised if the note you found has anything to do with Signora Pacelli's murder. Most likely, whoever killed her simply wanted her dead."

Chapter Twenty-Seven

HAYDN gazed thoughtfully at his untouched mug of ale. So it was the barber-surgeon who was the unwitting source of the news that Lucia was with child—the information cleverly ferreted out of him.

That Paolo was unable to do the deed was common knowledge. But how had Markos—if it was he who'd published the broadsheet—concluded that the father must be Archduke Ferdinand?

He raised his eyes. "How came he to hear of the Archduke's herbs being in Signora Pacelli's possession?"

Gerhard shrugged. "The singers were here last night as well as the stage-hands and some of the other servants. Signor Pacelli was in his cups and kept saying over and over that it was Frau Haydn's meddling that did his wife in."

The tavern-keeper glanced apologetically at Haydn, but the Kapellmeister gestured for him to continue. Paolo had made his views on the subject quite clear last night. He blamed Maria Anna.

"It was in vain Fiore explained there was nothing in the herbs that could've killed anyone—just a bit of chamomile, ginger, peppermint, and fennel, as far as he could tell."

"Fiore was right," Johann quietly asserted. "That was all sister-in-law put in the tea she brewed for Lucia before the performance."

"Aye," Gerhard agreed. "If anyone knew, it would be Fiore. We saw him go along with them when they left the auditorium last evening."

"But Paolo wouldn't listen to reason, I suppose," Johann said with a sympathetic glance at Haydn.

Gerhard shook his head. *"What about the bundle of herbs, we found?* he says to Hannah. *In her delicate situation, she should've consulted a midwife not some woman who fancies herself a herbalist.*" This with another apologetic look at the Kapellmeister.

"A midwife?" Haydn repeated, intrigued. Had Paolo known of his wife's condition, then? If so, he had as good a reason to kill her as anyone else.

Gerhard nodded. "Hannah just rolled her eyes. *What good would a midwife do?* she says. *It wasn't her health that was the issue.*"

He laid the broadsheet on the table. "Markos was sitting there with his mouth open, gaping first at one person then another. I suppose that's why he was here this morning, wanting to know if Signora Pacelli had trouble conceiving a child."

"Because Paolo had mentioned a midwife?" Luigi grinned. "As though it were her fault they had no children."

"Who was it who mentioned the Archduke's herbs?" Haydn asked again, realizing the question still hadn't been answered.

"It was Hannah. Signor Pacelli was adamant Frau Haydn's herbs had killed his wife. *Nonsense,* Hannah says. *Besides,* she says, *the herbs were made up for His Imperial Highness, not Signora Pacelli.*"

Ach so. Light dawned on Haydn's mind. The seamstress had merely been trying to defend Maria Anna and in so doing had inadvertently succeeded in casting suspicion on the Archduke.

Markos's ears, according to Gerhard, had immediately perked up at mention of the Archduke. Had His Imperial Highness given his herbs to Signora Pacelli, he'd wanted to know.

"His Imperial Highness must have held Tante Lucia in high regard, then," Fiore had said proudly, eliciting a sour look from his uncle.

"And Markos took two and two," Luigi began, "put them together . . ."

"And came up with six," Gerhard finished for him. "Although"—he flicked his forefinger at the broadsheet—"to give him credit, he never says it in so many words."

"No, he does far worse," Luigi responded wryly. "He implies it, letting his readers draw the aspersions he's too wily to print. He knows he'd lose his license instantly if he weren't circumspect."

⁂

Rosalie stared blankly at the door Hannah had just closed. Her chin rested on her hands as she struggled to come to grips with what the seamstress had said.

"She's right, you know," she said at last, turning to Greta. "Fräulein Leon may have been envious of Signora Pacelli. But she had no reason to cast blame on the Archduke. And I don't see why Herr Trattner would've murdered Signora Pacelli. What could he have had against her?"

"Unless one of them was the blackmailer, and Signora Pacelli found out about it." Greta stuck out her chin stubbornly.

"But think about it Greta"—Rosalie swiveled around in her chair to face Greta—"suppose everyone had considered the Archduke to be the killer and he'd been arrested. What would the blackmailer gain from such a situation?"

Greta pursed her lips. "Nothing, I suppose," she grudgingly admitted. She frowned. "Then, why . . .?"

"That's what I'm wondering," Rosalie admitted, her brow wrinkling as well.

What if Herr Groer had arrested the wrong person? Was the killer still roaming free? Who would be next?

"But someone was trying to lay Signora Pacelli's death at the Archduke's door," she said. "That much is certain. And Ulrike, poor girl, knew who it was."

They were quiet for a while. The dying rays of the late afternoon sun cast a dim glow over the room. It would soon be time to light the candles.

"You know," Greta said. "If Signor Pacelli thought his wife was having an affair with the Archduke—"

"He could've killed her in a jealous rage and made sure His Imperial Highness got blamed for the murder." Rosalie nodded. She turned to Greta. "Gerhard heard him saying something about Signora Pacelli needing a midwife last night. So he knew she was with child."

"He must have." Greta bobbed her head vigorously. "Can you imagine any man accepting a child not his own?" she asked.

Rosalie hesitated. It wasn't unheard of. Gerhard had been willing to do exactly that—not so very long ago. But still, Greta was right, few men would be willing to shoulder such a burden.

Gerhard had been so enamored of Marlene at the time, he'd have done anything for her.

Not for the first time, Rosalie wondered if Gerhard would have accepted such behavior from her. Then she scolded herself for harboring such a thought. As if she'd ever betray Gerhard's trust the way Marlene had.

Greta was saying something.

"What?" It was with an effort that Rosalie brought her mind back to the present.

"I was just wondering," Greta said, "how Signor Pacelli would feel if he realized it was someone else altogether that Signora Pacelli had betrayed him with."

"I wonder who it was." The words fell out of Rosalie's mouth before she was even aware of having thought them. They were closely followed by a sickening realization.

Could Signora Pacelli's lover have killed her? He may have thought nothing of risking his position by consorting with a married woman. After all, their dalliance could easily be kept hidden. But a pregnancy couldn't be kept secret. Signora Pacelli's growing belly would've given the matter away at once.

"If it's one of the other performers and His Serene Highness ever found out, he'd be out on the street immediately," she murmured.

***

Markos's printing shop was on the road to the village of Széplak, a few miles west of the palace. A carriage from Gerhard's tavern deposited Haydn, Johann, and Luigi on the rough, unevenly cobbled road outside the shop—a small building with a sign hanging over the door.

The words *Markos Papp, Printer* were printed in large white letters upon a black background. A thin red border outlined the whole. The door stood ajar.

"Let us hope we can learn something useful here," Haydn muttered as he led the way in.

A bespectacled, dark-haired man with ink-stained fingers and a black apron was inking the blocks of type set within a wooden box. A hinged lid with a sheet of paper affixed to it angled back. The jangling of the bell above the door caused him to jerk his head up. But to Haydn's surprise, he beamed when he saw them, wiping his hands on his apron as he came forward to greet them.

"You come from the palace, I suppose," he said, holding out a hairy arm stained with black up to the elbows.

"Yes." Haydn gingerly took the man's hand, allowing it to be shaken. "Are you Markos Papp."

"The very same." The slight fellow smiled widely. He rocked on his heels, surveying them with the delight of a connoisseur regarding a well-cooked pheasant. "What may I do for you, gentlemen? I take it His Imperial Highness, Archduke Ferdinand, has sent you?"

"You were expecting him, were you?" Luigi came forward, his eyes narrowed threateningly. "Is that why you published your lies?"

"Lies?" Markos raised his eyebrows, drawing back in a hurry. "What lies?"

Johann held out the broadsheet. "What would you call this? I assume this your work."

"Yes, it is. I've never denied it."

"Do you print every word of gossip that comes your way?" Luigi leaned into the man's face belligerently.

Markos's smile had faded; his features were white with anger. "I would hardly call it gossip. I take care to confirm every detail I can. It was Herr Hipfl who informed me Signora Pacelli was with child. And when I asked Fiore whether his uncle could've fathered it, he said it would be a miracle if he had."

Haydn's eyebrows rose. It was bad enough the man had chosen to spread rumors. Were they to stand by while he defended his actions?

"But to insinuate that His Imperial Highness was the father—" he began only to be interrupted.

"I did no such thing. I merely reported that his herbs were found in the unfortunate lady's changing room. They could not have made their own way there."

"So you let your reader believe that His Imperial Highness's kindness toward Signora Pacelli was somehow connected to her being with child?" Haydn persisted.

Markos was about to open his mouth, but Luigi spoke before he could.

"Don't bother denying it. There was no need to ask if the two events were connected unless you wished to spread the rumor that they were."

"What precisely were you hoping to accomplish?" Johann inquired, genuinely curious.

"I was simply printing the news," Markos muttered sulkily, retreating behind his press. He closed the hinged lid over the box and began to crank a handle that made the entire contraption move forward between a set of posts. "It's what I do."

"No," Haydn said. The truth had suddenly dawned upon him.

Chapter Twenty-Eight

"You were hoping to profit from the scandal, I'll warrant," the Kapellmeister said. "You thought the Archduke might read your vile lies and be persuaded to hand over a large sum of money. In return for which, you would graciously agree to publish a retraction."

It was how the broadsheet publishers in most of Europe operated, the Empress had warned him before they'd traveled to Prussia a year or two ago. "Beware of any rumors that may be published, Haydn. Once out, they are difficult to squelch, no matter how outrageous or untruthful. And when they are successfully stifled, one has only managed to confirm their truth."

Markos's swarthy features darkened. "If His Imperial Highness wished me to publish his account of the tale, I would naturally have done so. And if he saw fit to provide a small consideration . . ." The printer shrugged. "I cannot see the harm in it. The ink and the paper I use do not grow on trees, you know."

"How much were you hoping to receive?" Luigi demanded, following Markos to the printing press. "Enough to pay your debts to Gerhard?"

Markos raised his head. "My debts have nothing to do with it. Besides, I'm not the only one who owes Gerhard money." He turned to Haydn. "His Serene Highness's heir has run up a sizeable tab himself. As have some of your performers."

"My performers?" Haydn was stunned. Gerhard had mentioned no such thing.

"Signor Pacelli does, I know," Markos responded. He opened the hinged lid and inspected the paper on it.

"Paolo?" Haydn exclaimed. "The man is as sober as a judge."

"Well, his nephew, then," Markos snapped. "Everyone knows it's Fiore's uncle who pays his way. Fiore has no luck when it comes to—" He abruptly stopped short.

"Gambling?" Haydn asked, suddenly recalling the roosters he'd heard that morning. "Does Gerhard hold cockfights in the tavern?"

It was against the Prince's express orders that any form of gambling be allowed in the tavern.

No doubt, Gerhard had chosen to ignore the order to drum up business. And if Prince Toni and the Archduke had encouraged the activities, there would be even less reason to obey the strictures set forth in the license.

"And you gamble as well, don't you?" Haydn went on. Markos could ill afford to be in his cups if he depended upon gossip and rumors for his publication.

Markos glared at him defiantly. "And what if I do? His Serene Highness is well aware of what goes on in the tavern, and he turns a blind eye to it because his imperial guest and his own son indulge themselves. Were it not for that unfortunate fact, the rest of us would be hauled off to prison. Our betters do as they please, and then presume to police us."

Haydn glanced at Johann. They had come for information, but had only succeeded in baiting the man.

Johann turned to Markos. "Be that as it may," he said. "Our only interest is in the lies you've published. Are you sure no one paid you to publish them?"

Markos rolled his eyes to the ceiling. "Wouldn't I be a wealthy man if people deigned to pay me to publish my broadsheet? Besides, if I were of a mind to publish everything that came my way, wouldn't I have published this?"

He handed them a handwritten sheet.

"*The Nun's Confession*," Haydn read the title. He perused the sheet and felt the blood draining from his features. God have mercy, how could anyone have come to find out such intimate details of the Archduke's affair in Vienna?

That the woman was now a nun, her child taken from her?

He raised his head sharply. "Who gave this to you?"

Markos shrugged. "I found it when I returned from the tavern this morning. It had been pushed under the door. I meant to send a message to His Imperial Highness to see what he wished to do about it."

"It's someone who wants money, no doubt," Luigi remarked.

"Then let us by all means ensure they get what they're asking for," Haydn said grimly. He pulled out a pen and a piece of paper from his pocket and scribbled a note. "Be so good as to publish this notice in your paper. Have it ready by this evening. I will make sure you are paid for your troubles."

The extortionist was someone in the palace, it was clear. The notice would, he hoped, bring the individual out into the open.

"And as to this story"—Haydn waved the page the printer had handed him—"if so much as a word of it appears in your broadsheet, you'll find yourself behind bars."

His teeth gritted, Haydn strode toward the palace. He had sent Johann and Luigi back to the tavern with the carriage Gerhard had lent them. He himself intended to hasten to the palace to place the matter before His Serene Highness and His Grace, the Grand Duke of Tuscany.

He had every hope of apprehending the blackmailer that very night, but guards would need to be discreetly placed within the church to seize the fellow when he arrived. None of this could be done without His Serene Highness's express approval.

Head bowed, Haydn walked along the sunny, cobbled path when a voice loudly hailing him caused his head to jerk up and around.

"Haydn!"

"Your Grace?"

Haydn had heard the cantering of horses' hooves behind him, but his mind, mired in their thoughts, had barely registered the sound. He waited by the roadside while the Grand Duke, along with the Prince, emerged from a path in a thicket beyond onto the dusty ground by the road.

His Grace, mounted on a fine black horse, slowed to a trot alongside him. Cheeks flushed, he gazed down at the composer.

"You missed the hunt, my dear fellow. It was fine shooting."

Ach so, the hunt! It had escaped Haydn's mind. An outing had been arranged for the guests that afternoon. The wild ducks had been especially plentiful that summer, and the area by the lake was thick with the feathered creatures.

His Serene Highness followed at a slower pace. "Leopold here bagged several ducks. You should've been there, Haydn. You have certainly earned a respite. We could hardly believe it when Maria Beatrice informed us she had reconsidered her decision."

"What you can have said to persuade her to change her mind, I know not," His Grace added. "But your remarks clearly made an impression on her. The Emperor did well to put this matter in your hands. We are in your debt, my dear fellow."

Haydn felt his cheeks flushing. It was not just embarrassment at the encomiums being heaped upon him. He had disturbing news to convey and little idea of how to broach it. He was keenly aware of just how fragile his listeners' current good humor was—and how easily it could be shattered.

"I did no more than my duty," he replied, bowing his head. "His Imperial Highness appears to have made a most favorable impression upon Her Ladyship. It was merely some stray rumors reaching her ears that gave Her Ladyship pause."

"Stray rumors?" His Serene Highness frowned.

"Not about the affair in Vienna, I hope," the Grand Duke said at the same time.

Haydn shook his head. He threw a hasty glance at the thicket beyond before responding. Fortunately, no footmen were visible. Nor were any of the other guests behind them. Satisfied they were alone, he returned his attention to the Prince and the Grand Duke.

"It was a misguided remark or two in a local broadsheet that caused Her Ladyship to question the Archduke's fidelity in marriage."

"It was, was it?" The Prince gazed down at him, his eyes narrowed. "Who is the scurrilous villain behind the paper? He will lose his—"

Haydn held up his hand. "I have taken care of the matter. The man was under a misapprehension; he meant no harm. Besides, the remarks were easily proven to be false. The printer has, however, done us a great service."

It was certainly one way of regarding it. He thanked the stars that notion of the situation had occurred to him.

Hastily withdrawing the paper Markos had given them out of his pocket, he began recounting the details the printer had divulged. He handed the page to His Serene Highness, who perused it with a deepening frown before passing it to the Grand Duke.

The Grand Duke scanned the sheet. "Trattner is behind this, I suppose."

He raised his eyes, his features troubled and grave.

"I can think of no one else who would be privy to the details," Haydn replied quietly. Unless Lucia—who had certainly got wind of the facts—had confided in someone. Paolo, maybe? Or her mysterious lover?

But Haydn saw no reason to disclose his suspicions. After all, whoever it was, the scoundrel would soon be revealed.

"Nor I," the Grand Duke agreed. His voice hardened. "Something must be done."

"I have set a trap for him," Haydn assured his listeners. "He should be in our hands this very night. I took the liberty of arranging for a message to be circulated this evening."

He brought out the notice Markos had agreed to print, and read it out loud.

His Imperial Highness, Archduke Ferdinand Karl, has learned that some person or persons might be spreading scandalous stories impugning his character. Anyone with information on the subject should come forward forthwith. A handsome reward is promised to any individual who will help to put these rumors to rest and restore His Imperial Highness's good name.

"I have specified the hour as daybreak and the place as the village church," he said, raising his eyes from the paper. "I trust His Imperial Highness still means to spend the night in prayer there."

"He does," His Serene Highness replied. "I will have men discreetly posted there to apprehend the man as soon as he shows his face."

"But how are we to ensure that Trattner receives the notice—much less reads it?" the Grand Duke objected.

"Markos will endeavor to have several copies of his broadsheet delivered to us. The footmen must be directed to place one on every chair—that of the musicians as well as everyone in the audience. Although"—Haydn grimaced as the thought occurred to him—"we may safely omit Her Ladyship and the Duke of Modena as well as his companion. There's no need to alarm Her Ladyship any further."

The Grand Duke shuddered. "No, there's not. God forbid, she should change her mind again."

"We will have to recompense the printer for his work," Haydn added delicately, recalling his promise to Markos.

The money would ensure the printer was not tempted to print any further unsubstantiated stories about the Archduke. But it would be prudent not to put forward that perspective before his employer. Any whiff of extortion, and His Serene Highness would balk at paying the man.

"Certainly." The Prince waved a magnanimous hand. "Request the money from the paymaster and have it sent out at once, Haydn."

Haydn nodded. "I had better let Pfarrer Spalek know as well. He'll need to be prepared for what must take place."

Chapter Twenty-Nine

"We'll do it," Rosalie said resolutely. She realized she sounded a little more eager than was necessary. Had Gerhard been present, he might have surmised she had something up her sleeve. There was a telltale gleam in her violet eyes.

But Karl, fortunately, didn't know her quite as well as her husband. She and Greta had still been in the delivery room when Karl had hurried in—Miss Lidia close on his heels—wanting to know if a maid could be spared to clear out Signora Pacelli's changing room at the opera house.

"You will?" He now wavered, his gaze lingering hesitantly on Greta's rosy cheeks. "Are you sure you're up to it, my dumpling? There's really no need to trouble yourselves, you know."

"No need at all," Miss Lidia hastened to assure them. "Not after what you've been through. Besides, one person is all I need."

"It's all right," Greta said. "We can do it." Her blue eyes wide with curiosity flickered toward Rosalie. Rosalie raised her eyebrows ever so slightly to let her friend know she had a plan. Fortunately, Greta was following her lead.

"But I still don't understand why Signor Pacelli's insisting the work be done right this minute." Greta tilted her head to one side and regarded Miss Lidia inquisitively.

The singer's thin figure drooped. "I did suggest tackling the task tomorrow. But Paolo can't abide the thought of staying here another day. Not after what's happened."

"He can't, can he?" Rosalie remarked quietly. Why, she wondered, was Signor Pacelli in such a hurry to leave? His wife hadn't even been buried yet. Was he trying to flee the area before anyone realized it was he who'd killed his wife?

Greta looked at her strangely, but Miss Lidia fortunately didn't notice the note of suspicion in Rosalie's voice. Neither did Karl.

"Can't one of the other maids be sent, my sweet?" he asked Greta again. "I don't like the thought of your going back there after what happened."

Miss Lidia nodded, turning toward them apologetically. "I only need one," she said. "I'd do it myself, but Paolo's in a rush. And"—her dark eyes darted anxiously toward the clock—"there's the performance this evening. Lucia has—had, I should say—so many gowns and trinkets, it would take hours to get everything packed and ready."

"Oh, we can both go," Rosalie said with a reassuring smile at Miss Lidia. She turned to Karl. "It'll take our minds off . . ." She spread her hands wide in a vague gesture.

"Of course, of course," Karl said. "I should've thought of it myself. Very well, then, that's settled." Pulling Greta into his arms for a kiss, he turned toward Miss Lidia. "I had better go. There's much to be done."

"Yes, of course. Thank you, Karl." As the librettist turned to leave, Miss Lidia plucked at his sleeve. "Send for me, won't you, if we're not done by the time the performance starts."

He nodded.

While they were speaking, Greta crept closer to Rosalie. "Why are we doing this?" she hissed into her friend's ear.

"To see if there are any clues to be found in Signora Pacelli's room," Rosalie whispered back. "Don't you find it suspicious that her husband's so eager to leave?"

Who knew what kind of evidence Signor Pacelli had left behind in his wife's changing room? Small wonder, he wanted the room cleared out before anyone could get wind of his involvement in his wife's death.

"Besides," she continued, "we might even be able to figure out who her mysterious lover was?"

It was a heaven-sent opportunity. They'd be fools not to take it.

<hr>

"Shall we?" Miss Lidia smiled pleasantly at them after Karl left. She led the way to the opera house, chatting companionably all the while.

She might be a plain woman, Rosalie thought, tall and thin, but at least, she didn't give herself any airs and graces. Even Signora Pacelli, gracious though she'd been, had possessed an air of superiority, as though she were above the rest of the world.

But Miss Lidia was unpretentious. And nice.

"Paolo's taken Lucia's death very hard, you know." Miss Lidia looked over her shoulder at them as they walked along the tree-lined avenue. "It's not just losing his wife, poor man. But he's lost an heir, too. Well, at least, he hoped it would be an heir. Lucia might've had a girl, for all one knows."

Rosalie's mouth fell open. "He knew she was with child?"

Miss Lidia tittered. "Of course, he did. Oh, I know what you're thinking. It's best not to let on before you can feel the child quickening. But it was her husband. And she must have been so excited." She glanced over her shoulder again. "I don't know why Paolo never mentioned it to me, though."

She sounded disappointed, Rosalie thought, almost as though she'd been betrayed by a good friend. Was Miss Lidia just a tiny bit in love with Signor Pacelli? She doubted Signor Pacelli knew or cared how she felt.

"Paolo had given up all hope of ever fathering a child, you know," Miss Lidia prattled on. "He couldn't even with his first wife. She brought a son with her from a prior marriage. Paolo was so desperate for an heir, he adopted the child."

Greta looked at Rosalie, her eyebrows raised.

"Oh?" she said. "And what happened to the boy?"

Miss Lidia shook her head. "It's a sad tale. They went out fishing, the boy and Fiore. Fiore can't swim, you know. And he's completely lacking in any kind of common sense. Not his fault, I suppose, but there it is. Paolo's stepson insisted upon jumping into the river. The current was high that day, and he got swept out. Fiore, dumb as a brick, rather than rowing the boat out to him ran off to get help." Miss Lidia shook her head again.

"By the time, he found someone, it was too late. They found the poor boy washed up downriver several days later. Poor Paolo was devastated."

"It must've been hard for him to forgive Fiore," Rosalie commented. Small wonder, Paolo was forever snapping at his nephew.

"No, Paolo never held a grudge," Miss Lidia said. "What would be the point? What irritates him is Fiore's inability to take responsibility for his behavior. The debts he ratchets up, the incessant gambling . . . I think he's quite fed up with the boy."

Rosalie frowned, remembering Fiore's debts to Gerhard. Had the boy paid up? If Paolo were leaving tomorrow, Gerhard could say goodbye to his money. She doubted Fiore had the means to settle his debts.

Once again she found herself vexed by the entire situation. If only Gerhard had acted with greater caution. But he was never one to listen to her.

She tamped down her growing exasperation. There was nothing she could do about it—other than to send word to Gerhard that Paolo, and most likely Fiore as well, intended to leave town very shortly.

The door to the props room was ajar, and Signor Pacelli's enraged voice blared through it down the hallway. Startled by the avalanche of fury, Rosalie stumbled, nearly biting her tongue as she reached out to grab Greta's arm.

Dear Lord, what was the matter with the man?

"Your . . .?" Signor Pacelli bellowed. "What makes you think it is yours to command?"

Not every word could be clearly heard, so thick with rage was his voice. But he was clearly in a state.

"What have you done to . . .? For my sister's sake, I have put up with you all these years. But you have neither wisdom nor sense . . . I am—"

"Don't mind Paolo." Miss Lidia—walking briskly ahead—quickly pulled the door shut. Abruptly, the loud blast subsided into a muffled roar. "Fiore tries his patience more than you can imagine."

"What has he done to earn his uncle's wrath now?" Greta wondered, still looking as though she'd been struck by lightning. Fiore tried everybody's patience. And Signor Pacelli was easily vexed. But neither she nor Rosalie had ever heard him so incensed before.

"Incurred yet more debts and failed to pay them, I suppose," Miss Lidia calmly replied. Her heels clicked sharply on the wooden floor of the hallway and down another corridor.

Rosalie tried to ignore the flash of dismay that coursed through her being as she followed the singer. Would to God, Gerhard hadn't allowed Fiore to make any further purchases. As far as she knew, the lad had yet to settle the bills he already owed.

"And at this rate, those won't get paid either," she muttered to herself.

But before she could brood any more on the matter, Miss Lidia came to a halt in front of one of the doors.

"Here we are," she announced, thrusting it open and stepping in.

Rosalie and Greta were about to follow when, to their surprise, Miss Lidia suddenly staggered back.

"Lord have mercy, not again!" she cried.

"What is it?" Rosalie stood on tiptoe and peered over Miss Lidia's shoulder. The changing room was a hopeless mess. Clothes were strewn all over the floor, trinket boxes lay open, necklaces and bracelets streaming out in an untidy pile.

Chapter Thirty

"Look at the state of this room!" Miss Lidia cried. "Just look at it." She seemed ready to cry.

"Signor Pacelli and Hannah were going through it yesterday," Rosalie explained, hoping to calm the singer down. "They were looking for—"

"I know what they were looking for," Miss Lidia said, her voice shrill with outrage. "I tidied up after them last night. Then, this morning, it was in a mess again. I cleaned up again. And now look at this!"

Greta looked helplessly at Rosalie. It was unlike Miss Lidia to work herself up into such a lather.

"And over such a small matter, too," Greta hissed.

But was it really a small matter? Rosalie turned her attention back to the room. Clearly someone had scoured the room. Who? Signor Pacelli?

What could he have been looking for? Whatever it was, she hoped to goodness, he hadn't found it.

"Most likely, Signor Pacelli was looking for something," she said quietly. Evidence of his involvement in his wife's murder, if she wasn't mistaken. "It's no matter. Greta and I can tidy it up." She walked briskly into the room. "And the sooner we get started, the sooner we'll be done."

"I suppose you're right." Miss Lidia made a visible effort to calm down. "It's just so annoying. I have so much to do. And I've already tidied this room twice." Despite herself, her voice rose, shrill with indignation. "But at least, we're taking everything out this time."

She bent down, picked up a dress, and began to smooth out the wrinkles. Rosalie and Greta followed suit—neatly folding dresses, picking up trinket boxes and jewelry, packing everything into the large travel trunk Karl had left for them behind the door.

The clock loudly ticked the minutes away as the three of them worked in unison.

Rosalie kept a sharp eye out for anything out of the ordinary. But there was nothing. One last trinket box was left on the floor. She set it right side up and began gathering the jewelry that had spilled out of it.

She had just put away two rings and a necklace when a glint of gold caught her eye. She reached under the couch, her fingers searching the dusty ground until they touched a metal chain. She pulled it out—a thick braided gold chain with a large cross at the end of it.

"Does this belong to Signora Pacelli?" she asked, holding it up to the light.

It looked so familiar. But Rosalie couldn't remember ever having seen the prima donna wearing it.

"It must." Miss Lidia gave her a harried glance before quickly turning back to the petticoat she was folding. "There's nothing here that goes back to the props room. Lucia was always very good about returning her costumes and any jewelry that went with it."

Rosalie lowered her arm, frowning all the while. Should she put it in the trinket box with all the other things? She was quite sure it didn't belong to Signora Pacelli.

On the other hand, it didn't seem right to take it either.

Reluctantly, she laid it in the box.

"If it's not hers, Signor Pacelli will say so, I'm sure," Greta assured her.

Rosalie nodded. Unless, of course, it belonged to Signor Pacelli and he'd left it behind when he'd . . .

She pushed the thought away from her mind. It was too late now.

She should've taken it when she'd had the chance—before she'd drawn Miss Lidia's attention to it.

———◆◆◆———

Pfarrer Spalek was just emerging from the confessional when Haydn arrived. The door closed softly behind the priest, and he stood motionless before it—a stocky man of middle years with a shock of brown hair that fell over his forehead.

Haydn was about to hail him, but hesitated. Pfarrer Spalek's head was bowed, his hands clasped tightly over his stomach, and his features, what little Haydn could see of them, appeared unsettled.

Slowly Haydn walked down the nave, hoping his quiet footfall on the stone floor would attract the priest's attention. It did.

"Herr Haydn!" Pfarrer Spalek raised his head, his eyes widening in wonderment. He looked for all the world as though he'd seen a miracle. His hands still clasped before him, he turned, raising his head reverently toward the figure of the Savior on the crucifix above the altar.

"I was in two minds whether to send for you." The priest approached the Kapellmeister. "But your presence here has clarified the issue. Clearly, the Lord wishes to shed light on the situation and will not tolerate it being concealed any longer."

"What situation?" Haydn asked, struggling to understand. Had this something to do with Maria Anna?

Pfarrer Spalek bit his lip, looking uncertain again. He fingered his crucifix and looked once more to the figure of the Lord, as though seeking strength.

"I have heard"—he took a deep breath. "I have heard," he began again, "the most extraordinary confession."

Hope flared through Haydn's being. Had someone confessed to the murders? Or to blackmailing the Archduke? It was instantly deflated when he realized the confession meant nothing. Most likely, Pfarrer Spalek would have no idea who had made it. And even if he did know, he was forbidden to even hint at the truth.

"I thought," he began tentatively before pausing.

Pfarrer Spalek seemed to understand. "I wrestled with the issue myself —until I saw you, standing in the glow of the afternoon sun."

He gestured to a door on the right.

"Let us go into the sacristy. We can speak privately there."

Haydn nodded, following the priest through a small door on the left of the sanctuary. Pfarrer Spalek locked the door, gestured Haydn toward a chair, and took a seat himself.

"I cannot tell you who made the confession," he said.

"I understand. It goes against—"

"Not only that. I have in all truth no notion of who it was. But I could tell whom he was referring to. And since what he said did not involve himself, but could shed light on a murder . . ." He spread his hands wide. "I feel my duty is clear."

Haydn gazed at the priest in astonishment. "You are referring to Signora Pacelli's murder?"

"That is your prima donna, is it not?" Pfarrer Spalek waited for Haydn to incline his head before continuing. "I have heard of her untimely demise. Was she with child?"

Haydn frowned. How had the priest come to hear of that? And what did it have to do with her murder?

"She was. Was it her lover who killed her?"

"I believe it was her lover who came to confess. He was most distraught. He blamed himself for her death and the death of her child. But it was not by his hand that she died." Pfarrer Spalek swallowed. "I know not whether I should mention it, but your prima donna wished to marry the man. He has a wife, but being—"

"Away from her and close to a woman as seductive as Signora Pacelli proved too much of a temptation," Haydn finished for him grimly. So it was one of the musicians then who had fathered Lucia's child.

All the more reason for the men to be allowed to return to Eisenstadt. And once the festivities were over, he would ponder some means of persuading the Prince to that course of action.

"So he refused to marry her. But how does that make him responsible for her death? She did not take her own life."

Pfarrer Spalek shook his head. "No, but she feared her husband's wrath should he discover her secret. And, apparently, with good reason. She died the very night her lover refused her."

Haydn's hand shook. It was Paolo, then, who had taken Lucia's life? Had he also chosen to ruin the Archduke's good name and extort money from His Imperial Highness?

"Did the man offer anything other than his own conviction that it was her husband who killed her?" he asked.

"I fear not. But now that you know who it is, surely you can find a way to bring him to justice, can you not?"

Haydn drummed his fingers upon the armrest. Would a lover's confession hold up against the mountain of evidence pointing to Narcissa as the murderess? He would need something more concrete. But at least he knew where to look.

"So the child was conceived due to entirely natural means," he murmured to himself, recalling the story Lucia had fed Maria Anna.

"I beg your pardon?" Pfarrer Spalek's eyebrows were raised.

Haydn turned toward him. "Signora Pacelli insisted the child was conceived due to St. Gerard's intervention."

Pfarrer Spalek's lips twitched into a faint smile. "If that were so, she would've had no need to seek a man other than her husband to father it."

"She never lit a candle to the saint, I take it."

Pfarrer Spalek shook his head, amused. "No, she did not. The only person who seeks a miraculous conception, Herr Haydn, is—"

"I know. Maria Anna." He shook his head bitterly. "She has built her hopes up, and—"

"If God is willing, her prayer will be granted, Herr Haydn. But if He is not, then she must accept the Lord's will. As must you, of course."

"Of course," Haydn agreed. Had he not already accepted the good Lord's will on the subject? There was to be no child. There never would be—not for him and his wife. But that was beside the point. He had more pressing matters to attend to.

"There is one more thing," he said, beginning at last to relate the reason for his visit.

<hr>

The sound of the changing room door scraping against the floor had reached Rosalie's ears. But she hadn't thought much of it. It was the audible gasp that followed it that made her realize someone had entered the room.

Her head jolted up.

Master Gabriel, the dark-haired young cellist, stood at the door gaping at them.

"Wh—what are you doing?" He looked from Rosalie and Greta to Miss Lidia, who stood by the wardrobe with a dress in her arms. "Are you looking for something?"

"Of course not," Greta replied. "We're packing Signora Pacelli's things. What does it look like we're doing?" She put her hands on her hips. "Signor Pacelli asked us to, if you must know."

"Oh. Well, I suppose that's all right, then." Master Gabriel slid into the room. He hemmed uncertainly, his gaze drifting to the clock that stood by the wall.

Miss Lidia glanced at it as well. "Did Herr Haydn send for me? There's over an hour to go before the concert starts. He can't want me there already, can he?"

"Won't you have to change?" Rosalie pointed out. Miss Lidia was in her shabbiest gown. She could hardly go onstage wearing that.

Miss Lidia closed her eyes, harried. "Yes, of course. How stupid of me not to remember!" She opened her eyes, coming briskly forward. "Well, there's not much left to do. You girls can finish up here, can't you? I'll take these dresses and trinket boxes to Paolo. You can bring the rest by later."

The soprano picked up a stack of neatly folded dresses and piled a number of jewelry boxes on top. She hurried toward the door. Master Gabriel tried to step aside but succeeded only in bumping into her.

The dresses and trinket cases flew out of Miss Lidia's arms, falling to the floor in a tangled mess.

"Oh!" Miss Lidia cried in anguish. "How—?" she abruptly closed her mouth, pressing her lips tightly together.

"I—I didn't mean to . . ." Master Gabriel looked confused. He stared ruefully at the floor as though waiting for the mess to clean itself.

"An entire day's labor wasted," Miss Lidia grumbled, lowering herself to the floor.

She was about to say more when, blushing, Master Gabriel sank to his knees as well.

"Here, let me help."

He lifted up a couple of necklaces that had twisted together and painstakingly began to unravel them.

Rosalie and Greta glanced at each other. They'd never seen anyone quite so clumsy. Or so slow. If Master Gabriel stayed in the room any longer, they'd never get any work done.

In the time that it had taken Miss Lidia to arrange the dresses in a neat pile, all Master Gabriel had managed to do was untangle the first set of necklaces. He now reached for another.

"Oh, we have no time for that!" Miss Lidia cried. She snatched the necklaces out of his hands, swept the rest of the jewelry off the floor, and stuffed them untidily into the trinket boxes.

"Tell Herr Haydn I'll be there in just a minute," she commanded the hapless cellist as she strode out of the room, arms laden and muttering under her breath.

"I—er . . ." Master Gabriel looked at the maids, dismayed. "She seems upset. I didn't intend to—"

"It's not your fault," Rosalie assured him. "She's had a trying day."

"There's no need to stay and help," Greta added hastily, ushering the young man to the door. "Herr Haydn must be waiting for you. Rosalie and I can get this done."

"A-are you sure?" Master Gabriel stammered, glancing hesitantly around as Greta shoved him out the door.

"Very sure," Greta said. She snapped the door closed.

Chapter Thirty-One

HAYDN struck the middle C on his harpsichord and then, as his musicians tuned their instruments, craned his neck out toward the audience. Was the extortionist amongst them?

The stable yard had been transformed into a huge amphitheater—a replica of the Ballroom Grove at Versailles.

Beyond the circular platform where the Archduke and his bride would be performing their dance, were rows of tiered seats with boxwood hedges growing along the risers. The wooden treads—painted to look like gray stone—gleamed under the bright lights that flooded the arena.

"I had forgotten there were to be no chairs," he said to Johann, who stood beside him. There were none, unless one counted the semi-circular row of golden chairs right at the front where the Prince and his guests were to be seated.

"As had we all until Kertes reminded us of it," Johann replied.

The head gardener had apparently flown into a torrent of rage at the idea of newssheets being left upon each tread of the tiered seating. The wind would cause them to be blown onto his precious hedges, obscuring the effect entirely, he had complained.

"Have the broadsheet handed out to people as they come in," Kertes had suggested peremptorily.

"They will wonder why the Prince wishes them to take note of the paper," Luigi had protested in dismay.

Surely the extortionist would fear something was afoot if palace footmen began thrusting a broadsheet into the hand of every comer. It was one thing for Markos to leave his publication where people might find it. Quite another for the Prince to appear to be promoting his work.

"Then give them a basket of fruit as well," Kertes had said irritably.

Haydn smiled, recalling Luigi's account of the episode. But the head gardener's suggestion hadn't been entirely absurd. Footmen glided along the arena, offering copies of Markos's broadsheet along with a small basket of fruit to all the villagers and servants who had arrived to watch the show.

The small gift seemed to be welcome—and entirely in keeping with His Serene Highness's generosity.

"I do not see Paolo," Haydn muttered. Where was the fellow, he wondered? Fiore was fortunately there, sitting beside Hannah. They had their heads bent over their copies of the broadsheet. If Paolo was the extortionist, the message would reach his ears, at least.

"I expect he is preparing to leave," Johann said, unperturbed.

"Preparing to leave?"Haydn's head jerked toward his brother. "Who, Paolo? Are you certain?"

"So Miss Lidia informed us. Why does it matter, brother?" Johann stared at him puzzled. "Surely it is for the best. It saves you the trouble of dismissing the man as you most certainly would've been compelled to. His Serene Highness is unlikely to wish him to remain."

"I fear Paolo may have been responsible for Lucia's murder," Haydn confessed, recounting what he'd learned from Pfarrer Spalek that afternoon. "That he plans to leave—so abruptly . . . "

"Yes, I see what you mean. But—?" Johann broke off abruptly when Haydn withdrew his timepiece from his pocket and glanced at it. "Question him tomorrow, brother, if you must. You can hardly do it this evening."

"No, I suppose not," Haydn reluctantly conceded. The performance would begin in a quarter of an hour. He could scarcely depart now. Luigi would return any moment with the Archduke and Maria Beatrice.

"There'll be time enough tomorrow. Paolo has no reason to believe you suspect him," Johann reminded him gently. "I doubt he'll be leaving at the crack of dawn."

That was true enough, Haydn thought.

⁓•••⁓

The brothers gazed out in silence at the vast amphitheater that stretched before them.

Then Johann spoke. "Nevertheless, would it be worth alerting Herr Hipfl and the Bürgermeister to the situation?"

"On what grounds?" Haydn asked bitterly. "They're both satisfied the killer has been put away. It would take more than an anonymous lover's conviction to persuade them to the contrary. If only the man had thought to come forward ere this."

"Could he have been lying? The lover, I mean."

"In the confessional? I doubt it. According to Pfarrer Spalek, the man was most distressed about her murder. Besides, it's a plausible theory. Paolo murders his wife and then lays the blame at the door of the man he suspects to be her lover—the Archduke. I've wondered as well if he's the extortionist we're looking for."

"I suppose it's possible," Johann agreed. "Whoever it is, he has not made any demand for money. He seems to be intent only upon creating trouble."

"And in that, he has succeeded exceedingly well," Haydn said grimly. "He has caused quite a stir." Had Trattner been the source of Paolo's information as well? Or had Lucia confided in her husband?

He was about to share his musings with Johann when another thought occurred to him.

But an unpleasant interruption occurred before he could work out its significance.

Trattner strode up to the enclosure where they sat, broadsheet in hand.

"What is the meaning of this notice?" The publisher jabbed his forefinger into the newspaper. "What rumors does His Imperial Highness wish to put to rest?"

"I am astonished you need to ask?" Haydn responded with some acerbity. The man had some nerve, considering he was most likely the source of the scandalous tale himself.

Trattner drew back, his beady eyes roving suspiciously over the Kapellmeister's features.

"My papers spread no lies, Herr Haydn. I trust you are not insinuating that they do."

"You printed just this morning the falsehood that Signora Pacelli had crashed to the stage floor in a drunken stupor," Haydn countered.

Trattner bared his teeth in a wolfish smile. "Had you but informed me of the truth, Herr Haydn, there would've been no need for me to rely upon the sole information available to me."

Haydn gripped the golden rope that encircled the enclosure. How had Trattner the temerity to defend his lies?

"There was no information in your report, Herr Trattner," Johann interceded before Haydn's fury burst out of him in an unseemly remark. "You published an assumption."

"A natural conclusion based upon what my eyes saw," Trattner responded evenly. He waved the paper in the air, brushing the dispute aside. "That is not what I wished to speak about, however."

"You wish, no doubt, for us to provide you with more fodder for your gossip-mongering." Haydn gave the man an icy smile.

Trattner ignored his remark. He jabbed at the broadsheet again. "This notice should've been printed in my paper. I doubt anyone reads this Hungarian rag." He surveyed the amphitheater. A steady stream of people trickled in, met by footmen who handed out baskets and newspapers.

"If they did, the Prince would not have to hand it out." He turned his attention back to Haydn. "It is a desperate move, if you want my opinion. Whoever it is you wish to entrap will see through it, I am sure."

Thrusting the broadsheet under his arm as though it were a sword he was sheathing, Trattner walked away.

Haydn stared after him. Was Trattner their man? Or wasn't he? The encounter had left him with more questions than answers. Worse still, in his anger he had given the game away.

"I should not have accused him of scandal-mongering," he reflected ruefully.

⁕

Haydn was just wondering where Luigi was when he felt a sharp tap on his shoulder blade.

"Joseph?"

Recognizing his Konzertmeister's voice, Haydn turned around immediately.

"Ah, Luigi—" He broke off, seeing the expression on Luigi's face. He had rarely seen his friend in such a pother. Luigi's lips were tightly pressed together as though he feared a dam might burst out of them. His nostrils were flared.

"What is the matter?" Haydn demanded, instantly concerned.

Luigi took a deep breath. "It is the Archduke. I would box the ears of anyone who tried my patience as much as he has this evening. I managed to restrain my temper, but I assure you, it was with the greatest difficulty."

Haydn lowered his eyes to where Luigi's hands dug into his sides, his knuckles angry, white bumps on his clenched fists.

"I am at the end of my tether, Joseph. You must speak with him. His Imperial Highness refuses to see reason. A more stubborn, ill-mannered lad I have yet to see. If I have to deal with him any longer I fear I shall forget myself. I have—"

"But what has he done, Luigi?" Johann pressed gently.

Luigi swallowed several times—an effort to stem his exasperation—before responding.

"It is the sash he is supposed to wear for the performance," he said at last. "His Imperial Highness claims he has misplaced the golden one that is part of the uniform. Rather than replace it with an orange or red one or even allow me to send for Hannah to find another golden sash, he insists upon wearing black."

"Black?" Haydn repeated. What had come into His Imperial Highness? "That will not do at all."

"So I said."

"It is a most inauspicious color," Johann agreed. "Does he mean to personify the devil rather than a good Christian knight?"

"I tried in vain to point that out to His Imperial Highness. He would not listen. He will either ride out wearing black or not perform at all."

Haydn was aware of the crowd murmuring behind him. They had no more than ten minutes at the most before the performance began. What was to be done?

"I had better speak with him," Haydn said.

"He's behind the stables." Luigi pointed behind the building. "But I warn you, Joseph, he is quite adamant. He wittered on about his reputation and even went so far as to say you would agree with him on the issue."

"He must be addled if he thinks that," Haydn said, suppressing a sigh.

Was it not enough that he had to contend with extortionists and murderers? Was he expected to coax his imperial performers into submission as well?

Chapter Thirty-Two

THE candles in the sconces on the back wall of the stables threw a dim pool of light on the grassy area behind it and the dusty road beyond.

The Archduke—gloriously attired in the costume of a knight of the Order of the Golden Fleece—was frenetically pacing the area when Haydn arrived. His slim form covered in a red cloak was all that was visible at first. It was only when His Imperial Highness turned that Haydn saw the black sash— a dark, unsightly stain upon the young man's otherwise rich attire.

"Herr Haydn!" Relief was audible in the Archduke's voice as he hurried toward the Kapellmeister. "I am glad you are here. Your Konzertmeister, I fear, is a blockhead. A stubborn fool."

Haydn ignored the insults to Luigi.

"Luigi meant well. The black, unfortunately, does not become Your Imperial Highness," he said as calmly as he could manage. "My Konzertmeister was right about that. But I am sure a more suitable color can be found."

The Archduke shook his head, his expression desperate. "I do not have a choice in the matter, Haydn. It is a question of my reputation. When it seemed the wedding was not to be, I saw no reason to care. But now that Maria Beatrice has seen fit to accept me again, I must do what I can to ensure the nuptials go through."

His features hardened. "I have no desire to take up Holy Orders, Haydn. I will do anything I can to avoid that fate."

Haydn nodded cautiously. "A wise decision, indeed. But how does the black sash enter into it?"

Archduke Ferdinand Karl bit his lip. His youth had never been more evident than in this moment of disquiet.

He reached into his cloak and withdrew two folded sheets of paper. He handed one to Haydn who unfolded it.

"I found that among my correspondence this afternoon," His Imperial Highness said.

"*Don't think to rid yourself of your troubles so easily. You must pay for your sins*," Haydn read the note out loud. Frowning, he raised his eyes. "This is of a piece with the first note discovered in your study. Who could've written it?"

"Clearly not your prima donna," the Archduke replied unhappily. "Unless she has returned from the dead to plague me."

His Imperial Highness mustered a grim smile as he spoke. Haydn returned it.

"I very much doubt ghosts can pen notes." He looked down at the note. "No, someone else is responsible for this."

Paolo, perhaps, but he kept the thought to himself. Although, now that he considered the matter, if Lucia had been so eager to leave her husband, would she have confided what she knew to him? Wasn't it more likely, she had entrusted the matter to her lover?

But what could her lover hope to gain by threatening the Archduke? No, most likely, it was Paolo, convinced the young Archduke had made a cuckold of him and enraged as a result of it.

The Archduke's black sash fluttered in the wind. Reminded of the issue at hand, Haydn raised his eyes.

"There is nothing here about a black sash, Your Imperial Highness."

"No, there's not." The Archduke smiled wanly. "But not content with sending one warning, the extortionist sent another with more specific instructions." He handed the second folded sheet of paper over.

"I am to wear the black sash as a sign that I am willing to deal with the villain," he explained as Haydn carefully unfolded the note. "Otherwise . . ." His Imperial Highness exhaled heavily.

Place an offering by the baptismal font tonight—no less than 2,000 gulden—and all rumors will be laid to rest. Wear a black sash in place of the golden one if this proposal is acceptable.

Two thousand gulden! Haydn nearly staggered back in disbelief. What kind of person could think to make such an outrageous demand?

"The instructions could not be more precise," he conceded, striving to keep the stupefaction out of his voice. Nor more business-like, he thought. The extortionist appeared to have no qualms at all.

The man either had no conscience or had rightly sensed the Archduke's extreme desperation.

The Kapellmeister perused the message again. If he didn't know any better, he would think they were dealing with two individuals. One content with making idle threats; the other more eager to profit from the situation.

Most likely, of course, it was the same individual who had sent both notes.

Was it Trattner who had made the demand? How fortuitous, then, that Haydn had thought to place a similar offer in Markos's broadsheet—anticipating, as it were, the demand for money.

But having seen the notice—and divined its purpose—would Trattner still succumb to his greed? Haydn could only hope so. If, on the other hand, it was Paolo—seeking compensation for his wife's infidelity . . . Well, it was even less likely then that the fellow would leave Eszterháza before dawn.

"Wear the black sash, Your Imperial Highness," Haydn said decisively. "It is our only hope of nipping this affair in the bud." He gestured toward the arena. The performance was about to begin and they were expected out there.

But as he followed the Archduke, Haydn wondered how Paolo—if he was the extortionist—would come to find out His Imperial Highness had agreed to his proposal. The man had not even deigned to show his face at the performance.

Could he be working with someone else? Miss Lidia, perhaps. Only a fool would entrust Fiore with such a delicate matter.

Then again, was Paolo likely to take anyone into his confidence? It hardly seemed plausible.

And as for Miss Lidia, Haydn had no reason to believe she was anything but honorable. It was unlikely the Englishwoman would involve herself in such a disreputable venture.

No, no, the extortionist had to be Trattner. Who else could it be?

⁕⁕⁕

"Why is His Imperial Highness wearing a black sash?" Greta leaned over to whisper into Rosalie's ear.

"I don't know," Rosalie whispered back, peering at the stage.

The performance had just begun. The orchestra had struck the first notes of the ballet. Soon after, the Archduke and Her Ladyship had come riding out on their mounts. The dance itself was beautiful, the two riders circling each other gracefully. Rosalie marveled at the way the horses moved—keeping perfect time to the beat.

But His Imperial Highness's costume was marred by the black sash he had chosen to wear. Even his bride—glancing quizzically at his chest from time to time—seemed puzzled by his decision.

Rosalie shifted on the wooden seat. It had no backrest and was uncomfortable. The bushes along the risers scratched at her ankles and the ones behind her caught against her hair. The tiered seating looked magnificent but she would have preferred ordinary chairs.

As she shifted again, the paper sitting between her and Greta rustled. Rosalie glanced down at it. It was the broadsheet a footman had given them when they entered the stable yard. It was the same broadsheet that had insinuated that the Archduke had fathered a child upon Signora Pacelli.

Why His Serene Highness had consented to having the thing handed out to all comers at the performance, Rosalie didn't know. She and Greta had both caught sight of the notice in it. It was hard to miss, prominently positioned as it was at the top center of the newspaper.

"Wouldn't it have been best not to mention the rumors at all?" Greta had asked, puzzled.

Rosalie had agreed. "I know, it makes no sense to call attention to them." Why hadn't Herr Haydn insisted His Imperial Highness ignore the matter altogether? It only fed the gossip to acknowledge it.

Hannah, who was sitting in front of them, had turned around. "Besides, how should anyone here know whether they're rumors at all? For all we know, they're true."

But Fiore, who sat beside her, shook his head vehemently. "They must not be true. Why else would His Imperial Highness offer a reward to squelch them? I only wish I knew something of the matter. I could do with a little more money." He'd grinned at Rosalie. "All of mine has gone to your husband."

"To pay the debts you owed, no doubt" Rosalie had reminded him tartly. She wouldn't have believed him if Gerhard hadn't mentioned it. They'd passed by the refreshment tent Gerhard had set up a few yards from the stables.

She'd told her husband about Paolo's intention to leave. "Fiore will go as well, most likely," she'd said. "You'd best get your money while you can."

"I already have, lass." Gerhard had grinned down at her as he arranged bottles of wine and plates of food on the white-cloth-covered tables. "Whether it was Signor Pacelli who gave him the money, I know not. But the boy's paid up in full."

"Mind you don't sell him anything else," Rosalie had cautioned him before she and Greta had continued on their way.

Now as she stared at the Archduke's sash, she recalled the extortion note His Imperial Highness had received. Had he received another one—with a demand for money perhaps?

The rumors about His Imperial Highness and Signora Lucia might be false, but was there something else in his past that the extortionist was aware of? Why else would the person be so relentless in their demand for money? What if His Imperial Highness had fathered a child—out of wedlock—in Vienna?

She glanced at the tier beneath her. If only Fiore weren't here, she'd ask Hannah about it.

"Mark my words, there's no smoke without fire," the seamstress had sagely remarked when Fiore had foolishly insisted every rumor about the Archduke was bound to be false.

"They'd better not lay that at my door," Hannah now muttered. "I left the golden sash with His Imperial Highness. And I took care to keep a second in my store in case he misplaced the first."

"I'm surprised Herr Haydn allowed His Imperial Highness to ride out wearing that," Greta said in a low voice. "It doesn't go with the reds and oranges of the rest of his outfit."

"And they'd better not say they couldn't find me," Hannah grumbled on defiantly. "I've been here the whole while."

"Why should anyone blame you?" Fiore asked. "If His Imperial Highness is wearing a black sash, it's because he wants to. No doubt he wants to convey an appropriate air of strength and authority to his bride. Did you know she's four years older? He could end up a henpecked fool if he's not careful." Fiore leaned back and folded his arms. "If you ask me it's never too soon to put a woman in her place."

"Never too soon, is it?" Greta cuffed him on the head. "What would you know of such things?"

But Fiore remained unmoved. "I know it's best to send out the right message before you're wed than to wait until after the vows have been said—when it's too late to do much about it."

Send out a message? Was that what the Archduke was doing, Rosalie wondered.

She glanced down at the broadsheet again. Was the notice a message as well? After all, who but the blackmailer would have the power to stifle any unseemly stories?

It must be that weasel of a person Trattner who was the extortionist, then.

Or at least, Herr Haydn suspected that was the case. Why put the notice in a Hungarian broadsheet instead of the more prestigious Viennese publication?

The tales had been printed in the broadsheet as well—no doubt placed there by Herr Trattner. He was much too clever to use his own publication to circulate such tittle-tattle. He'd lose his license if he were discovered.

She tugged on Greta's arm. When her friend leaned closer, she whispered: "Remember how we saw Herr Trattner having words with Herr Haydn before the performance?"

When her friend nodded, she continued, "I think he might be the extortionist."

Chapter Thirty-Three

H AYDN played the last phrase of the ballet, lifting his hands with a flourish off the keyboard. The performance had gone remarkably well. The Archduke and Her Ladyship were at the front of the stage now, hands joined together and upraised, still mounted on their horses.

As the applause died down, His Imperial Highness cleared his throat. "I wish to say a few words," he announced.

Sitting beside Haydn, Johann shifted uneasily. "Is that wise?" he murmured nervously.

"He will say no more than he needs to," Haydn responded with more assurance than he felt.

He had schooled His Imperial Highness on what to say. He could only hope the words would elicit their desired response.

"I am deeply honored," the Archduke began, "that Her Ladyship Maria Beatrice D'Este has agreed to be my wife."

"It prevents Her Ladyship from breaking off the alliance," Haydn explained hastily, feeling Johann stirring once more beside him. "Besides, I wish to see if the fact of the marriage going ahead as proposed causes consternation in any quarter."

No doubt, whoever was trying to thwart the nuptials would show their dismay at being upended.

He scanned the faces of the audience—noisily cheering its approval at the Archduke's tidings—looking for any signs of displeasure at the news. But everyone he looked at was smiling broadly.

Only Trattner sat unmoved, his hands tightly folded across his chest.

His Imperial Highness was now speaking of his desire to be worthy of his wife. He would spend the night in prayer and in confession at the Heiligen Kreuzes, he said.

"There I will make penance my sins to the Lord"—Haydn waited with bated breath for the next words—"and place an offering, as he has requested."

Johann was about to turn toward him, his mouth opening to ask a question. But Haydn held up his hand, staying his brother's curiosity.

"I will explain later," he whispered as he searched the crowd again for any sign of comprehension.

Her Ladyship's eyes had widened at the mention of an offering requested by the Almighty. Everyone else seemed equally stunned.

Haydn's eyes traveled to where Trattner sat. The newspaperman's eyebrows rose slightly, but he soon recovered his composure, and stared straight ahead, stone-faced.

Haydn released his breath. It was just as he'd expected. The minor change in the placement of the offering—the confessional rather than the baptismal font—had caused some surprise. But that was only to be expected.

"One can only hope the bait has been swallowed," he said.

Surely, the prospect of receiving no less than two thousand gulden would overcome any objections the extortionist might have.

<hr>

In the tiered seats at the back of the stable yard, Greta's voice rang out in surprise.

"An offering? In the confessional?"

"It's an odd place for an offering, to be sure," Rosalie replied.

Why had His Imperial Highness made such a public announcement of his intentions, in any case? Why state exactly where the offering would be kept? Surely that was a matter between himself and Pfarrer Spalek.

On the seat below hers, Fiore leaned back.

"In the confessional, eh? Why there, I wonder?"

"He must have misspoken," Hannah said, her gaze riveted on the stage.

"Could he have meant the altar?" Greta turned toward Rosalie.

"I suppose it's possible." An altar would be the best place for a silver figure or a robe fashioned out of cloth of gold. "Unless—" Rosalie paused. Her eyes fell on the broadsheet between them.

Greta's gaze followed hers.

"Oh!" she said. "You think it's that kind of offering?"

"What else could it be?" Rosalie pursed her lips. "Most likely Herr Trattner has some means of stopping the rumors and expects to be rewarded for his cooperation."

She was about to continue when she became aware of Hannah's eyes on her. The seamstress gave them a disapproving glare that sent a chill down Rosalie's back.

Squeezing Greta's hand, Rosalie clamped her lips shut. It was best not to speculate about things they didn't know in public. But why—she couldn't help wondering—did Hannah look so outraged?

Wasn't it plain to see the Viennese publisher was a weasel and would stop at nothing to line his pockets with gold?

Chapter Thirty-Four

Rosalie stirred restlessly in her bed. Was there to be no hope of sleep tonight?

Her eyes, alert and watchful, followed the shaft of moonlight that came in through the window, slashing across the thin coverlet that covered her form and Gerhard's. She stirred again and sighed, her mind roaming over the events of the day.

Was it just yesterday that Ulrike had called out to her and tipped her basket over? That's when she'd found the extortion note and all the trouble had started. If only she'd kept her nose out of it. Ulrike might still be alive.

Gerhard's arm lay across her form, feeling heavy. She moved gently, sliding out from under its weight.

Who had killed Ulrike?

The same person who'd murdered Signora Pacelli, that much was clear. But who had poisoned the soprano?

Most likely, the same person who'd left behind the braided chain with a crucifix she'd found in the prima donna's changing room.

"It must belong to Signor Pacelli," she thought. "But I've never seen him wearing it."

In her mind's eye, Rosalie could see the chain and the crucifix hanging from someone's neck. A man's neck. But for the life of her, she couldn't recall who it was. It was as though a thick gray fog shrouded the mysterious individual's features.

If only they knew why the prima donna had been murdered. That might furnish them with a clue.

"It can't have been for what she knew," Rosalie murmured to herself.

Whatever the prima donna knew had to do with Vienna. Only the Archduke would care about that, and he hadn't done away with Signora Pacelli.

So who had?

It wasn't hard to believe Fräulein Leon was the culprit. But the murderer had deliberately sought to involve the Archduke. Fräulein Leon would have no reason to do so.

That only left Signor Pacelli. But would he have killed Ulrike? He'd barely exchanged two words with the girl. His anger at being cuckolded might cause the irascible old man to lash out at his wife. But would he kill a young girl in cold blood?

Had he even been anywhere near the opera house that afternoon? Ulrike's body had hardly been cold when they'd found her.

If only the girl had thought to come to her or Greta. What had she been thinking, confronting a killer all by herself? Hadn't she known she was putting herself in harm's way?

Rosalie's mind returned to the chain. It was the only clue they had. After all, anyone could've taken the bottle of pennyroyal oil from the supply closet.

She wished she'd had more time to examine the braided chain. But Master Gabriel had come barging into the room.

"It's a good thing that he did," Karl had said when she and Greta had told him about it. "It had slipped my mind altogether. And Herr Haydn arrived too late himself to send after anyone."

Rosalie yawned, wondering what had made Master Gabriel come for Miss Lidia. How had he even known where to find her?

Her eyelids drooped. She was just drifting off to sleep when a memory startled her into wakefulness.

She knew where she'd seen the crucifix and the chain. And it didn't belong to Signor Pacelli. No, it did not.

She must remember that.

Sleepy now, she closed her eyes. She must remember to tell Herr Haydn. Anyone could've taken the poison.

"But not everyone had . . ." a voice in her head began to object. But Rosalie was too tired to listen.

The distant crowing of a rooster brought Haydn out of the fitful sleep he'd fallen into. He opened his eyes, instantly awake, and arose.

Dawn had yet to arrive. A gray darkness filled the room.

His eyes adjusted to the gloom, and he made out the chair by the bed. His livery, neatly folded, hung upon the backrest. He reached for his clothing, quietly and swiftly dressing himself as he stared unseeingly out the window into the last vestiges of night.

The Archduke must by now have returned to the palace. Any moment now the summons would come from Johann.

Picking up the candle by his bedside, he left his bedchamber, careful not to make a sound. Maria Anna was fast asleep, but she was a light sleeper. The slightest noise could awaken her.

In the kitchen, he stoked the fire and lit his candle before making his way into the parlor. His hands tightly clasped together, he sat in his armchair and prepared to wait.

Would to God, the affair was proceeding as expected.

Drumming his fingers on the upholstered wooden armrest, he tried to still the apprehension that gripped his being. Dear God, what if the extortionist had seen through their plan? What were they to do then?

A quiet knock sounded on the door.

Haydn frowned, glancing at the clock. He had not expected the blackmailer to venture into the church until shortly before dawn. Was something amiss?

The knock sounded again—louder, this time. Haydn hurried to the door, willing himself to stay calm.

"Pfarrer Spalek?" A mixture of relief and puzzlement coursed through his veins.

"We did not mean to disturb your rest, Herr Haydn." The priest shrugged apologetically. "But His Imperial Highness insisted—"

"I wish to confront the individual, Haydn, whoever it is," the Archduke explained, stepping out from behind Pfarrer Spalek.

Haydn nodded, gesturing for them to follow him into the parlor.

"I understand your desire," he said, sitting down. "But is it wise to involve yourself in this affair?" He didn't have to spell out the consequences.

It had been decided that Prince Nikolaus should be sent for once the blackmailer had been apprehended.

"If anyone should see Your Serene Highness," Haydn had explained, "they will merely suppose you to be acting in your capacity as High Sheriff of Sopron County, dealing with a routine felony in the vicinity."

The Grand Duke of Tuscany had voiced his objections, but Prince Nikolaus had agreed with his Kapellmeister.

"It would be best not to draw attention to this sordid affair, Leopold. Your presence, I fear, will broadcast to all and sundry that it concerns the imperial household. And, by definition, the Archduke's marriage."

His Grace had reluctantly assented.

But Archduke Ferdinand Karl now jutted out his chin stubbornly.

"I wish to know what the man's demands are," he asserted firmly. "And why he feels he has been injured." His Imperial Highness bowed his head, sighing.

"I am not proud of my actions, Haydn. I wish to do what little I can to set things right."

Haydn pursed his lips. He could hardly argue against that sentiment. On the other hand—

Pfarrer Spalek coughed. "The sum demanded is so outrageous, Your Imperial Highness, I doubt it is any perceived sense of injury that motivates the criminal."

"It is not," Haydn agreed, feeling himself on firmer ground at the reminder. "We are dealing with avarice rather than need or desperation."

Once again he wondered if they were dealing with two different individuals. One who felt himself to be injured—as the Archduke surmised; the other motivated by plain greed.

And what—if anything—did all this have to do with Lucia's murder? It would simplify things greatly if it turned out the extortionist was also the murderer.

But money didn't appear to be the motive behind his prima donna's death. No, most likely, it was a colleague's envy or a husband's jealousy that had taken her life.

Haydn would've considered an adulterous lover's fear of discovery as well were it not for what he'd learned from Pfarrer Spalek the previous day. A man as distraught over her death as Lucia's lover had been could surely not have caused her death.

He wondered idly who the man might be when an urgent rap sounded upon the door.

Haydn raised his head expectantly.

"That will be Johann," he announced to his visitors, propelling himself out of his armchair and striding toward the door.

———•••———

But it was the barber-surgeon who stood at the door, his features white and anxious.

"I fear we may have erred in apprehending Fräulein Leon." Herr Hipfl crossed the threshold.

"Erred?" Haydn repeated, reluctantly stepping back to allow him into the hallway. "How so?"

What had brought the barber-surgeon to his door—and at this hour in the morning? The blackness of night had lightened to a cold gray, but the sun was not yet up. Johann would soon arrive as well.

Where was his younger brother, Haydn wondered. Surely it was time for him to return with news of some kind.

The barber-surgeon followed Haydn in, his eyes traveling toward the open parlor door. His Imperial Highness's heel and a corner of Pfarrer Spalek's cassock were visible.

"You have visitors, I see." He turned toward Haydn, his expression a mixture of curiosity and consternation.

"It is merely Pfarrer Spalek and His Imperial Highness, on their way back from the church."

The barber-surgeon nodded. But he made no move to join the other two men in the parlor. "Then it would be best we spoke in the kitchen."

Haydn led the way into the kitchen and glanced pointedly at the clock upon the mantel.

"What leads you to believe now that Fräulein Leon is innocent?" He struggled—in vain—to keep the annoyance out of his voice.

Neither Herr Hipfl nor the Bürgermeister had seen fit to question their conclusions yesterday. Yet, here Herr Hipfl was at a most ungodly—not to mention, inconvenient—hour, wishing to reconsider the decision. Could it not have waited until morning?

The barber-surgeon nervously clasped and then unclasped his hands.

"There has been another murder."

Haydn gaped at him, stunned. "Another murder?"

"Another attempt," Herr Hipfl clarified unhappily. "In the same manner. He will survive, but—"

Chapter Thirty-Five

"W̲ʜᴏ is it?" The Kapellmeister demanded roughly.

Fear gripped his heart. God forbid, anything should have happened to Johann. Why in the name of heaven had he allowed Johann to keep vigil at the church, exposing himself to danger?

"Signor Pacelli."

"Paolo?" In his anxiety, Haydn had seized the barber-surgeon's shoulders. Now he released them—relieved beyond measure but bewildered as well.

He had considered Paolo to be guilty of either murdering his wife or attempting to extort money from the Archduke—or both. That someone might wish to do away with the old man had never entered his mind.

Paolo was clearly not the blackmailer either. Who was it, then?

"Fräulein Leon has been behind bars this entire time," the barber-surgeon pointed out. "Clearly, she is not to blame."

"No, I dare say not. But"—Haydn frowned—"how came you to hear the news? At this hour?"

"Miss Lidia sent for me. Just in time, I might add. Any later, and the poor man would've met his Maker."

Haydn struggled to understand the situation. "And it was in the same manner, you say?"

"Pennyroyal. I am certain of it. Signor Pacelli had been complaining of a discomfort in his stomach when Miss Lidia returned to her rooms this evening."

He had apparently seemed well enough for Lidia to retire to her bedchamber. But later at night, she had heard loud groans coming from the aged violinist's room and hastening there found him doubled up with a severe stomach cramp.

"And you arrived in time to administer an antidote?" Haydn had not realized the poison had one.

"There is no antidote. Signor Pacelli had fortunately not ingested very much of the wine. I gave him an emetic to purge his system of the toxin."

"The poison was in the wine?" That was surely no coincidence.

The barber-surgeon nodded grimly.

"The same variety as that which killed his wife and the young maid. It was from Gerhard's tavern, flavored with mint just like the others."

"Suggesting the same hand might have killed all three." Comprehension dawned upon Haydn at last.

"I can see no other explanation, Herr Haydn."

"But why kill Paolo?" Haydn found himself at a loss to understand the motive behind the attempt. "What could he have known?"

"He may have discovered the identity of his wife's killer." Herr Hipfl withdrew an item from his pocket and held it out to Haydn. "I found this clutched in his palm."

It was a thick braided chain with a crucifix at the end of it. Haydn reached out for it. He had seen it before. But where?

He turned it over in his palms, scrutinizing it. "Have you any idea to whom this belongs?"

"I thought it might be Miss Lidia's at first. It has not escaped my notice that she bears a most tender affection for him—a sentiment Signor Pacelli doesn't seem to return. She may have expected an offer of marriage when he found himself widowed—and not receiving it . . ." The barber-surgeon shrugged.

Haydn smiled, amused. "Would she not have had to kill Signora Pacelli first to ensure that happy event?"

"I thought she may well have," Herr Hipfl replied in all seriousness. "What better reason to kill them both? But since she showed no sign of agitation or guilt when I showed her the crucifix, I was forced to conclude that she is entirely innocent in the matter."

Haydn lowered his eyes to the crucifix. As he gently passed his thumb over it, feeling the cold metal, his skin snagged against something sharp. It looked to be a clasp of some kind.

He pushed against it. Immediately, the crucifix sprung open, revealing a tiny image of a woman.

Dear Lord! Haydn closed the locket, clasping it tightly within his palm. So that was who Lucia's lover was. How had he not guessed at the man's identity?

"Do you know who it belongs to?" Herr Hipfl gazed at him curiously.

"No," Haydn lied, raising his eyes with difficulty. "But I intend to find out."

He placed the chain in his coat pocket, his mind racing over the events of the past few days. Certain odd incidents and stray behaviors were now beginning to make sense.

Had Lucia's lover taken matters into his own hands—avenging his mistress's murder? Or had Paolo discovered the identity of his wife's lover, confronted him and threatened him with exposure, only to have the man turn against him?

Or had her lover killed Lucia, cleverly tried to blame her husband, and then turned upon him as well?

If that was the case, the man had duped them all.

"I shall need to make some inquiries," he told the barber-surgeon. "After that, if Paolo is in any condition to speak, I'd like a word with him as well." With any luck, Paolo had set eyes upon his opponent.

The barber-surgeon nodded. "I've had him transferred to a room at the tavern that I may better attend to him. Frail and infirm though he is, he is recovering nicely. I will send for you when he seems strong enough."

He prepared to leave but turned just as he got to the door.

"I am still inclined to believe someone wanted both the Pacellis gone. And the poor young maid had an inkling who it was and had her life snuffed out as a result."

⁂

Standing behind the stone pillar, Johann shivered. The day had been warm enough, but in the absence of the sun, the temperature had rapidly plummeted. It was as cold now as a winter's day.

It had been some time since the Archduke had left, accompanied by Pfarrer Spalek. Only Johann, along with the two palace guards the Prince had sent with him, remained.

From where he stood in the narthex, he could see the open outer doors of the church. One panel of the double inner doors was open. He fixed his eyes on the slender shaft of light that spilled out from within, emanating from the brightly burning sacristy lamp.

It illuminated a narrow path on the stone floor and fueled his fast-flagging expectations. For brother's sake, he held fast to the hope that the affair would be brought to a close tonight. But it seemed unlikely.

Even the guards were growing impatient.

"How much longer must we stand guard here, Master Johann?" Igor, the bald, burly palace guard beside him, grunted in a low voice. "It is nearly dawn."

"And it grows uncommonly cold," Konrad, the second guard, grumbled from his position on the other side of the inner doors.

"Until dawn," Johann reminded them quietly. "His Serene Highness wishes us to stay until dawn."

He held back a sigh, not entirely unsympathetic to the guards' complaints.

It was doubtful the extortionist would reveal himself tonight. The notice in the broadsheet must have served to put him on his guard. Or perhaps Markos—working in conjunction with the man to profit from the Archduke's sin—had cautioned him away?

The notion troubled Johann, but he put it out of his mind. It was too late to remedy the matter now.

Besides, he had vowed to lie in wait the entire night. It made no sense to leave before the sun had even risen. Who knew, the promise of two thousand gulden—a vast sum that even a king would not sniff at—might serve to draw out the man.

"The man may yet make an appearance," he said in a low voice to the palace guards, "and we would look like fools were we to leave at this juncture."

He trained his eyes on the darkness outside. Igor was beginning to clear his throat when Johann's ears, straining to hear the slightest noise, detected a sound. Holding up a hand to silence the guard, he listened intently again.

Muffled footsteps? Was someone approaching?

The sound came nearer. The shaft of light upon the cold stone floor darkened noticeably near the threshold and around the walls of the outer doors.

Johann pressed himself back against the pillar, determined to remain unseen.

A figure appeared at the door. Johann frowned. It was not Trattner, as they had expected.

In fact—his frown deepened—it was not even a man.

Had one of the villagers come by to light a candle or offer prayers to one of the saints? But surely no one would venture out at this ungodly hour.

He hesitated as the woman stepped in, gliding swiftly past the baptismal font. Should he attempt to stop her? Or better still, send her on her way?

He was still considering the issue when the woman entered the nave. Stepping out from behind the pillar, he hurried noiselessly after her toward the door.

The woman—a plump matronly figure—was striding down the nave.

Johann was about to follow her when she stormed her way to the confessional and flung open the door. His eyes widened in horror.

Dear God, it was the blackmailer, after all! Only the extortionist would've realized what the offering was—a guarded reference to money, not a figure made out of silver as was customary among the ruling classes.

"Quick!" He beckoned toward the two guards. "Lock the doors. I will get brother and send word to His Serene Highness."

"Be sure not to let her out," he warned as he set off.

Chapter Thirty-Six

"I cannot for the life of me imagine who she could be?" he said to Haydn as they approached the church.

Johann had found brother waiting for him at their quarters in the Music House. To his surprise, Pfarrer Spalek and the Archduke were there as well and had insisted upon accompanying them back to the church.

"Did it look like Lidia?" Haydn asked, recalling the disturbing news the barber-surgeon had brought him.

Johann shook his head. "Lidia is taller by far, and lanky as well. This woman, whoever she might be"—he cast a surreptitious glance over his shoulder at the Archduke—"seems far too old to have been dallying with a man as young as His Imperial Highness."

Haydn glanced over his shoulder as well. "He claims not to have indulged in any dalliances here."

"Do you suppose I would make the same mistake twice?" His Imperial Highness had demanded irritably when Haydn had confronted him before they set out.

"No," Haydn shook his head, turning back toward Johann. "Most likely, Trattner sent a woman in his stead to collect the money." But the explanation made little sense.

Would any extortionist be willing to draw in an accomplice at the last minute—one with whom any gains might have to be shared?

They were barely a few yards away when the hammering on the church doors assailed them. The ruckus was fit to wake the dead, Haydn thought.

"She's a veritable spitfire," Igor, one of the two waiting palace guards, grimly informed them as they drew near. "She's been beating her fists on the door for a good ten minutes, screeching all the while to be let out."

"Unlock the doors, then," Pfarrer Spalek said, alarmed. "She'll batter them down if we wait any longer."

At a sign from Haydn, Konrad, the second palace guard, inserted the huge key into the lock and pulled the doors open.

The woman must have had her person pressed against the door for she immediately tumbled forward—a force of tumultuous energy.

Quickly Haydn reached out, catching hold of her before she could fall. Braced by his hands, but struggling to wrench herself free, she jerked her head up.

"Hannah?" He gaped at the seamstress's disheveled features.

<hr>

The seamstress ignored the Kapellmeister. Her eyes, blazing furiously, darted toward the Archduke. She drew her head back and spat at him.

"For shame!" she cried. "Would you cover up your sins, pretend they are just so many rumors, while a young girl languishes in a convent? Forced to give up her child."

"That is enough!" Haydn admonished her sharply. There was no need to bandy about the Archduke's past in the presence of servants and palace guards.

"Shackle her!" he ordered the guards. "And wait here," he continued when the seamstress had been restrained, her wrists tightly cuffed behind her back. "Whatever you need to say," he said to Hannah, "may be said within."

Pfarrer Spalek led them into the sacristy. When they were all seated, Haydn turned toward Hannah.

"Signora Pacelli confided in you, I see. However she came by her knowledge, she had no business talking to you."

"Signora Pacelli was never one to blab," Hannah retorted. "I didn't need her to tell me what had happened. I knew."

"How could you possibly have known?" the Archduke asked wonderingly. "Bettina—"

"You remember her name, do you?" Hannah turned to him, furious.

Wearily, the Archduke ran his hand through his hair. "Of course, I remember her name. I wished to marry her. But the Empress . . ." He broke off.

"Whatever His Imperial Highness's sins," Pfarrer Spalek interrupted gently, "it is not for you to judge him, Hannah. *'Who is without sin?'* says the Lord."

"Worse still," Haydn said, "you sought to profit from his sins. Where is the leather purse His Imperial Highness left behind? Have you not found it yet?"

To his astonishment, he saw tears pricking at Hannah's eyes.

"For shame, Herr Kapellmeister! Would you add insult to injury? I never sought money. What good is it to me when my daughter wastes away in a convent, separated from her child?" She turned to the Archduke. "She never expected marriage. Bettina knew her place."

"Your daughter!" Haydn exclaimed in unison with the Archduke. They sought each other's eyes.

"Then it was you who urged Signora Pacelli to speak with the Archduke," Johann said.

Hannah nodded. "She said she could prevail upon His Imperial Highness. If I'd thought it would get her killed, I would never have allowed her to step in."

"His Imperial Highness did not kill Signora Pacelli, Hannah," Haydn assured her.

But who had? And who had made the demand for money?

He felt the weight of the braided chain the barber-surgeon had found in Paolo's cold hands. It was in his coat pocket, its substance making the garment sag. Had Lucia's lover compounded his sins with extortion and murder?

He withdrew the extortion note the Archduke had received and held it before Hannah.

"Do you swear—upon your daughter's soul—that you did not write this?"

She stared at the note, and then at him. "I did not. It is not even my hand." She sank deeper into her seat, head bowed in dejection. "All I ask is for my child to be released. She is all I have in this world."

The Archduke looked despairingly at Haydn. "Mother will not listen to a word I have to say. I have tried."

"I will raise the matter with Her Majesty," Haydn promised before he could stop himself. He was aware of Johann staring at him. His younger brother was no doubt convinced he'd taken leave of his senses. Haydn himself half-suspected he had.

God in heaven, what had compelled him to make such a rash promise? He squelched the feeling of unease that snaked through him.

"Surely, a position can be found for the girl here with her mother," he said. "And if she vows to relinquish any claims she or her child might have with the Archduke . . ."

"His Serene Highness can be quite persuasive as well," Johann added with an understanding smile that buoyed Haydn's spirits. With his brother's support, he was certain the thing could be accomplished.

Chapter Thirty-Seven

THE next morning, Haydn was seated at his desk in the Music Room when he heard a knock on the door. Fighting the morose spirit that threatened to overwhelm him, he swiveled around just as the door opened.

Gabriel Krause, the young cellist, entered the room.

"You sent for me, Herr Kapellmeister?" The young man stood respectfully before him.

Wordlessly, Haydn gestured toward the empty chair that stood beside his desk. The Kapellmeister regarded his musician as though he'd never seen him before. Gabriel was a tall young man with tightly curling dark hair. A handsome enough lad.

Young, too, Haydn thought, the boy's smooth, unlined features causing him to feel his age.

Under his steady regard, Gabriel fidgeted uncomfortably.

"Is anything the matter, Herr Kapellmeister?"

"I fear there is, Gabriel." Reluctantly, Haydn reached within his pocket.

He had lost an astoundingly talented soprano. And after her humiliating arrest, who knew whether Narcissa would stay on with the Esterházy troupe either?

Now it appeared he was about to lose an exceptionally talented cellist as well. Gabriel would've gone far. But what was mere talent without either morality or integrity?

"Besides, what am I to say to his wife when she learns I have left her bereft of her young husband?" Haydn muttered to himself. The couple, he recalled, had been wed for no more than a few months.

"Something of yours has come into my possession," Haydn began. He held out the braided chain with the crucifix at the end of it.

Deliberately, he opened the crucifix revealing the miniature portrait of Gabriel's beautiful young wife.

Mortified, the young cellist flushed a deep red.

"It is mine," he admitted. "B-but where did you—?" he swallowed, unable to continue.

"It was in Paolo's hands," Haydn said remorselessly.

To his surprise, Gabriel's head sunk lower onto his chest.

"He knows, then?" he mumbled.

"That you and his wife were indulging in a passionate interlude?" Haydn demanded sternly. "It appears so." Although, truth to tell, he had no notion whether Paolo had divined the truth.

"But I expect you were aware of that?" Haydn continued. "Why else would you have confronted him?"

"Confronted him?" Gabriel's voice rose. His head jerked up instantly. "Why would I confront the man?"

Haydn gritted his teeth together. Was his cellist about to deny he had killed his paramour's husband? Despite the evidence against him?"

"How else do you suppose he got hold of your chain?" Haydn demanded, outraged. God in heaven, did the question have to be asked?

Gabriel swallowed, his eyes widening in confusion. "I-I suppose it was amongst Lucia's things in her changing room. I saw the maids gathering them up yesterday."

He lowered his head again. "It was there that I lost it the day she died. She threw herself at me and—"

"You were consorting with her up to the moment of her death?"

Haydn found himself sickened by the notion, although he knew not why. He'd already suspected Lucia of cavorting with the Archduke. Why was this so much worse?

Gabriel shook his head. "She asked me to meet her that morning," he said dully. "She was with child, she said. She'd hinted at the possibility before, but now she claimed it was mine. It brought me back to my senses like nothing else could. That and the realization that she expected me to leave my Adella and marry her.

"I—" He flushed dully again. "I never loved Lucia. It was just—" He turned aside. "God forgive me, were Adella with me, I would never have succumbed."

The lad sounded sincere, Haydn thought. A question occurred to him, and he frowned.

"Lucia wanted you to marry her?"

Gabriel nodded. "She said her husband could never know she had conceived a child out of wedlock. I supposed at first it was just a pretext to get me away from Adella."

A natural enough conclusion, Haydn mused. Lucia was nothing if not determined, and she had never—God rest her soul—balked at anything to get her way.

"But then when she died, I realized she was telling the truth. She was with child."

"Is that why you thought she had killed herself?" Haydn asked, recalling how unusually distraught Gabriel had appeared that evening. It was Gabriel, too, who had convinced Friberth and the others that Lucia had taken her own life.

The cellist nodded again.

"And then the barber-surgeon said she'd consumed pennyroyal. I naturally thought . . ."

Haydn cupped his chin thoughtfully.

"Then you realized she'd been murdered?"

"I thought Paolo must have done it—in a rage."

"Is that why you sought to kill him—to avenge her death and that of her unborn child? Your child as well, if truth be told."

The question had to be asked even though Haydn was beginning to doubt his original conclusion.

"No, no, Herr Kapellmeister!" In his agitation, Gabriel half-rose out of his seat. "Why do you say that? I have sinned against my wife. I've betrayed my vows. But, as God is my witness, I am no killer."

"No," Haydn said pensively. "No, I don't suppose you are."

<hr>

For some time after Gabriel left, Haydn sat at his desk, staring sightlessly out the window. The palace gardens stretched out in an immense vista before him. From where he sat—well above the grounds—the ornate pattern in which the gardens were laid out could be easily distinguished.

"But when one walks through the gardens, one seems to wander through a disorienting maze of paths and grassy areas and nooks," he murmured to himself.

He chewed pensively on his lower lip.

If only he could stand back, thus, and view the conundrum they faced from a distance. Despite his best efforts, they were no closer to finding the extortionist. Nor had he discovered the hand that had taken two lives and attempted to take a third.

Hannah had no reason to murder Lucia. The seamstress had confessed to doing her utmost to thwart the Archduke's alliance—to the point of sliding Markos's broadsheet under Maria Beatrice's door—but she had never once demanded a kreutzer.

The hand that had penned the demand for money was different. Haydn had compared it to the ones Hannah had acknowledged writing.

As for Gabriel, Haydn had discreetly sounded the cellist out as to his knowledge of the Archduke's dalliance. But Hannah was right; Lucia hadn't so much as whispered a word of the scandal to him.

"She sought a position for herself in Milan," Gabriel had replied, confused, when Haydn asked him about Lucia's pursuit of His Imperial Highness.

The excuse had served their purpose well. It was, apparently, the very tale Lucia had fed her husband on the nights she left him for her clandestine meetings with Gabriel.

Moreover, the cellist's tale that his crucifix had been amongst Lucia's belongings could easily be confirmed. Intending to do just that, Haydn got up, strode toward the bell pull, and tugged it. With any luck, it would be either Rosalie or Greta who responded to the summons.

Returning to his seat, he reviewed the events of the past few days.

Ulrike had been killed likely because she knew who had murdered Lucia. But what had his prima donna done to lose her life?

Why, for that matter, had the killer gone after Paolo?

The killer, whoever it was, had sought to blame Lucia's murder on the Archduke.

But why? Was it for the money?

His Imperial Highness had stood ready to hand over as much as two thousand gulden to silence the rumors of his liaison with Hannah's daughter in Vienna. How much more would he have coughed up to suppress the lie that he had dallied with—and murdered—an opera singer?

But why get rid of Lucia? Or Paolo?

Clearly, avarice had incited the extortionist to his deeds.

Had greed provoked the murders as well?

Chapter Thirty-Eight

A sharp rap on the door interrupted Haydn's musings. He looked up as Rosalie entered the room.

Haydn beckoned her forward. "You and Greta helped to gather up Signora Pacelli's belongings yesterday, did you not?"

When she nodded, he continued: "Did Master Gabriel come by while you were about your task?"

"He did, indeed." Rosalie seemed more than a little eager to share the news. Haydn wondered why. He was about to continue with his questions when, after a momentary hesitation, she plunged on.

"He let us believe you'd sent him. But Karl told us you hadn't. Greta and I think he was there to look for—"

"A chain with his crucifix on it?" Haydn interjected.

"Yes." She seemed puzzled that he knew.

"Herr Hipfl retrieved it from Signor Pacelli," he explained. "I have just returned it to him."

Rosalie's brow furrowed. "But that must mean—"

"I'm afraid it does," Haydn interrupted her again. The girl was intelligent. It was only natural she'd discovered the significance of her finding. There was no need to discuss it any further.

"It would be best to keep the news quiet," he cautioned her. "Master Gabriel is well aware of what he has done. There's no reason to shame him any further." Or his wife, for that matter, although Haydn saw no need to belabor the point.

"I didn't think he'd done much more than . . ." Rosalie's voice trailed off, subsiding into silence, when he directed a quelling glance at her.

"The pennyroyal oil," she began after a few minutes, "is in the storage cupboard where anybody can find it."

"True enough," he agreed. Anyone in the opera house could have got their hands on the stuff.

"It occurred to me—" She hesitated.

Haydn looked questioningly at her. "Yes?"

Rosalie took a deep breath. "It occurred to me that not everyone knew about the wi—"

"The wine!" Haydn's eyes widened. The girl was right. All three victims had partaken of tainted wine. But—

Snippets of what he'd learned in the past few days slid into his mind.

"It's possible, we've found our killer," he barely breathed the words out loud, astounded. "I will need to speak with Paolo."

He glanced at the clock. He trusted Paolo was awake and in a condition to answer his questions.

But he stayed his haste. There was another topic he needed to bring up with Rosalie. The sooner the better, in fact. After all, there would very soon be a new maid working under her and Greta.

⸻ ❧ ⸻

"Herr Haydn knew about Master Gabriel?" Greta's mouth dropped open. "How could he possibly know?"

"Signor Pacelli found the crucifix. It wasn't his wife's, just as I surmised," Rosalie replied. She glanced surreptitiously over her shoulder.

She and Greta were alone in the kitchen, washing the breakfast dishes.

"I wonder why Signor Pacelli gave it to Herr Hipfl?" Greta frowned down at her soapy hands. She lifted the silver coffee pot up and rinsed the soap off it before carefully handing it to Rosalie.

"Possibly because he thought it belonged to her killer," Rosalie said as she dried the coffee pot.

"But Herr Haydn doesn't think Master Gabriel did it?" Greta scrubbed gently at a porcelain cup.

"No. Although you'd think he'd have reason enough to if he fathered Signora Pacelli's child."

Rosalie's eyes narrowed as she thought back to her conversation with the Kapellmeister.

"You know, Gerhard told me that Herr Hipfl had Signor Pacelli brought into the tavern last night. I thought it was because the poor man had taken ill. But now I'm wondering—"

"If someone tried to kill him?" Greta turned to her aghast.

Rosalie nodded. "And come to think of it, there was something strange about the way Herr Haydn asked whether Master Gabriel had been by Signora Pacelli's changing room. As though he'd already heard the news and wanted to make certain it was true."

"He must've thought Master Gabriel did old Paolo in," Greta said knowingly. "He knew why Master Gabriel came by the changing room as well, didn't he?" Greta handed her the ceramic cup.

"He did. I was about to tell him about it when he interrupted me."

Rosalie rubbed the drying cloth over the cup, soaking up the droplets of water on its surface. It wasn't the first time he'd spoken over her that morning, either.

Why, the Kapellmeister's eyes had nearly bulged out of their sockets when she'd mentioned the wine. Only the singers, stagehands, and the few servants who tended to the opera house would've known where it was kept—let alone how to get hold of it.

"It's not much to go upon," she conceded to Greta. "Still, it does point to one of the performers being the culprit."

But Herr Haydn had reacted as though he'd been granted an epiphany. Then before she could even set forth her thoughts, he'd abruptly changed the subject.

"He wanted to know whether anyone owed money to Gerhard. Whether anyone had paid their debts recently."

"That is odd," Greta agreed, rinsing a saucer. "I don't see what that has to do with anything."

"I told him Prince Toni still owes Gerhard a substantial amount. But I doubt Prince Toni could've got his hands on the wine."

"And he wasn't anywhere near the opera house when Ulrike was killed," Greta agreed. "It's not him."

"We're getting a new maid, though." Rosalie had yet to break the good news to Greta.

"About time, too," Greta huffed. "When is she coming?"

"Not soon enough. His Serene Highness will have to send for her. She's in Vienna. Hannah's daughter."

"Hannah's daughter?" Greta's voice rose. "She's never mentioned a daughter."

"The girl has a child, too. She's no more than sixteen."

Greta turned to look at her. "You don't think, do you—?"

Rosalie nodded before her friend could complete her question.

"It wouldn't surprise me if Hannah was behind that letter His Imperial Highness received. Did you see how she was looking daggers at me last evening?"

Greta bobbed her head. "There's no smoke without fire, she kept saying." She grinned at Rosalie. "That notice His Imperial Highness put in the broadsheet must've been meant for her."

Greta frowned as another thought occurred to her.

"But how will the girl get any work done with a child to look after?"

Rosalie smiled. "Frau Haydn has offered to help raise it. She's been lighting candles for a child all this while. It's not quite the same as having your own, of course."

"But it's a child, nevertheless." Greta's cheeks dimpled. "And she'll likely be as much or more of a mother to it than Hannah's daughter. Well, that's good."

Chapter Thirty-Nine

"O f course, I knew the child wasn't my own, Herr Kapellmeister," Paolo said gruffly. "Do you take me for a fool?"

It was not a question Haydn wished to answer, so he remained silent. He was sitting on a pressback chair by Paolo's bedside. The old violinist lay under a quilt pulled up to his chin—a thin, frail figure in the large feather bed. Two plump pillows supported his grizzled head.

The Kapellmeister's silence must have made Paolo uneasy.

"What was I to do?" he growled impatiently. "Put her away for infidelity?"

"Most men would not be willing to accept another man's child as their own," Haydn pointed out in an even tone. It was unlikely Paolo had anything to do with his wife's death, but the Kapellmeister needed to assure himself of the fact.

He had fallen prey to speculation and formed far too many assumptions already.

Paolo sank lower into the depths of his bed.

"I am old, Herr Kapellmeister," he said wearily, "with no hope of fathering an heir. Lucia's child would've been an unasked-for blessing—someone to leave my wealth to. A child who—raised in the right manner—would not squander my life's work."

"Would Lucia have frittered away your wealth?" Haydn wanted to know. He had not known his prima donna to be a spendthrift, although she had never seemed especially frugal either.

The question was like a prod to Paolo, goading him into irritability.

"That's not what I said. Lucia wasn't extravagant—no more than a woman of her beauty had any right to be. But she lacked the capacity to take charge of Fiore and restrain his wayward behavior. Without someone to hold the reins, the money would soon be gone. But the responsibility of motherhood might have served to instill some firmness in her."

"I've heard of Fiore's debts. He owed a substantial amount to Gerhard, did he not?"

"He can take care of that himself." Paolo's lips pressed into a thin line. "I told him yesterday I'd had enough of his shenanigans. Gerhard had best not look to me for his money."

So it was not Paolo who had supplied Fiore with the money. That did not surprise Haydn. He had an inkling of who had.

"I don't suppose he will," Haydn responded to Paolo's remark. "Fiore managed to procure the money from somewhere. He's discharged his debts fully."

Paolo grunted. "I would not have thought the boy had it in him. He has no sense. He was my widowed sister's only child, and she spoiled him. By the time I took him in, it was too late." He sighed. "God forgive me, many a time, I've wished it was he who'd drowned instead of Uwe."

"Uwe?" Haydn was unfamiliar with the name. "Was that your stepson?" Lucia had mentioned something about Paolo adopting his first wife's son.

Paolo nodded. "He was like a son to me. They went to the river one day, Fiore and he. Only one of them came back."

Haydn quietly listened as Paolo recounted the details to him. When the old man eventually subsided, he waited awhile before gently broaching another topic.

"Was Fiore with you last evening?"

Paolo plucked at his quilt listlessly. "Why would he be? Hadn't I threatened to disinherit him?"

Haydn frowned. It was not what he'd expected to hear. He asked about the wine. Where had that come from?

"I expect it was from the supply delivered to the opera house. Lucia liked drinking it. Now that she's gone, Fiore must have let Lidia take it. Lidia had it with her when she came to see me." Paolo gripped his quilt. "Poor Lucia! Gone before she could finish her wine; the bottle had barely been touched."

"But you had some yesterday?"

"I would've preferred a concoction of peppermint, but there was none in the house. Lidia suggested the wine. It is flavored with peppermint. Foolish woman! I should not have heeded her. I had barely taken a few sips when I felt my insides twisting. The pain was excruciating. Had Herr Hipfl not arrived in time—"

"You would've been dead, I fear," Haydn said grimly.

"I doubt Lidia was trying to kill me, Herr Kapellmeister." Paolo wasn't too feeble to roll his eyes. "She has money troubles to be sure, but how would killing me help?"

"I don't say she was," Haydn replied. He would need to ponder what he'd learned, but the details of what had happened were becoming clearer to him. The murderer would have to be apprehended. But how?

"Was Lucia to inherit your estate?" he asked Paolo.

"In the event of my death." The old man sighed. "I never thought to outlive her, Herr Kapellmeister. But now that she's gone . . . I suppose a new will must be drawn up."

"The sooner the better," Haydn agreed, a plan forming in his mind.

When he left Paolo's side an hour later, he made it a point to meet with Herr Hipfl.

"Keep an eye on him," he warned. "I suspect there will be another attempt on him this very evening."

⁕

Greta hesitated outside the opera house. "I can hardly bring myself to go in there," she confided.

Rosalie glanced at her friend. Greta's lips were pinched together.

"I know what you mean," she said quietly, squeezing Greta's hand.

The thought of seeing Ulrike's killer and behaving as though nothing had happened made her stomach clench up as well.

"But we're doing this for Ulrike's sake." Still looking at Greta, Rosalie reached for the door handle. "It will bring her some measure of justice."

At least, Rosalie trusted that it would. It all depended upon how well they played their part, helping Herr Haydn spring his trap.

"I know, but—" Greta bunched her palms into fists.

Nevertheless, she followed Rosalie into the vestibule. The double doors leading to the theater were open, and the rich sound of the orchestra and of Miss Lidia's voice—in Vespina's role—singing with Jakob Friberth reached their ears.

Herr Haydn had deliberately sent them to the opera house in the midst of a rehearsal. Now that Fräulein Leon had been let out of prison—and the troupe once again had two sopranos—the Prince had called for a second performance of Karl's opera.

It would be given not tonight but on the next evening.

"The entire troupe will be in the auditorium," the Kapellmeister had told the maids. "Be sure everyone receives the message."

Firmly clutching the bottles of wine Gerhard had sent over from the tavern, Rosalie composed her features.

Turning to her friend, she whispered, "Are you ready to go in?"

Greta nodded. Together they marched toward the stage. Herr Haydn was right, Rosalie thought as she looked around her. The entire troupe was here.

Master Luigi was conducting the orchestra. Master Johann and Karl stood in the wings, poring over a copy of the libretto as they monitored the performance.

The stagehands and Fiore were sitting on chairs just behind the orchestra.

"Ah, there's the wine at last!" Jakob Friberth broke off in the middle of his recitative.

"Thank heavens!" Miss Lidia stepped forward and reached down for the bottles Rosalie held out to her. "Now we can do the scene properly."

Straightening up, she looked uncertainly at the maids. "Any news of Paolo?" she asked softly. "Did Gerhard say . . .?"

Before Rosalie could respond, Fiore sat up, shaking the hair off his forehead.

"Why, what has happened to Onkel Paolo? I thought he was at home. Where is he?"

"He took violently ill last night." Miss Lidia's lips trembled. "I sent for Herr Hipfl. I couldn't think what else to do. But . . ." She glanced down at the maids.

"It was the wine he had," Rosalie explained. She glanced over her shoulder. "It was tainted. Your Onkel Paolo nearly died last night, Fiore."

Fiore's eyes narrowed. "Who gave him tainted wine?" he demanded. "Never say, Onkel tried to kill himself. He would never do that."

"Of course, he didn't try to kill himself. I suggested he have some," Miss Lidia said, more distressed than ever. "I even poured him a glass. I didn't know there was anything wrong with the wine."

"This is your fault, then!" Fiore shot out of his chair, nostrils flaring. "Shouldn't you have tasted some before giving him any?" he yelled, furious.

He would've jumped up onto the stage to confront the soprano had Karl not hastened to restrain him.

"For heavens' sake, it was Miss Lidia's quick thinking that saved your uncle's life," Greta admonished the lad.

"It's true. She called Herr Hipfl, didn't she?" Rosalie vigorously bobbed her head in agreement. "Where were you when Signor Pacelli needed you? You weren't even around."

Unable to counter her accusations, Fiore hung his head. *So he should, ungrateful wretch*, Rosalie thought.

Lips pursed, she turned her attention back to Miss Lidia. Worry creased her plain features. She was clearly anxious to learn Signor Pacelli's fate.

Rosalie gave Greta a surreptitious nudge. It was time they got on with it. They'd just received the perfect opening.

"He's ever so much better, Miss Lidia," Greta quickly began. "And very thankful to you, he is, too, for saving his life."

"As well he should be," Master Luigi commented. "Joseph tells me that had Herr Hipfl not arrived in time to administer an emetic, Paolo would be gone."

"And I've heard he means to give you more than thanks, Miss Lidia," Rosalie added with a smile.

"Why, what does he mean to do?" Jakob Friberth winked at Miss Lidia. "Marry her? That would make you happy, wouldn't it?"

Miss Lidia blushed but said nothing.

"How can you say such a thing?" Fiore muttered. "Tante Lucia is barely cold in her grave."

"From what Gerhard says," Greta said, "Signor Pacelli wants to leave his entire estate to Miss Lidia."

"His entire estate?" Fiore repeated as Miss Lidia's mouth dropped open. "Whatever for?"

The other singers onstage, Karl, and even Master Luigi and Master Johann looked astounded.

"He says it's the least he can do," Rosalie explained, "after the way Miss Lidia saved his life."

She turned to Miss Lidia, recalling the information the Kapellmeister had told her to be sure to provide.

"I expect that's why he wishes to see you this evening. He doesn't want you to have to worry about money anymore."

"Oh!" Miss Lidia turned redder still but didn't seem to have the words to respond to this news.

"You won't be needed at the masked ball this evening, will you?"

"Wh—oh, no," Lidia stammered, "No, I won't. I'll be sure to visit Paolo —if he wants me there."

"His entire estate, eh?" Jakob Friberth whistled. "If Paolo were to die tonight, Lidia, you'd be a wealthy woman. That would be even better than marriage, what say you?"

He grinned and clapped her on the shoulder.

"You won't forget your friends when that happens, will you, my dear?"

Chapter Forty

Paolo plucked at the thick quilt that covered him. The loud ticking of the clock on the shelf above his bed had an oddly unnerving effect on him. It seemed to underscore the nervous thumping of his heart.

The killer would soon be here. The Kapellmeister had explained who it was to Paolo, but Paolo still couldn't believe it. Greed he could understand. Envy as well. But this—why, this was pure evil. It was incomprehensible.

A sharp rap sounded, causing the wall behind him to rattle. Jolted by the sound, Paolo's bony knees jerked up.

"Herr Hipfl," he hissed, twisting his head around. "Is that you?"

The barber-surgeon was posted in the room behind him.

"They are here, Paolo. Are you prepared for what is to come?"

Paolo grunted. "As prepared as any man can be for death, Herr Hipfl."

"Be sure not to drink any of the wine," the barber-surgeon warned him. "Or anything else, for that matter."

Paolo grunted again. The clatter of footsteps ascending the wooden stairs outside echoed within the room. His fingers grasped the quilt. If he were to die, at least he would not die alone.

The barber-surgeon would be privy to everything that went on within his bedchamber.

He glanced up at the shelf above his headboard. It held a small glass panel.

Brightly lit by four candles on either side of it, it appeared to be nothing more than a mirror. But for Herr Hipfl—sitting in a darkened room on the other side of the wall—it would be like a window into Paolo's room within the tavern inn.

Even though he was waiting for it, the knock on the door startled him.

Lidia entered the room, bearing a small tray. She smiled at him.

"Paolo." She hurried to his side, followed by his nephew. "They told me you were on the mend. I'm glad to hear it." She set the tray down on a table by the bed. "Although you still look a little pale."

"I'd no notion you'd taken ill, Onkel Paolo," Fiore exclaimed as he sat down on the bed. His hand rested on the quilt. Paolo could feel the weight of it on his leg. "Why didn't you send for me?"

Paolo refrained from rolling his eyes. "How could I, when I knew not where you were?"

He glanced at the tray. There was a bottle of wine on it, along with three wine glasses. It was the same *kékoportó* that Lucia had favored. The same wine that had taken her life—and nearly taken his as well.

Unable to help himself, Paolo grimaced.

Lidia must've noticed, for she immediately said, "It's an unopened bottle, Paolo. It hasn't been tampered with. It couldn't have been."

"No, I suppose not." Paolo agreed reluctantly. Nevertheless, the warning that both the Kapellmeister and the barber-surgeon had impressed upon him reverberated in his mind.

"The killer will strike this very day," Herr Haydn had warned. "Accept no drop. Ingest nothing."

"I hear it was thanks to Miss Lidia that you're still alive, Onkel," Fiore said. "We should drink a toast to her, don't you think?"

He brought out a corkscrew, pulled the bottle of wine to himself, and inserted the worm into the cork. Paolo watched him, riveted.

"Oh, there's no need to drink to me," Miss Lidia laughed. "Let's drink to Paolo's health, instead."

"There's no reason we can't do both," Fiore said as he poured a generous quantity of the *kékoportó* into one of the glasses. He handed it to Paolo, who accepted it as gingerly as though it were a viper.

A cough sounded. The barber-surgeon, no doubt, Paolo thought. It was time to play his part.

Paolo coughed as well and noisily cleared his throat.

"I am very grateful to you, Lidia," he began. "It is thanks to you that I'm still alive. Herr Hipfl was quite clear about that."

"Oh, Paolo, I did no more than any friend would've done."

"Yes, well." Paolo waved his hand, impatiently dismissing her remarks. "I owe my life to you, and as a mark of my gratitude, I wish to leave my estate to you."

"Yes, so I heard, But that's not necessary," Lidia said at once as she accepted a glass of wine from Fiore.

"Cease your protestations, woman!" Paolo dismissed her demurral again. "It's been done already. But the old will must be destroyed. It favored Lucia, and she's no more. And I wish to make a small change to the new will as well."

He turned to Fiore, forcing a kindly smile upon his lips. It did not come easily. He had always been a brusque, impatient man.

"Gerhard tells me you've taken care of your debts, my boy."

His nephew shrugged. "What else could I do but discharge them?"

His heart aching, Paolo took hold of his nephew's arm. He recalled the day he'd taken the poor orphaned boy in. Would to God, the Kapellmeister was wrong in his conclusion.

"I had no doubt you would do the right thing. Anger raged in my heart, Fiore, when I rewrote my will to favor Lidia. But now I want to make sure you're taken care of as well. You'll receive a stipend while she's still alive and when she's gone, she's to leave the entire estate to you."

Paolo turned to Lidia. She had not lifted her wine glass to her lips, he noticed.

"Both documents are on my desk. Will you go to my quarters and take charge of them?"

Lidia seemed taken aback. "Y-yes, of course, Paolo."

"At once, if you please," he commanded. "And return here tomorrow with both sets of papers. The Bürgermeister has arranged for a lawyer to visit me."

She seemed hurt. Looking uncertainly from him to Fiore, she set her glass reluctantly down.

"Of course, Paolo. I'll do it at once."

"Be sure to attend the masked ball as well," he gruffly instructed as she left the room. "Lucia would've gone had she been here. She was looking forward to it."

When she'd gone, Fiore gestured toward Paolo's untouched glass of wine.

"Won't you sip your wine, Onkel?" He smiled. "Or do you not trust Lidia? It was the wine she poured you that almost killed you, I hear."

Paolo shrugged. "I trust her well enough." He tipped his chin at the third glass. "I see you haven't poured yourself any."

Fiore grinned. "I'd never hear the end of it from Karl if I went into the ballroom reeking of wine. You know how he is!"

Paolo nodded, bringing the wine glass to his lips. He was careful not to take a sip, although he couldn't see how the wine could have been tainted. The strong flavor of mint—so closely resembling the pennyroyal he'd ingested earlier—made him retch. His stomach turned.

"What is it, Onkel?" Fiore leaned forward.

"Nothing." Paolo pretended to take another large swallow of his wine. Then, grimacing and clutching his stomach, he leaned back against his pillows and shut his eyes. "I wish to rest now, Fiore. Come and see me tomorrow, won't you?"

He heard Fiore quietly leave the room. The door closed behind him. A few minutes later, it opened again.

"Herr Hipfl?" Paolo sat up.

"I have the rats here." The barber-surgeon carried a small cage in either hand.

Setting them down, he took a small quantity of the wine and poured it into two small bowls that he proceeded to give to the rats. The rats eagerly lapped up the liquid and instantly began writhing and squeaking in pain.

To Paolo's horror, they were dead within minutes. He stared at the creatures, aghast. God Almighty, he had very nearly met the same fate himself.

The barber-surgeon emitted a low whistle. "Herr Haydn was right!"

"So it seems," Paolo gasped. "B-but how?"

Chapter Forty-One

Aquarter of an hour later, the barber-surgeon was putting the self-same question to the Kapellmeister.

Haydn studied the tray, the two wine-filled glasses, the third empty one, and the opened bottle of wine. He had hurried forth as soon as the barber-surgeon had sent for him. Paolo, he was aware, was avidly watching him.

"The bottle was unopened, you say?" His eyes roved over the contents of the table once more.

"It was, indeed," Paolo assured him. "Could you have been mistaken in your surmise, Herr Kapellmeister?" he continued hopefully. "There was no way for anyone to taint the wine. You must see that."

"Yet tainted it was." The barber-surgeon stroked his chin pensively. "Could the bottle have been contaminated before it was filled? Or the wine poisoned in the barrel?"

Haydn shook his head.

"It must have been the corkscrew! It is the only thing missing."

"The corkscrew?" Paolo and Herr Hipfl exclaimed together. In unison, they turned toward the little bedside table. But the Kapellmeister was right. The object was nowhere in sight.

"The cylinder beneath the handle is usually quite wide," Haydn explained. "It may have been used as a receptacle to store the pennyroyal oil."

It was in just such a manner that an Italian traveler had eliminated a rival of his in England. The story had been widely publicized in the English papers. Haydn's friend, Charles Burney, had shared the account with him in a recent letter.

"I suppose it is possible." Herr Hipfl let out a heavy breath. "And now that you mention it, I do recall seeing something of the sort in the next village. They are used to infuse cheap tavern wines with tinctures and other herbal flavors."

"Maria Anna has one," Haydn said. He turned to Paolo who reclined white-faced against his pillows, about to ask a question, when the barber-surgeon interrupted.

"But Paolo had two visitors. Either one of them could have brought the corkscrew in."

Haydn looked down at the old man. "Was it still here when Lidia left?"

Paolo shrugged. "How should I know? I paid the thing no mind."

"I still say it was Miss Lidia," Herr Hipfl said adamantly. "Given her pecuniary circumstances, she has more reason than anyone else to wish Paolo dead."

"That may be so." Haydn glanced down at Paolo, who sat with his bony fingers clasped together. "But I fear it's your nephew who's behind this, Paolo."

"And if you are wrong?" Paolo refused to meet his gaze.

"Then I will gladly acknowledge my mistake."

There was a moment's silence. Then Paolo said quietly, "I hope to God your judgment is faulty. If it's not, I have harbored evil by my side—nay, encouraged it."

"I doubt that's true," Haydn tried to reassure him, but Paolo was in no mood for encouragement.

"I could have been a better father to the boy. But he was prone to tears, wont to cling to my side, and I had little patience with that. God forgive me"—he bowed his head—"I was habitually condescending and contemptuous."

Haydn had heard the recriminations before. Paolo blamed himself for having stoked the evil. "Could any of it have been avoided?" he'd asked miserably.

Paolo looked up at him now, his eyes blazing. "But when Uwe died, Fiore was no more than a child himself. He was only fourteen."

Haydn was aware of the barber-surgeon gazing curiously at them, but he saw no reason to air the story before him. Nor did he see any reason to harp on his conclusions.

The truth was self-evident, and Paolo was aware of it. It was greed that had incited Uwe's drowning; and greed that had caused Lucia and her unborn child to die. It had almost sent Paolo to his grave. It would likely send Lidia to hers as well, if they weren't careful.

After all, she stood between a young man and what he considered his rightful inheritance.

All the pieces had fallen into place once Haydn had realized that.

A period of silence had followed Paolo's outburst. Now Herr Hipfl cleared his throat.

"Still, most people would suspect Miss Lidia," he pointed out. "Paolo here is more useful to her dead than alive."

"Don't you think Fiore knows that as well as anybody else?" Haydn responded quietly. "He'll find a way to implicate Lidia, mark my words. We must stop him."

Chapter Forty-Two

FROM his seat at the harpsichord, Johann's eyes kept flitting toward each of the doors that led into the concert hall. How long would it be before brother returned?

Luigi, mistaking the reason for his anxiety, leaned toward him and whispered, "Never fear, Johann. No one will know it is you and not Joseph beneath that mask. Even the musicians are unaware of the fact."

Johann nodded, tight-lipped, although it was not the fear of being discovered that was causing his anxiety. Few of the guests who swept into the Great Hall adjoining the concert hall where the orchestra was stationed had so much as glanced his way.

Even if they had, who would know it was Haydn's younger brother who sat in his place, conducting the orchestra? God be praised, it was a masked ball, and Johann was wearing the very mask Haydn was supposed to wear. Sister-in-law had stitched him one of the same design.

Although despite her best efforts, brother's spare livery still hung loose upon his frame.

Searching his surroundings again, Johann took a deep breath, seeking to calm himself. Visitors milled into the room, headed toward the Great Hall. But there was still no sign of brother.

Johann was aware of his fingers feeling like frozen sticks of ice. During a brief respite in the music, he reached out for the glass of wine a passing footman had left upon the harpsichord for him.

The strong red wine fortified him somewhat, sending some of the blood rushing back into his icy fingers. But it could not entirely calm his spirits.

"What if brother is in danger?" he muttered, worried.

Luigi shot him a quick, quelling glance. "He is not. Never say such a thing!"

"The boy has not hesitated to kill three times. What's to prevent him from taking a fourth life? He appears to have no conscience."

"Joseph is not alone, Johann," Luigi reminded him.

That was true enough. The Bürgermeister had accompanied brother—as had a few palace guards. Nevertheless—

Nevertheless, trepidation seeped into Johann's blood, flowing through his veins. He should've accompanied brother. Better still, he should've taken brother's place. A man with a wife could ill afford to put himself in danger. Yet that was what brother had done.

Brooding over the past won't change it, Schani. Johann heard his father's matter-of-fact tone admonishing him. *No, it won't*, he agreed, firmly casting his anxiety away. The music quickened, and he gave himself up to the notes.

He had barely managed to quash his fears when they returned again. A woman was headed his way, her petite figure determinedly weaving a course through the crowd. Despite the mask that covered most of her features, it was clear who the woman was.

Her Ladyship, Maria Beatrice D'Este.

Dear God, she must want to speak with brother.

Luigi had caught sight of Her Ladyship as well. "Be sure not to address her, Johann," he warned. "Your voice will give you away. I will venture to deal with her."

But Her Ladyship was not to be so easily thwarted. Ignoring Luigi's protestations—that Haydn was needed at his post; that his voice was too hoarse for him to speak—she plucked at Johann's sleeve, nearly lifting him to his feet.

"I must speak with you," she insisted. "At once."

Reluctantly, Johann followed her outside, down the staircase, and into a sequestered corner of the Court of Honor. A stone fountain in the nook obscured them from view, and the babbling of the water—Johann hoped—would prevent his voice from giving him away.

"I thought it exceedingly strange, Herr Haydn," Maria Beatrice began without preamble, "that the Archduke chose to wear a black sash during our performance last evening. I might've dismissed the fact as a curiosity had he not also mentioned leaving an offering—in the confessional of all places."

She paused. Johann remained silent as well. There was no contradicting the details she'd cited. He considered it best to hear more of what she thought before rushing to assuage her concerns.

"Clearly, something odd was going on, Herr Haydn. Something I am not privy to. Do not attempt to deny it. Those two details have been preying on my mind. I demand to know the truth."

Johann coughed. "I take it His Imperial Highness has not had an opportunity to explain the matter to you himself?"

"I stayed up all night for him, but he returned far later than I expected. And what with one thing and another we have not had much time to ourselves."

"No, I expect not." Johann coughed again.

"We didn't wish to alarm you, Your Ladyship, but br—" Johann stopped himself just in time. "We, er, uncovered an attempt to thwart your alliance. The rumors floating in the broadsheets had persuaded an unscrupulous individual to try to extort money from His Imperial Highness."

Maria Beatrice's lips tightened. "What rumors might those have been?"

"The ones that br—er—that I discussed with you yesterday. The story was entirely false, as I explained. Even the seamstress—a close friend of Signora Pacelli—discounted them."

"Oh, I see." He could see her lips pursed together pensively.

"Rather than pander to the extortionist's demands, we sought to trap him."

"How?"

"Using the very details you noticed, Your Ladyship." Johann allowed himself a small smile. "The black sash was a message that His Imperial Highness consented to the egregious demands being made. The offering was an oblique reference to the sum demanded."

"And has this man been apprehended?"

Johann sighed. "I fear not. The extortionist unfortunately saw through our attempt."

"But you know who it is, do you not?" Maria Beatrice sounded concerned now.

Johann nodded. "It appears to be the same individual who murdered Signora Pacelli as well as a palace maid."

"Dear God! A palace maid has been killed as well?" The furrow that formed on Maria Beatrice's brow was visible above the mask she wore. "I had not heard that."

"I'm afraid so. But I have every confidence that the man will be apprehended this very night. Another trap has been set, and the Bürgermeister himself is monitoring it."

Maria Beatrice nodded. "And that is all there is to it?"

It was clearly a question, not a statement. Johann paused before responding. It was not his place to reveal the Archduke's sins, he decided.

"As far as I know, Your Ladyship. Only His Imperial Highness can say if there's anything more."

Maria Beatrice seemed to hesitate, looking out at the brightly lit courtyard beyond the stone fountain.

"You once told me, Herr Haydn," she said, turning back to him, "that I should put my questions to the Archduke himself."

It was excellent advice brother had given her, Johann thought.

He chose his words carefully.

"A good marriage is built upon mutual trust, Your Ladyship. But trust must be nurtured. And it must be freely given to those we profess to love. It is fostered by openness and a willingness to communicate with each other."

He paused, considering the wisdom of uttering his next remarks, before gently adding:

"It is hardly encouraged when one spouse relentlessly doubts the other. Nor when one goes behind the other's back to seek answers to nameless suspicions."

Maria Beatrice had the grace to blush. She lowered her head.

"You are right, Herr Haydn. I have demanded trust." Her voice was low and mortified. "But I have been grudging in my own bestowal of it."

They stood in silence for a while. Then she raised her head, reaching out to clasp Johann's hand in both of hers.

"Her Majesty was right about you, Herr Haydn. With your unfailing wisdom, you have put my mind to rest more surely than my confessor could have. I thank you!"

Impulsively, she reached up to kiss him on the cheek.

Then before the blood could even suffuse Johann's cheeks, she was gone.

Chapter Forty-Three

THE ticking of his timepiece sounded so loud in the darkness, Haydn placed his palm against his chest to muffle the sound. He stood within a closet in Lidia's quarters. The apartment consisted of a single bedchamber with a small room beyond it that served as both parlor and study.

Through a chink in the double doors of the closet, he could see the halo of light cast by the thick candle on the desk. Behind it—against the back wall of the room—was another closet. There the Bürgermeister hid. Two more palace guards—armed with swords—waited in Lidia's bedchamber.

When would Fiore arrive, Haydn wondered. He could hear the Bürgermeister growing restive in the other closet. Herr Groer's muted footsteps shuffling on the closet floor and the faint rasping of his throat, as he cleared it, were audible in the quiet room.

Fortunately, the window was thrown open. An intruder could just as easily conclude the sounds came from the courtyard below.

Haydn had no doubt that Fiore would come. With the Bürgermeister and the two palace guards, he had searched Paolo's quarters. Nothing had been found there. No corkscrew. And, as expected, the wills had been nowhere in sight either. The corkscrew was not in Lidia's quarters either.

Despite all that Herr Groer had been skeptical. "I see no evidence to conclude that Miss Lidia is innocent, Herr Haydn. The corkscrew—if indeed that is what she used to poison the wine bottle—might still be on her person. Any killer of sense would've long since discarded it. She may have as well."

Nevertheless, the Bürgermeister had reluctantly agreed to proceed with the plan.

They had made their way to Lidia's quarters, where Haydn had made his preparations before they'd taken their hiding places.

Haydn was just about to pull his timepiece out of his pocket when the muted sound of approaching footsteps caught his attention. Placing his ear as close as possible to the crack in the double doors, he listened carefully.

The footsteps grew louder. He thought he saw the door handle turning. Then the door opened, and a tall, slim figure quietly stepped into the room. Despite the candle on the desk and the low fire burning in the porcelain stove, Haydn could barely make out the intruder's features.

It was a man. That was as much as he could tell.

Treading carefully, the newcomer quickly crossed the room and approached the table. Glancing surreptitiously all around, he reached into his pocket, withdrew an item, and lay it upon the desk.

Then, picking up the candle, he began to rifle through the papers scattered on the writing table. Haydn had helpfully put a cover on one of the wills, marking it so the intruder wouldn't feel the need to open it all the way and read the words inside.

He held his breath as he watched the prowler lay his hands upon the will. He released it in relief when he saw the man viciously tear it in two and toss it into the embers of the dying flame.

The interloper rummaged through the papers once more, growing increasingly desperate in his search.

"Where is the accursed thing?" he muttered, loud enough for Haydn to hear.

"Is this what you are looking for?" Haydn emerged from his hiding place and held aloft the document he'd confiscated from the desk earlier.

Fiore spun around. "Herr Kapellmeister!"

His shock was palpable. His gaze tore around the entire room. The young man must've stolen out from the ballroom, confident the Kapellmeister was too preoccupied with the business of conducting the orchestra to notice.

"What are you doing here?" he demanded, his eyes swiveling back toward Haydn.

"I could ask the same of you?"

Fiore glanced at the door again, no doubt wondering if Haydn had followed him in through the door.

"Onkel wished me to retrieve his wills," he said at last. "He had changed his mind about leaving his money to Lidia."

"Had he?" Haydn's eyebrows rose. Fiore was speaking as though Paolo were already dead.

Fiore nodded. Oblivious to Haydn's reaction, he plowed ahead with his lies.

"She tried to kill him, if you must know. I was there. Onkel had no sooner taken a sip of the wine she brought up to him than his stomach twisted. But not before he was able to instruct me to burn his new will and retrieve the original."

He held his hand out, reaching for the document in Haydn's hands.

Haydn pulled it back out of reach.

"Who's to say it wasn't you that tried to kill Paolo?" he asked.

Fiore stepped aside, pointing to an object on the desk. "But the corkscrew that contained the poison is here in Lidia's quarters," he said.

Sickened by the man's inveterate lies, Haydn's fingers closed tightly around the will. He hoped the Bürgermeister had been paying attention, although it was still not time for Herr Groer to reveal himself.

"Enough with your lies, Fiore!" he thundered. "Only the killer would've known how the poison was administered. Only the killer would have reason to take the corkscrew out of Paolo's room."

His nostrils flared as he inhaled sharply.

"You were seen and you were heard. Paolo had not changed his mind about the will at all."

For a moment, Fiore's features darkened and a black storm seemed to twist them out of shape. Then he recovered his equilibrium. His lips curved into a slow smile.

"Be that as it may, Herr Kapellmeister." He glanced at the porcelain stove. "There's only your word for it that Onkel meant to change his will. The new will—favoring Lidia—is all but ashes now."

It was Haydn's turn to smile now. "Had you taken the trouble to read what you so hastily burned, my boy," he said, "you'd have realized you were about to destroy the original will. The one that favored you in the event that both Lucia and Paolo died."

He held up his hand.

"This one in my hands is the new will. It is in Paolo's hand and has his signature on it."

"No!" Fiore burst out sharply. His eyes widened in disbelief.

Then, realizing Haydn spoke the truth, they narrowed in fury.

"Give it to me!" he roared.

"No." Haydn stepped back as Fiore stalked closer.

Something gleamed in his hand. The dangerously sharp blade of a stiletto.

Where was the Bürgermeister? Had he any intention of coming forth?

"You were a fool to come here by yourself, Herr Kapellmeister." Fiore came ever closer. "When your body is found in Miss Lidia's study, everyone will think it was her desperation that drove her to stab you."

"Drop the dagger!"

The Bürgermeister's peremptory tones were as music to Haydn's ears. He'd emerged from the closet behind Fiore as soon as Haydn had taken a quick step back, allowing his heel to clatter onto the wooden floor.

The long, curving blade of Herr Groer's sword pressed against Fiore's neck. A trickle of blood spouted forth from where it penetrated the skin.

"Drop your dagger, boy," he commanded again. "I warn you, I will not hesitate to slash your throat if you take so much as one step more toward Herr Haydn."

Glaring balefully at Haydn, Fiore relinquished his hold on the stiletto. It clanked onto the floor by his feet. Herr Groer thrust his boot out instantly, kicking it far out of Fiore's reach.

Then with a snap of his fingers, the Bürgermeister summoned the palace guards who'd accompanied them.

While they shackled Fiore, Haydn thought to resolve another question.

"It was you attempting to extort money from His Imperial Highness, wasn't it?"

Fiore's eyes blazed defiantly at him.

"You will never prove it. It wasn't I who presented myself at the church this morning, eager to get my hands on His Imperial Highness's offering, was it?"

Haydn stared at him for a moment. Then he smiled.

"It is just as I surmised, then." His smile widened. "But I would not have been able to prove a thing had you not spoken."

How Fiore had managed to persuade Hannah to confront His Imperial Highness, they would never know. But only the extortionist would've understood the implication of the Archduke's delicately coded communication.

Only the extortionist—having taken care to incite Hannah into accosting His Imperial Highness—would be aware that someone had responded to the Archduke's covert message.

"I will leave you to it, Herr Groer," he said to the Bürgermeister as he turned to leave. "It is long past time that I returned to my duties and relieved Johann from his post."

Chapter Forty-Four

"H USBAND!"

Haydn twisted around to see Maria Anna peeking in through the parlor door. Her voice had startled him, but the interruption was not entirely unwelcome.

He had sat for the past half-hour at his desk that morning, chewing on the end of his silver pen as he mulled over the report he was to write for Her Majesty, Empress Maria Theresa.

But other than the date and the greeting, he had managed to write nothing at all.

He looked at his wife, eyebrows raised. She was dressed to go out.

"What is it, Maria Anna?"

"I need some money," she replied, coming to stand by his desk. "Thirty gulden ought to suffice."

Haydn swallowed. "Thirty gulden!" It was a large sum of money. "Whatever for?"

She rolled her eyes.

"A portion of it is needed as an offering for answered prayer—"

"Your prayer has been answered?" Haydn's gaze dropped to his wife's belly. Had she conceived a child? Already?

"Of course, it's been answered. I asked for a child, and I am to receive one. Did Pfarrer Spalek not inform you of the matter?"

"Ah, the child!" Haydn suppressed a smile of amusement. So, Pfarrer Spalek had raised the issue with Maria Anna as an answer to prayer, had he?

"The child will need a bed, besides," Maria Anna continued. "There's a good cabinetmaker in Széplak, I'm told. Hannah has offered to sew some suitable clothing, but I can hardly expect her to pay for the fabric."

"No, of course not." Haydn reached into his pocket and pulled out some coins, which he dropped into his wife's hands.

He watched her go before reluctantly turning his attention back to the unwritten report on his desk. He lowered his nib to the sheet of paper and then raised it again. Dear God, what was he to say? Was there any way of providing an honest account without including the sordid rumors that had swirled around in the past few days?

Perchance, Johann could help. Gathering up his papers, Haydn rose to his feet, determined to find his brother.

He found his brother in the Music Room, preparing a fresh set of scores for the second performance of the opera that night. There had been a few more changes to the cast.

Narcissa was to take Vespina's part since Lidia had asked for a few days' leave to attend to Paolo. A soprano from Meninger's traveling opera troupe would take on Sandrina's role.

"Narcissa was threatening to leave," Johann explained the changes apologetically. "And Meninger could only spare one soprano. I thought letting Narcissa have the part she craved would induce her to stay."

"It was a good decision." Haydn smiled at his brother. He drew a chair up to the desk and sat down.

But before he could broach the subject of the report, there was a knock on the door and a footman entered.

"From His Imperial Highness and Her Ladyship," he said, handing Haydn two small boxes and two folded sheets of paper.

The footman had barely closed the door behind him when Haydn tore open the first letter. He perused it with a satisfied smile.

"I see His Imperial Highness took my advice to confess his past indiscretions to his bride."

"A wise decision," Johann commented. "There'll be no reason to fear any future attempts at extortion."

"So I told him," Haydn said with a nod.

He set the paper down on the desk and opened the small box. It contained a gold snuffbox, inlaid with lapis lazuli.

"It is exquisite," Johann exclaimed, leaning over to look. "And certainly well-deserved."

But Haydn, reading through the second letter with a puzzled frown on his brow, made no reply.

"His Imperial Highness has done me the doubtful honor of confessing his past indiscretions to me. I cannot say I was pleased to hear of his behavior"—Haydn glanced up to briefly lock eyes with Johann before looking down again—*"nor that you might have intentionally kept the details from me."*

Haydn raised his head, about to ask what Maria Beatrice could possibly mean, when a stream of words burbled out of his younger brother.

"I had the most uncomfortable conversation with Her Ladyship last night," Johann confessed. He recounted the details. "I hardly knew how to address her questions."

He looked anxiously toward Haydn. "She doesn't refuse to marry him, does he?"

"Not at all," Haydn assured him. "Her confessor took the trouble to point out that"—he glanced down to read the relevant portion—*"a man's sins are his own to confess."* He raised his eyes. "She also realizes it took His Imperial Highness a great deal of courage to be honest with her."

Johann nodded as he absently twirled the pen in his hand. "Nevertheless, I felt dreadful about pointing out her mistrustfulness to her, knowing full well she had cause. But"—he shrugged, spreading his hands wide—"what could I do? It hardly seemed my place to inform Her Ladyship about the affair in Vienna."

"It was not," Haydn said firmly. "Besides, your advice must have been timely. She says it encouraged her, along with the Archduke's assurances, of course, to"—he lowered his eyes to find the pertinent section—"ah, here it is. *I have been persuaded to grant His Imperial Highness my everlasting trust. I believe this is the man God intended for my husband, and I thank you sincerely, dear Herr Haydn, for clarifying my path."*

He set down the letter and held out the second box to his younger brother.

"Her Ladyship says she sends you a token of her appreciation."

Johann drew back. "But the letter is addressed to you, brother."

"That may be so. But it was your advice that set her mind at peace." Haydn pushed the box closer to Johann. "Her Ladyship's gift rightfully belongs to you."

Johann sighed. "Very well."

Reluctantly, he drew the velvet-covered box closer and opened it. Inside, within a bed of satin, rested a large gold ring set with a deep blue sapphire.

His eyebrows shot up. "Dear God, it is more than I deserve!"

Haydn leaned forward, urgently.

"That sentiment does you no justice, Johann. Her Ladyship might well have rejected His Imperial Highness were it not for your words. The alliance would've fallen through. She says as much herself."

He pushed the letter across to his brother.

He waited until Johann had finished reading the letter before beginning to broach the matter of his report. He had barely gotten the words out of his mouth when a knock interrupted him yet again.

The same footman entered the Music Room.

"His Serene Highness wishes to see you," he informed Haydn. "In his capacity as High Sheriff of the county," he added.

Haydn sighed as he pushed himself out of his chair. At this rate, he would never get Her Majesty's report done.

⸺⸙⸺

Prince Nikolaus was in his study. To Haydn's surprise, Leopold, Grand Duke of Tuscany was present as well. His Grace, staring restlessly out the window, barely turned when Haydn entered the room.

The Prince threw a quick glance at the Grand Duke's rigid back and then gestured Haydn toward a gold-framed seat.

"The young man apprehended—" His Serene Highness began, only to be interrupted.

"Are you quite certain he is the extortionist, Haydn?" His Grace swiveled around to face Haydn. "We can ill afford any more incidents of this nature."

"Not a shadow of a doubt, Your Grace," Haydn responded. "I—"

"He seemed a most benign individual," His Serene Highness interposed.

"A lad of extremely limited intelligence as well," the Grand Duke added. "I can scarcely credit him to have been an agent of the Prussian King. How would King Frederick even have had the opportunity to get in touch with the boy?"

"He was not working for the Prussian King," Haydn felt obliged to clarify. "I am quite certain of that."

The Grand Duke's brows drew together. But rather than openly contradict Haydn, he leaned against the window sill. "What then was his motive?"

"His inordinate greed for money." Haydn turned toward the Prince. "Fiore had no desire to thwart His Imperial Highness's nuptials. The only person who wished to do so," he continued delicately, "was after justice, not gold."

"And you can assure us," the Grand Duke pressed him, "that we can expect no further trouble from that quarter, either?"

Haydn glanced at Prince Nikolaus again before responding. "Hannah's only desire was to be reunited with her daughter and grandchild. Both women understand that their position is contingent upon releasing His Imperial Highness from any further obligations."

His Serene Highness nodded his head in vigorous assent. "Never fear, Leopold, the contract is iron-clad. If there's so much as a whisper about the affair, they'll lose their positions."

His Grace still looked doubtful. "I am not sure of the merits of rewarding a troublemaker," he said with a grimace.

Haydn suppressed a sigh. "It was much the best way to ensure the sins of the past did not overshadow His Imperial Highness's future, Your Grace."

He left unvoiced the thought that had the sin itself not been committed, there would have been no trouble to avert.

"Yes, yes, I see." The Grand Duke paced back toward the window, his head bowed, his hands locked behind his back.

"How did you even come to suspect the young man?" His Serene Highness inquired after a while.

Chapter Forty-Five

HAYDN sat back, considering the question.

"Lucia's killer had deliberately tried to cast blame on the Archduke," he said at last. "I asked myself why. Hannah had no reason to kill Signora Pacelli. After all, Lucia had espoused her cause. Lucia's husband—despite her betrayal—did not wish her dead either."

His Serene Highness gazed quizzically at Haydn.

"But judging by the scurrilous account in the broadsheet," he said, "the killer wished us to believe His Imperial Highness had engaged in an illicit relationship with your prima donna."

Haydn nodded. "And the situation, had it been true, would've provided the Archduke with a plausible motive to kill her," he replied. "Even the smallest whiff of a rumor, however untrue, would have been damaging. But almost everyone who knew Signora Pacelli thought she was pursuing His Imperial Highness to procure a position for herself in Milan."

"Not Fiore," the Grand Duke objected. "It was he who pointed the couple out to us."

"Intentionally making us believe there was a romantic entanglement," Haydn agreed. Anyone else, he reflected, would've simply held his tongue about the matter. But Fiore had taken pains to draw their attention to it.

"I believe he truly thought his aunt was involved in an illicit affair with the Archduke. Fiore kept bringing up the supposed affair before Paolo as well, hoping to egg his uncle onto jealousy."

"But instead the old man chose to accept her child as his own," Prince Nikolaus commented.

Haydn nodded. "Fiore was so certain his uncle would cast Lucia aside, it never occurred to him that Paolo, eager for an heir, would forgive her. That decision unfortunately spelt Lucia's demise. She and her child stood in the way of Fiore's inheritance."

"But that I suppose," the Grand Duke said, standing by the window once more, "didn't bring Fiore any closer to his inheritance, did it?"

"No, it did not. Paolo, fed up with his gambling and the debts he'd ratcheted up, threatened to disinherit him. That must have sealed Paolo's fate."

"Was that what tipped you off to him, Haydn?" His Serene Highness leaned forward to ask.

"Yes." Haydn turned to face Prince Nikolaus. "Anyone could've killed Lucia. But none of her colleagues had reason to do away with Paolo."

He decided not to mention his suspicions regarding Lidia. Her only fault was being overly fond of Paolo, and that had saved his life.

"In all three cases, the poison had been administered in wine," Haydn resumed his account. "The maids reminded me that anyone could've gotten their hands on the pennyroyal oil. But the wine was always kept under lock and key, and Fiore was in charge of both. He adamantly denied even a sip to the other singers, but he was only too willing to let his aunt consume as much of the wine as she wanted."

"He was poisoning her on a regular basis?" His Serene Highness asked, horrified. The Grand Duke looked aghast as well.

"So it would appear," Haydn replied grimly. It chilled his soul to realize that a man could be so self-obsessed, so utterly devoid of pity. "Certainly Hannah seems to think so."

Judging by the symptoms—dizziness and persistent nausea—that Lucia had exhibited in the days before her death, Hannah's surmise likely was not far from the truth.

"And that he was the extortionist?" the Grand Duke pressed him. "How came you to that conclusion, Haydn?"

"The extortionist was motivated by greed, that much was clear. The murders, too, appeared to have the same motive. The more I considered it, the more likely it seemed that the same person was behind both crimes.

"Besides, Fiore's debts to Gerhard were extensive. But he was able to repay them even though Paolo had steadfastly refused to give him the money."

The Grand Duke's eyes narrowed.

"How was he able to do that?"

Haydn hesitated. There was no concrete evidence of what he was about to say.

"I believe Markos, the publisher of the broadsheet, may have shared the money we paid him. They both paid their debts at the same time." Haydn paused again. "I expect it was Markos as well who warned Fiore about the trap we were setting."

That was yet another unverified surmise, but it was the only thing that made sense.

"But"—His Serene Highness frowned, leaning forward—"Fiore expected to blackmail the Archduke for his supposed entanglement with your prima donna, did he not? How came he, then, to find out about the affair in Vienna?"

"He must've overheard Hannah and Lucia talking," Haydn said, shaking his head. "Or perhaps Hannah, in her agitation, let fall some comments that led him to that conclusion."

The latter supposition was not entirely implausible, he thought. The "nun's confession" Markos had fortunately refrained from publishing had been extraordinarily detailed. Haydn was convinced it was Fiore who had supplied the story. Privy to these sordid details, Fiore had been only too ready to believe the Archduke had fathered yet another child out of wedlock—this time upon Lucia.

The Grand Duke exhaled heavily.

"All's well that ends well, I suppose." His Grace withdrew a small leather pouch from his pocket and held it out to Haydn. "A small reward for your efforts, Haydn. Were it not for you, I doubt Maria Beatrice would have accepted Ferdinand."

After a small pause, His Grace continued: "I see no need to mention all the sordid details to the Emperor, do you, Esterházy?"

"Not at all," Prince Nikolaus agreed. He cleared his throat. "And Haydn, it would be best to keep the details out of your report to Her Majesty as well."

Haydn started. How had His Serene Highness known about that?

Before he could wonder too much about the question, his employer pushed a leather pouch toward him.

"A well-deserved reward," His Serene Highness began to say, but Haydn gently pushed the pouch away.

"I would prefer something else, if Your Serene Highness doesn't object."

Prince Nikolaus frowned, displeased. "What else could you possibly want?"

Haydn thought of Gabriel and his temptations and of his other men, patiently biding their time in this backwater without their wives.

"To say farewell to Eszterháza. The men wish to return to Eisenstadt, Your Serene Highness. As do I." He bowed his head. "If you could graciously grant this request. . ."

The Prince harrumphed irritably. "Very well, Haydn. Tell your men to make preparations to return."

He snorted again.

"Although I can't see why anyone would wish to leave this paradise. And to turn down a bag of gold over it. Utter folly!"

The End

Want more **Haydn Mysteries**? Visit NTUSTIN.COM/BOOKS. Sign up to **get two complimentary Mystery Anthologies**—one featuring your favorite eighteenth-century sleuth and the other set in California.

And, while you're waiting for the next Haydn Mystery, why not try the **Celine Skye Psychic Mysteries**? If you enjoy **art heists laced with psychic detection and suspense,** you'll love this series as well.

Read an Excerpt Or Grab Your Copy From NTUSTIN.COM/BOOKS!

Author's Note: The Soprano Who Died

YEARS ago a brief entry in the Oxford Composer Companions volume on Haydn stirred my imagination. Barbara Dichtler, a longtime soprano at the Esterházy court, had died during a performance of an opera.

The entry itself is rather undramatic: "She died on stage during a performance of Sacchini's *L'isola d'amore*." But as soon as I saw it, the wheels in my mind started spinning.

Had Frau Dichtler—she was married to Leopold Dichtler, a fellow singer, and Haydn had acted as witness—crashed to the stage floor while singing an aria? How had the audience reacted?

More importantly, was her death an unfortunate accident—the result of faulty rigging? Or had it been a carefully planned murder? My mind, as you can imagine, veered toward murder. How could it not? I'm a mystery writer.

Who, I wondered, could have murdered the poor woman? A fellow singer? A jealous husband maddened by her infidelity? A lover frustrated by her unwillingness to commit to him? The possibilities were endless.

And so was born yet another Joseph Haydn Mystery. This one that I've enjoyed writing so much and which I hope you've relished as well. So, all those years ago, I jotted down a few notes, saving them in a file on my computer until last year when I was ready to start writing *Death of a Soprano*.

Because I was writing in September, I decided to set the novel in September as well.

Yet even the choice of that month is strangely fortuitous. Years ago when I'd read the entry about Barbara Dichtler in my book I hadn't noticed the date of her death. In fact, until I re-discovered the entry—a few moments before sitting down to write this—I couldn't even remember where I'd read it.

I scoured every book on Haydn I had until I found it at last in the volume edited by David Wyn Jones.

So you'll imagine my surprise when I realized that Barbara Dichtler had died in September—the very month in which Lucia Pacelli, the murder victim in my novel, is murdered. She died on the nineteenth of the month in 1776.

But that's not the only strange coincidence. When I was plotting the novel, trying to figure out who had killed Barbara's fictional counterpart and the reason for their actions, I decided that the action would take place against the backdrop of a wedding.

It would take place in Eszterháza, where I'd long intended to set a Haydn Mystery. Now the couple getting married—Archduke Ferdinand Karl and Maria Beatrice D'Este—were actually wed in Milan. But it wasn't out of the realm of possibility—in my opinion—that they should have first met under the auspices of Haydn's employer, the powerful and immensely wealthy Hungarian magnate, Prince Nikolaus Esterházy.

Here the couple would meet and formally agree to marry. Haydn—just to complicate matters for the hapless composer—would not only have to furnish the music for the festivities but would also have to keep an eye on the situation and make sure the couple did as their elders expected.

Now as far as I know, Haydn was never charged with anything like this. However, it could have happened. In her keen desire to know everything about her children's lives—their relations with their spouses, their conduct in their respective courts, their religious devotions, and general behavior and lifestyle—Empress Maria Theresa frequently demanded reports from those surrounding them.

Confessors, ambassadors, and ladies-in-waiting were frequently pressed into service. These in turn might pay servants and other attendants for more detailed reports that could then be compiled and sent on to the Empress.

Moreover, a wedding did take place in Eszterháza in the 1770s in the month of September. The wedding of Countess Lamberg, the Prince's niece, to Count Poggi was celebrated in Eszterháza in September 1770. This I didn't know until I was halfway through the book!

Three years later, Empress Maria Theresa visited Eszterháza in September as well—accounting for an imperial presence in the place in that month.

It really was a backwater—at least at the time. Haydn and his musicians hated it there. Haydn because it was so far from the exciting cosmopolitan life of Vienna. The musicians because it meant being away from their wives for long periods of time. The story goes, in fact, that Haydn's Farewell Symphony was written as a subtle message to the Prince, pleading with him to let them return to Eisenstadt.

One by one, each musician apparently snuffed out his candle and walked away, until the music reached its final cadence.

I liked the story but thought the message too subtle to be understood, which is why I have Haydn refusing a bag of gold in exchange for the favor of being allowed to pack their bags and leave. It seems entirely in keeping with the magnanimous and Christian character of the composer I so admire.

The more I learn about the faith that I've recently embraced, the more I realize that Haydn was in so many ways a unique and inspirational exemplar of it.

With God's blessing upon you all!
Nupur

www.ingramcontent.com/pod-product-compliance
Lightning Source LLC
Chambersburg PA
CBHW031031310726
48969CB00007B/1935